Death by Candlelight
How we succumb

Written by

Kevin Goodman

Grosvenor House
Publishing Limited

This book is published by
Grosvenor House Publishing Ltd
Link House
140 The Broadway, Tolworth, Surrey, KT6 7HT.
www.grosvenorhousepublishing.co.uk

This book is a work of fiction. Any resemblance to
people or events, past or present, is purely coincidental.

A CIP record for this book
is available from the British Library

Paperback ISBN 978-1-83975-977-2
Ebook ISBN 978-1-80381-059-1

Dedication

I dedicate this book to my mother; we had some tough times while I was growing up. The past is the past, you will always be missed. Wish you were still here so that you could see the person I have become. Taken from us too early. Even though we had our differences and arguments, you always inspired me to be the best I could be. You always said to me, when describing anything I need to pad and pad some more, give life to the things I am describing. That lesson has stuck with me throughout my life. I love and miss you, Mom.

turns purple and eventually black, as the stars start to twinkle and the moon its nightly dance across the sky.

The front yard stretches from the house to the roadside, encased by a metre-high red brick wall in a large L-shape, mirroring the outline of the house. The great oak tree stands at the bend of the L. To one side of the great oak tree is a well-manicured lawn, surrounding by a variety of evergreen flowers, creating a rainbow of colour. To the other side are a few tropical evergreen trees and two small banana trees, leaving enough space for a two-door garage. There are two red-bricked paths leading to the front door, one starting from the front gate at the boundary wall, the path snaking its way between the great oak tree and the well-manicured lawn. The other path hugs the side of the house leading to the front door from the garage, and there is an electric gate which opens onto the driveway from the roadside. There is enough space to park a car between the garage and the boundary wall without the split gate hitting the car.

The two paths meet at the bottom of a staircase leading up to a porch which is made from the same long oak beams as the patio and stained in the same colour varnish. The porch is one metre in height, the same as the patio in the backyard. Three short steps from porch to the pathway and the inviting lush garden drawing you in. The porch is two metres in width from the exterior wall to the edge of the

garden, with a wooden railing stretching half the length of the long side of the L to protect anyone from falling off the porch. The edge of the lounge windows at one end is where the railing starts, and it finishes just beyond the front door at the other end. There is a two-seater white wicker bench, with a cream-coloured pillow set covering the seat and backrest, and a small wooden table on either side. The wicker bench and tables nestle between the railing and the front door.

The outside of the house is in keeping to the same raw feel as the boundary wall and the two paths. The deep red varnish of the porch and patio blend seamlessly with the red brick exterior, as though they are one. It is a two-storey house which has a flat roof with a slight slope from the middle towards the edges, allowing the water to drain away when it rains. There is a retractable awning which covers the porch. During the summer, it is open to shade the porch from the summer heat, and closed in the evenings to view the stars in a clear night's sky.

The front door is stained in a caramel colour to offset the deep red of the porch. There is a wooden post-box to the right of the front door, with the word Morley engraved on it; to the left is a wooden plaque with 36 Strawberry Grove engraved into it. Both are stained in the same colour varnish as the front door. A brass knocker on the door is in the shape of an eagle's clawed foot gripping a sphere, and it sits

just below and in the middle of two small yellow stained-glass panes. From a distance it looks like two eyes and a nose.

Throughout the entire inside of the house the walls are painted in a creamy white to compliment the cream carpets, and all wooden surfaces are stained in the same caramel varnish as the front door, bringing a soft warmth to the wood. To the left of the front door is an arched doorway with a split panelled wooden door which opens onto the lounge. The wall the front door opens onto has a wooden rack with hooks to hang coats, and next to the hooks is a small piece of wood with tiny hooks to hang keys. Below the hooks is a thin but long wood table, with a white crochet cloth draped over it, upon which are some ornaments, a bowl with loose change, and some post. To the side of the long thin table, stuck in the corner below the coat hooks and the front door, is a tall cylindrical tube used to house umbrellas. The long, thin table sits up against the wall to the guest toilet, which fits into the corner of the L-shape of the house, the guest toilet door just left of the long thin table.

Opposite the front door is a staircase that leads to the upstairs portion of the house. To the right of the staircase is the open plan dining room and kitchen which make up the small side of the L-shape of the house. The lounge is long and narrow with a working fireplace at the back wall

opposite the arched door, and there are three couches – a three-seater and two two-seaters – in a U-shape, with the three-seater facing the fireplace. A wooden table sits on either side of the three-seater couch, linking the other couches into the U-shape with enough space on either side of the tables to walk in between. There is a large Persian rug centred between the couches, its bright colours creating an intricate pattern to offset all the cream and white in the room.

Above the fireplace, mounted on the wall, is a flat screen television, below which is a built-in set of three shelves. The first shelf is for the Blu-Ray player, the second for the digital television control box, and the third for a soundbar. The first and second shelves are side by side, with the soundbar below, and there is enough finger space to pull the devices out with ease. Either side of the fireplace are shelves for films.

The side wall of the lounge has family photos mounted on it, as well as some hanging artifacts, among which are tribal masks, shields, short and long spears. The walls on either side of the arched door have fitted bookcases filled with books, and the light switches. The windows are framed by heavy cream curtains to block out the light when closed. They are usually open to let in the natural light, which is becoming less and less over the years as the great oak tree grows larger with each passing season and casts its shadow

over the house. A built-in dropped ceiling has spotlights to give extra light. They are on a dimmer to move from ambient light while watching television or films, or brighter to even out the light on days when the natural light is low. In the corners of the room are tall stemmed standing lamps with cream lampshades, brightening up the lounge when having guests around for coffee, tea, or drinks.

The family photos are in nice picture frames of varying sizes with a high gloss black border to them; some are square, others are rectangle, and a few are circled. The rectangle frames house multiple photos of a loving family of three. A wife, husband, and a daughter. Most of the photos are of the daughter through different ages of growing up, from a young toddler to teenager, school prom and graduation from university, all grouped together in the rectangle frames. Some of the photos were professional family portraits, others taken on an old school camera using spools of film. They have a grainier feel than the high gloss, extremely sharp look that digital gives.

The walls of the guest toilet are painted in a light grey with a matt black finish on the wooden skirting boards, and a lightweight black roller blind to cover the window above the toilet. The window of the guest toilet sits above the post-box and is above eye level so that no-one can peek in. The toilet area has a handbasin, towel rail, and a toilet. The basin and toilet set are a darker grey than the colour of the

walls, giving varied levels of colour to the room. To the left of the basin, attached to the wall, is a high gloss chrome soap tray which holds a bar of lavender soap. There is a black hand towel hanging over the towel rail. To the left of the toilet is a toilet brush hidden in a tall silver metallic cylindrical tube; to the right another metallic tube to hold extra rolls of toilet paper.

A round flat light cover, placed in the centre of the ceiling, throws off a deep warm light, more golden than white. Also, on the right side of the toilet is the toilet paper holder made from chrome with a rounded piece of wood to hold the roll. Close to the door is the light switch.

The open plan dining room and kitchen are broken only by a bank of low cupboards, with their white backs facing the dining room, while the counter surface is made from a black and white speckled marble. The dining room isn't very large and has more artifacts hanging on the walls. A square wooden table with four chairs is placed in the centre of the room, with a small diamond-shaped crocheted doily in the centre of the table and a vase of sweet-smelling flowers sitting upon it. When walking into the dining room, on the right-hand wall is a large canvas painting of animals around a watering hole in Africa; there are zebras, water buffalo, some springbuck, elephants, and giraffes eating the shrubs nearby, drinking and bathing at the water's edge. In the watering hole you can see the heads of three crocodiles

waiting to pounce upon their unsuspecting prey. There are some tall trees not too far in the distance from the watering hole, and lying under the trees is a pride of lions. The sun shimmers off the water in golden sparkles.

An island in the centre of the kitchen has a washbasin and work area for preparing food, and underneath the counter is more cupboard space for storage. On one side of the island is space for rubbish bins – one for waste and the other for recycling; on the other side of the island is space for a dishwasher. Above the island is a bank of lights, throwing its glow in different directions, lighting up the whole kitchen. One side of the island is the folding sliding doors onto the patio, and the other side is the back wall of the kitchen, with a stove inlaid within the marble counter top. An extractor fan is mounted on the wall, and on either side of the stove at eye level is an oven. Medium-sized black and white tiles line the back wall like a chess board.

The side wall from floor to ceiling is a mosaic mural of the ocean, with dolphins swimming and a whale breaching the water. Off to the side of the mural is a tropical island with a lush forest, while wooden huts line the beach. The huts are on an open green patch of land – a barrier between the beach and forest. There are fishing boats anchored on the beach using rope tied to wooden poles deep in the sand. Smoke bellows upwards from two fire pits behind the huts.

Stretching either side of the huts are rows of coconut and palm trees.

Next to the staircase going upstairs is a door leading to the basement, which lies below the kitchen and dining room, with the back wall of the basement stretching partway into the rear of the garage. The washing machine and tumble dryer are kept in the basement, and line one wall along with boxes of old photo albums, books, and kids' toys. Lining part of the opposite wall is a large, tall square metal box from floor to ceiling, which houses chopped wood for burning in the fireplace. In the back of the garage is a trapdoor, half the size of the metal box, to be used when wood is delivered. The trapdoor has a hinge and is held open with a latch on the wall.

Two chest freezers sit between the metal box and the washing machine. A folded-up table tennis table is stuffed into the corner next to the metal box, while wine racks take up most of the open space in the centre of the basement. There is a single hanging light from the ceiling, the switch located at the top of the stairs as you enter the basement.

On the walls going up the staircase are more framed photos of the close-knit family, yearly portraits of love and happiness, adoration beaming off the parents' faces towards their daughter. This is a family grounded in their love for each other. The loving embrace portrayed in the

photos varies year by year – the parents arm-in-arm in one photo, looking at their daughter with nothing but love in their eyes; another shows a long cushioned low bench made from oak – varnished in a dark brown stain, the cushion covered in a red wine burgundy coloured leather, attached to the bench with brass studs – on which the family is sitting, daughter in the middle, both parents kissing her on the cheeks in a hugging embrace like a crescent moon.

To the left at the top of the stairs are the family bathroom and the daughter's bedroom, which is above the open plan kitchen and dining room. To the right is a passage leading onto the master bedroom. Hanging on the outside of the daughter's slightly ajar bedroom door is a large wooden heart, which takes up the top half of the door. It is painted in rainbow colours, with a big S J carved into it – an arrow going throw the S and the J, joining them together. On the inside of the room there is a small double bed in the corner, almost against the wall. Above the bed are shelves stocked with sports trophies for hockey and athletics.

Next to the bed is a desk, which sits under the window, with frilly cream curtains to kiss the edges of the sash window. A wardrobe fits into the recess on the other side of the desk. It has sliding wooden doors. Just behind the bedroom door is a plank of wood with hooks attached to the wall. A nightgown and jumpers used to hang from them.

The family bathroom has a separate shower cubicle and bath on the opposite side to the door, and behind the door is a basin, with the toilet in the corner. The bathroom suite is a combination of cream and white. To the left of the toilet is a frosted glass window to obscure the view of anyone passing by the house. It is square and has a small, hinged section to allow the window to be opened. The bathroom is tiled with cream and white tiles; on the white tiles are images of wild birds, with a short description of each one. There is a cream roller blind attached to the wall above the window. The toilet roll holder is made of white porcelain and is flush with the wall. It has a round piece of wood fitted in place to house the toilet paper, and there is a peach-coloured toilet roll on the holder. A toilet brush sits in the corner, obscured by the toilet.

A dropped ceiling with spotlights brightens up the bathroom with warm light. From the basin to the toilet are cupboards for storage, and above the basin is a rectangular mirror, ending just above a chrome soap dish. The basin is embedded in a tall but narrow white cabinet with two doors that have chrome handles. Between the basin and the door is a chrome towel rack. On the wall by the shower cubicle are hooks placed quite high to hang dressing gowns and other clothes, with a set of three rails to hang towels below the hooks. On the floor are two mats – a small square one outside the shower, and a longer one the length of the bath; both are cream in colour.

The hallway is brightly lit, with evenly spaced hanging lights. On the wall are shelves, hanging artefacts placed between them. There are other trinkets and ornaments on the shelves. There are warm caramel runner carpets in the hallway, the corners of which are turning inwards with fraying ends.

The master bedroom is quite minimalist in its furnishings, nonetheless they are a matching set, made to order. On the far wall opposite the door, either side of the chimney from the lounge below, are floor-to-ceiling built-in deep wardrobes with sliding doors made from oak with a deep brown gloss finish. In the corner between the double windows and the door is a dressing table with a swivel mirror. It has a large drawer in the centre, and two smaller ones on either side – all with tiny brass handles. A small rectangular stool with a caramel leather finish sits in front of it. On top of the dresser is an assortment of makeup, perfumes, and jewellery boxes, kept neat; everything in its place.

On the other side of the door is a bookcase filled with rare editions from long deceased famous authors and poets, geology and archaeological books, others on natural history and primitive tribes from around the world. In-between the bookcase and the bed, a long-standing mirror boxed in wood hangs on the wall. There is an ornate chandelier hanging in the middle of the ceiling. Opposite the windows is a large wooden bed with a carved headboard. The bed is covered by

an oversized cream duvet with matching pillows and a caramel blanket, with a bedside table on either side. On one bedside table is a lamp with a caramel-coloured shade. Under the bed is a large caramel rug, stretching beyond the borders of the bed to blend the cream carpet and the deep brown of the bed. The windows are cradled either side by heavy cream curtains to drown out the world outside, but today they are open, letting in the late afternoon sun.

Asleep on the bed is Sarah-Jane, covered by the caramel blankets as the afternoon sun slowly slinks it way down the bed, leaf-shaped shadows from the great oak tree dancing on the cream duvet and carpet in the disappearing light. Sarah-Jane is 5 foot 8 inches tall, athletic in build, with long dark brown hair. Today is her 31st birthday; she is meeting friends for dinner, a night out for a few drinks and a lot of laughs, and maybe in the early hours of the morning some silly antics when getting drunk-hungry munchies. Sarah-Jane has been a librarian at the local library since she graduated from university aged 24. Six years is a long time; co-workers become friends, and eventually they become family, too. Though Sarah-Jane is her birth name, she prefers to be called Sarah by friends and family. When being introduced to someone new, she politely answers my name is Sarah-Jane, but Sarah is fine.

This birthday is an important one. It is just over a year-and-a-half since her parents died. She misses them and is just

beginning to get over mourning them, and starting to live again. Sarah-Jane moved out to be close to work and was renting a one-bedroom apartment which was walking distance from work, but she gave up the furnished apartment when her parents died.

She moved back into the family home she had grown up in, and her bedroom was once her parents. Now reliving memories of her childhood since their death, the house is too large for one person, but there are too many happy memories to pack it all in and sell the house. Eventually she will have to get round to making the house more her own and less her parents', but the hurt is still too fresh in her heart and mind to sell all the artefacts to museums and private auction.

As both of her parents were scientists and archaeologists, a lot of the tribal masks, shields and spears, plus other artefacts, were collected over their many years of travelling the world collecting and cataloguing their archaeological finds. Before Sarah-Jane was school age, she used to go with them, but when school started, they took turns being away until she grew up, then they resumed going on finds together.

Chapter 2

Lying on the bed next to Sarah-Jane is her mobile phone. It starts to ring and vibrate; the ringtone is Darth Vader's imperial march from *Star Wars*. As a librarian, she is not only a fan of the written word but loves cinema too, especially science fiction films. The vibrating of her phone wakes Sarah-Jane up, and she opens sleepy eyes to see who is calling her. It is Agnes from work.

Sarah-Jane answers her phone in a raspy voice. "Hi, Aggie, what time is it?"

"It's close to half five," says Agnes. "God, you sound strange, what have you been doing?"

Sarah-Jane replies, "Since coming home from work, I haven't done much. Did some laundry and had a nap."

Agnes asks, "What time do we have to be at Giorgio's this evening?"

"I will be arriving for eight o'clock," replies Sarah-Jane, "but I said to everyone they can start arriving from eight o'clock.

I booked one of the booth tables at the back of the restaurant for the five of us. They are nice sized tables, as you know, and the staff don't mind how loud we get," continues Sarah-Jane.

"Ah, ok," replies Agnes. "See you there."

By the time they ended their conversation, it was quarter-to-six. Sarah-Jane lay till six, thinking of the things she needed to do before leaving for her birthday celebrations, making a mental list.

She gets up, folds the caramel blanket, and lays it neatly at the foot of the bed. Walking over to the wardrobe, sliding open the door, Sarah-Jane takes out a black evening dress, black high heeled shoes, and a smart black slim ladies dinner jacket. Carefully placing the clothes on the bed and shoes on the floor, she takes a matching black lace bra and panties from a drawer. As the sun is close to setting, Sarah-Jane switches on the lights before closing the curtains.

Walking over to the dressing table, she gets undressed before putting on her dressing gown. Sarah-Jane walks to the bathroom, putting her clothes in the laundry basket housed inside the cabinet under the wash basin. Turning around, she runs a bath. On the inner corners and the outer corner at the foot of the bath are three large white vanilla fragranced candles. Sarah-Jane drops a large lavender bath

bomb in the water before she lights the candles as the bath is almost three-quarters full. Testing the temperature of the water, Sarah-Jane adds cold water while turning off the hot tap. Checking the temperature for a second time, she turns off the cold tap, swirling the water around in a continuous figure of eight, mixing the cold with the hot, and churning up the foam from the bath bomb.

I've got about an hour and a half before I have to leave for Giorgio's, she thinks to herself. *That gives me time to relax in the bath before I have to get ready.* Working out in her head how much time she has to allocate to each step of getting ready, she decides that 45 minutes to relax in the bath is well deserved after the long tiring week at work. *Thank God I'm not working tomorrow. At least I have my birthday weekend off.*

Sarah-Jane plays some classical music on her phone before setting a timer for 45 minutes. Laying her phone down on the hand basin countertop, she climbs into the hot bath awaiting her. Leaving her phone on the countertop will force her to get out the bath and switch it off when the timer ends.

She lies back in the bath and puts a hot, folded facecloth over her closed eyes. Dozing in the water, listening to music, soothes her. After 20 minutes, the music builds to a crescendo, pulling Sarah-Jane out of her doze. Feeling refreshed with energy in her being, Sarah-Jane conducts

the closing of the classical piece, her arms moving in the air, soapy water dripping down her arms. She knows it has only been 20 minutes, as the piece of classical music she chose was around 20 minutes in length.

Taking the facecloth off her face, Sarah-Jane sits up, pulling the plug as she gets out the bath, and steps onto the long cream rug. *I still have 25 minutes left before I need to get ready*, she thinks. Sarah-Jane prefers having a bath to relax but a shower to get clean, as she has this thing about lying in her own filth after soaping up in a bath.

Starting the shower, she moves the mixer handle till she gets her desired temperature before stepping under the water. Sarah-Jane pours a large amount of shampoo into the palm of her hand before putting the bottle back. Lathering up the shampoo, she washes her hair, then takes the bar of soap and washes her face before rinsing the shampoo out. Conditioning her hair next, she massages her scalp, then takes the bar of soap again to soap up her body. She combs out her long hair before she rinses the conditioner and her soapy body.

Switching off the shower, Sarah-Jane wrings the excess water from her hair before opening the shower door and grabbing her towel. She dries herself off before she wraps her hair in the towel, then puts on her dressing gown just as the timer starts to chime. Reaching for her phone, she

unlocks it before she can end the timer. Normally, Sarah-Jane leaves her phone on the dressing table at night, making her get out of bed in the morning to switch off the alarm. The annoying alarm tone is ear piercing, otherwise she would just let it continue and stay in bed.

Before leaving the bathroom, she opens the small hinge window to let the steam out; she had forgotten to open it before having her relaxing hot bath. Walking back to the bedroom, steam bellowing out into the hallway behind her, she sits down on the dressing table stool and takes the towel off her head. Dropping it on the carpet, she reaches for her hairdryer, humming the classical piece she had been listening to in the bath. She rough dries her hair a bit before she puts some anti-frizz serum in and brushes it through with a large paddle brush, using the brush and hairdryer to smooth out her hair as it dries.

Picking up her phone to see the time, Sarah-Jane books a taxi to take her to Giorgio's, which is a half hour drive away. One of the bonus features of the app is you can prebook a taxi for a specific pick-up time. Having finished with her hair, Sarah-Jane starts doing her makeup. She doesn't need much, as she has a natural beauty – a little base and blusher, eye liner and mascara, and lastly a deep red lipstick.

Walking over to the bed, Sarah-Jane takes off her dressing gown, laying it on the bed before picking up her black lace

panties and shimmies them on. Next, she puts on the black lace bra, then picks up her evening dress and slips her legs in one at a time as she pulls it over her waist, putting her arms through the long sleeves; Sarah-Jane wants to avoid getting makeup on the dress.

Placing a nice matching black strapped watch on, she slips on a pair of slippers to walk around the house before leaving for Giorgio's. Clutching her purse and high heels in one hand, the dinner jacket in the other, Sarah-Jane switches off the bedroom light and walks down the hallway. Turning the lights for the staircase and entrance hall on, she goes downstairs to wait for the taxi. Hanging her jacket on the coat rack by the front door, she leaves her purse on the long thin table and her shoes below it. She still has almost 15 minutes before the taxi is meant to arrive.

She walks into the kitchen and over to the fridge, thinking to herself, *I've got time for a cheeky glass of wine.* Pulling the cork and pouring herself a small glass of dry white wine, she switches the lights off in the kitchen and dining room before going to the lounge to wait. Turning the lounge lights on, she dims them to get some ambient light. Sarah-Jane sits on the couch facing the windows, placing the wine glass on a cork coaster to avoid leaving a liquid ring on the table next to her.

Scrolling through her social media, occasionally taking a sip of her drink, Sarah-Jane has almost finished her glass of

wine when she sees a taxi pulling up in front of the house. She will wait for the driver to phone her, just in case the car is for one of her neighbours. Her phone rings and she answers, "Hi, I will be right out." The driver replies, "Ok, don't rush. I arrived early."

Sarah-Jane downs the last of her wine, leaving the glass on the coaster and switching off the lounge lights as she leaves. Quickly, she runs upstairs to brush her teeth. On her way back downstairs, she remembers to turn off the upstairs hallway lights. Putting on her shoes and jacket, Sarah-Jane takes her keys from its hook, turning on the porch and footpath lights that frame either side of the path leading to the front gate. She sets the alarm, locks the front door behind her, and leaves the entrance hall and porch lights on.

Walking down the path to the front gate, Sarah-Jane's phone rings. It's Giorgio's. "Hi, this is Sarah." A voice in an Italian accent at the other end explains, "Evening, this is Sergio. I just wanted to let you know we received your birthday cake from Gino's bakery. We didn't know if it was going to arrive, as Gino's oven broke down two days ago and it was a mad scramble to get cakes made and delivered."

Closing the front gate behind her, Sarah-Jane replies, "Thanks, Sergio, for letting me know. I'm about to get into a taxi. See you at eight o'clock."

As she climbs into the taxi, the driver says to her, "Evening, my name is Carl, you must be Sarah-Jane."

She answers, "Yes, I'm Sarah."

Carl asks, "Which Giorgio's am I taking you to this evening?"

"We are going to Giorgio's on Park Lane," she replies before continuing, "Yes, it can be confusing, as they have now opened their ninth location, although the one on Park Lane is the original location."

Carl turns the engine on and, before pulling away, turns to Sarah-Jane. "Would you like the radio on or off? Or maybe you would like to chat while we drive to the restaurant?"

Sarah-Jane replies, "If you don't mind, I would prefer the radio on. Could you find either a classical or jazz radio station, please?" Then she adds in a friendly tone, and with a smile on her face, "We can chat, too."

The drive to Giorgio's seems to fly by and Sarah-Jane enjoys their small talk. Pulling up in front of Giorgio's, Carl turns off the engine. "Sorry we are a few minutes late. Traffic, what can you do?" He adds, "Have an awesome birthday dinner, and the rest of the weekend."

"No worries. Thank you so much for the birthday wishes, Carl, and it was really nice chatting with you. You are very

knowledgeable on a variety of subjects," she replies, opening the door to leave. Before closing the door, Sarah-Jane hands Carl a large tip, "Hope this helps towards getting your medical degree."

Carl accepts the tip graciously. "It's too much. Are you sure?"

Nodding, with a friendly smile, Sarah-Jane replies, "Pay it forward is the philosophy I believe in. Everyone can use a little help now and again." She waves goodbye and heads towards the front door of the restaurant.

Giorgio's is their favourite Italian restaurant, and the staff are very welcoming. The first time they went out as a group of five was to this Giorgio's – that was four-and-a-half years ago, when Jenny joined the library. Since then, they try to go at least once a month; more often, if they can.

The door to Giorgio's opens as Sarah-Jane approaches and Sergio greets her with an open-mouthed smile, showing off his pearly white teeth. "So nice to see you again, Sarah. Please follow me to your table."

"So nice to see you, too. I hope we didn't make too much noise last time we were here," Sarah-Jane replies, following Sergio to the back of the restaurant. As they get closer, she sees her four friends already seated, and immediately they stand up and start singing "Happy birthday to you".

Agnes had gotten to Giorgio's an hour early to decorate their booth, and there are two rows of balloons, one on either side of the seats. The balloons are alternating colours of black and gold, and are attached to a black streamer, vertically from the back wall to the edge of the booth, with adhesive tape to keep them in place. On the wall, hanging from the lampshade, is a '31' made of dassies and encircled with colourful flowers.

Sarah-Jane takes off her dinner jacket and places it on the leather seat of the booth as they finish singing to her. One by one they come forward to give her a hug before sitting down again. There is cold champagne on the table, open ready to pour. Sarah-Jane looks at her four friends with great affection – Jenny Jones, Patsy Heart, Amanda Stone, and finally her best friend, Agnes Smith.

Jenny is a short woman, just 5 foot 2, with short, curly, blonde hair, a curvy figure, smouldering features, and a sassy attitude to match. She gives as good as she gets, and never takes no for an answer. Jenny is wearing a gold and silver strapless dress with silver high heels. The youngest of the group at 28, and single, she recently split from her boyfriend of three years.

Patsy is 6 feet, the tallest in the group, with a lanky, almost stick-figure frame, and dead straight, long, black hair. Even with average looks, she still turns heads. Patsy is wearing a

black, knee-length dress to avoid drawing attention to her long legs. She is 33 and has been with her boyfriend for five years; they are busy planning their wedding for next year, and are still deciding on a venue but have narrowed it down to two.

Amanda is 5 foot 6, with an athletic build. She still plays hockey once a week and goes to gym twice a week. She has striking features and could have been a model, but didn't want all the attention. Amanda is wearing a mid-thigh, red dress, matching her hair colour. She is 35 and single.

Agnes is 5 foot 5, with fine, strawberry blonde, straight hair, and of average build. She is not overweight but not a gym person either. Tonight she is dressed in women's black slacks with a purple, lacy shirt. She is the mother figure in the group at 40, married for five years, and has a son named Ronald.

Sarah-Jane has met them all through work. Agnes has been there the longest, while the others have joined the library over the years. Friends for life.

Smiling at her friends, Sarah-Jane says, "Thanks for joining me on this special birthday in remembrance of my parents. Only a year-and-a-half ago they were taken from me, but all of you have been there for me. You are my rock, my family." They all lift their glasses and take a sip of champagne.

Jenny says, "We love you, Sarah, and we will be there for you, no matter what."

Turning to Agnes, Sarah-Jane says, "Aggie, thank you so much for the lovely decorations. I really didn't expect any fuss."

Her friend smiles. "Anytime, my love."

They are chatting amongst themselves when Sergio appears. "Would you like any other drinks while you look at the menu before ordering, or just the champagne?"

Amanda replies, "Just the champagne for now, thanks. We have a long night ahead of us."

"I'll come back in a few minutes to get your food orders," says Sergio with a smile before walking away. Ten minutes later, he returns to take their order. "Who would like to go first?" he asks.

Agnes says, "Sarah, as it your birthday, you go first."

Sarah-Jane replies, "Ok, let's see. Can I have the calamari as my starter, and the four-cheese pizza with bacon and pineapple as my main?"

Patsy gives her order next. "I will have the garlic mushrooms as my starter, and seafood pasta as my main."

Jenny follows her. "For my starter I would like the garlic snails, and spaghetti bolognaise for the mains."

And Amanda is next. "I think I will also have the calamari starter, and a medium-rare rump steak with a baked potato, instead of fries, thanks."

Lastly, Agnes gives her order. "For my starter, can I have the salmon pate on your fresh ciabatta, then a lasagne with extra cheese on top for the mains, thanks?"

Sergio repeats the order back to the ladies, making sure everything is noted correctly. "Thanks, your starters shouldn't be too long," he says, just before walking away.

He has only gone about four steps when Sarah-Jane calls to him, "Can we please have a round of gold tequila while we wait?"

"Most definitely," replies Sergio.

Off in the distance they can hear him asking another employee to take the tequilas to their table. A few minutes later, Mario arrives, tray in hand with 5 tequilas. "Here's your tequilas," he says. "Enjoy, ladies."

"Thanks, Mario," replies Agnes.

After ten minutes, their starters arrive, and all you can smell is the garlic from the mushrooms and snails. Behind Sergio is Mario and Maria, each carrying two starters. Sergio places the first starter in front of the birthday girl, then serves the rest one by one in a clockwise direction.

"Enjoy your starters," Maria says as they leave the table.

There is nothing but silence while the friends are eating, savouring every bite. Eventually Jenny breaks the silence. "Nothing better than great Italian food," she comments,

Amanda and Patsy say simultaneously, "Never a truer word said." Then they look at each other and start laughing; it happens all the time when they are together.

Patsy says, "Great minds think alike."

Amanda replies, "You know it."

Agnes takes her butter knife and clinks it against her champagne glass to draw everyone's attention at the table. "I would like to make a toast in honour of our beloved friend Sarah," she says, and they all raise their glasses before she continues. "Six years ago, you came to work in our sanctum, the place we call home during working hours. You were shy, unsure of yourself, and unapproachable. But

over the years I have seen you grow as a person, become sure-footed, more approachable, more outward, and easy going, especially since the death of your parents. Some people would just shut down losing both parents at the same time. We five have become a family; we would die for each other, and do anything to help each other in tough times. We love you, Sarah." She smiles. "Right, let's dispense with the serious talk."

They all take a sip of their champagne then Agnes continues. "Now for the fun surprise. We want to get this out the way before our main course arrives. Sarah, please don't be mad, but we all chipped in for your present and we got you a six-month subscription to a sex site, 'We Play'."

Jenny interrupts, "We all know you haven't been with anyone since Connor, when you broke up at the end of university."

Patsy adds, "This site isn't a dating website; it's a sex site. People on there are only looking for sex. Some do end up in relationships, but it is rare."

Finally, Amanda says, "I'm not ashamed to admit I have used the site myself – some of the best sex I have ever had."

Sarah-Jane at first has a puzzled look on her face, then slowly her cheeks turn a light pinkish red as she blushes,

before she bursts into laughter. "Not sure if I will use it," she tells her friends, "but we'll see."

Agnes quickly explains, "We set up your account and all contributed to building your profile. As the people who know you best, we can answer all the personal questions objectively."

Amanda interjects, "Don't be too shocked when you are browsing the website. There are a lot of different people looking for many different things. You've got people like us who are just looking to have great sex, to people who have extreme kinky sides, to people into BDSM." Amanda finishes explaining that BDSM stands for Bondage/Domination and Sadomasochism just as Sergio, with Maria and Mario at his back, bring their main courses.

The air is filled with the aroma of fresh herbs and garlic; at Giorgio's, their philosophy is "never enough garlic". Their motto is: "After eating at Giorgio's, you won't have to worry about vampires."

Sergio serves Sarah-Jane first, then goes clockwise again to serve the rest of the group.

"Would anyone like freshly ground pepper and extra parmesan?" asks Maria. They all confirm they would, and Mario works his way around the table, grinding pepper

onto each of their dishes. "If you need more, please feel free to ask," he tells them.

Maria returns with two medium bowls filled with parmesan, and places them in the centre of the table. "Please help yourselves," she says.

While they are enjoying their food, the conversation is light-hearted. Unfortunately both Patsy and Agnes can't drink too much as they have to be at work in the morning; it's their weekend on shift. But they are all going to Jonestown after the meal, to have a few drinks and see some live blues.

Sergio appears. "Is everything ok with the food?" he asks. "Would anyone like anything to drink?"

Sarah-Jane replies, "Would it be possible to have a couple of bottles of sparkling water, please? And I'd also like a glass of orange juice, please." She adds, "As always, the food is delicious."

Amanda asks, "If you don't mind, could I have a diet soda, please? Thanks."

The rest of the ladies reply that they are alright, and the women carry on eating.

When Maria returns with a tray carrying the sparkling water, orange juice, diet soda, plus five empty glasses for

the water, she hands out the drinks then asks if she can clear away some of the empty plates.

Having all finished eating their main course, they decide they need some time for their food to digest before the cake comes out. After a while, Sergio and Mario appear and clear away the rest of the plates, then Sergio returned with the cake and a hot drinks menu. Three of the ladies are having cappuccino, while two decide on tea to go with the cake from Gino's bakery.

The cake itself has layers of white and brown chocolate sponge with a sweet chocolate buttercream filling and strawberry jam between the layers. The icing on the outside is white chocolate, with coconut flakes sprinkled over the top, and the words "Happy Birthday Sarah" have been written in brown chocolate icing with a heart made from sliced strawberries.

Mario comes back with the teas and coffees, placing them in front of each person, while Sergio cuts the cake and presents Sarah-Jane with the first slice. Thanking him, she adds, "Please give Mario and Maria some of the cake, and don't forget to cut yourself a slice as well." Then she adds, "On second thoughts, please share what is left of the cake with the rest of the staff working tonight."

Sergio smiles. "You are too kind. Thank you for the cake. The staff will enjoy it once their shift has ended."

The ladies are silent as they eat the cake and enjoy their hot drinks. The cake is very rich, not quite but almost bordering on being sickly sweet. The layers are very moist and spongy, melting in their mouths along with the buttercream and jam, and the coconut is a subtle aftertaste. Gino's bakery is known for their lovely but super calorific cakes.

As Jenny finishes her portion, she says, "My God, I'm stuffed. I couldn't eat another morsel. That was one of the best cakes I have ever eaten."

The others nod in agreement. Patsy sighs, "Another great meal with great friends."

Sarah-Jane adds, "I don't think we have ever had a bad meal here."

It is almost ten o'clock and they have to get to Jonestown for 11pm. They still have to organise the taxi taking them on the half hour drive. None of the ladies had decided to drive to the restaurant or to Jonestown, as they knew they would be drinking. A quick phone call allows them to order a minibus taxi, which is arriving within 15 minutes.

Sarah-Jane quietly slinks off to the front of the restaurant to take care of the bill, paying by card, and leaving a large cash tip for Sergio, Maria, and Mario. When she gets back to the table, she announces, "Ok, ladies, the bill has been taken care of. Let's finish up our dessert and drinks."

Agnes tells them, "If anyone needs the toilet before we leave, now would be the time to go, as the taxi will be here in about ten minutes."

They go to the toilet one by one, and are getting their coats on when Sergio comes to the table to inform them that the taxi has arrived. As the women leave the restaurant, they individually hug their host for the evening and thank him.

Sergio says, "Hope to see you all again soon. Enjoy the rest of your night ahead."

The taxi is a large 16-seater minibus in black – a lot larger than they need, but more sensible than taking two cars. Their driver gets out the front and opens the sliding door, greeting them as they get in. She closes the door and gets back in the front.

Before starting the minibus, she turns around to face them. "My name is Donna," she informs them. "Where are you ladies off to this evening?"

Patsy shouts out, "We are heading to Jonestown to watch some live blues."

Donna replies, "I know Jonestown well. Been there myself to see some live music." She adds, "The traffic isn't too

heavy at this time of the evening, so I should have you there in half an hour, maybe sooner."

The journey to Jonestown seems to pass in a blur as they are all deep in conversation, not realising that half an hour has flown by. There is a short queue of people waiting to get inside before the main band goes on stage. As they get out of the minibus, the friends can hear the last song of the support band. It's slow, dirty sounding, bluesy rock.

They wish Donna a great evening, and hope that the rest of her shift is pleasant and not too long.

In turn, she tells them to enjoy the music, and adds to Sarah-Jane, "Enjoy the rest of your birthday. Hopefully, you won't be too badly hungover in the morning."

They walk up to the back of the queue as the support band finishes playing. The jukebox plays some tunes before the main band comes on stage, and they can hear Aerosmith's *Sweet Emotion* playing while they wait to get in.

Chapter 3

Jonestown is not your typical music venue. Friday and Saturday nights showcase live blues and rock bands, giving local artists a platform to attract new fans, and giving them the chance to play live. It has also housed the greats like B.B. King, Muddy Waters, and slow hand himself, Eric Clapton, when they have toured. Some big rock bands have played there over the years, too.

Jonestown is more a home away from home. The building is made up of different sections, all offshoots from the main area housing the live music. The other sections are a pool hall with an outdoor smoking area, a restaurant, and a nightclub. The outside of the building is painted matt black. Above the entrance, in changing colours, is a neon sign *JONESTOWN*, and on either side of the sign are large guitars – the necks of the guitars stretching away from the sign in a diagonal direction. Over the double door is an awning to keep the door staff dry when it is raining.

The owner is in the process of extending the awning around the outside of the building into the parking lot on the right side of the building. It will keep the queueing patrons out of the wet winter weather, which is on its way in the coming months. There is a wall to the left of the front door. Mounted on the wall is a black, wood framed glass cabinet with flyers highlighting future live music. During the week there are no live bands, but the other areas are still full of people having a few drinks, enjoying their night out.

Going through the large, red leather covered doors, you walk into the main area; opposite the front door is the stage, which is raised a metre from the ground. It is a fairly large stage, comfortably allowing a five-piece band to play. To the left of the front door is a spiral staircase leading to a metal platform with railings, which is bolted to the wall for safety. The metal platform sits above the door and houses the spotlights that shine onto the stage – there are two, manned by one person each.

To the right of the front door is the cloakroom. Running the length of the wall on either side of the venue is a well-stocked bar, with cold lager on tap, as well as some craft beers. Some fridges stand against the wall, built out of stainless-steel to create a work surface and storage space, with shelving above for spirits. Under the bar counter is where the glasses are kept, while the built-in electronic till

system sits on top. Hanging on the walls is lots of music memorabilia and guitars; some are antique-looking acoustic guitars, others are shiny electric ones used by the pioneers of blues and rock.

Looking out from the stage at the rest of venue where the tables are placed, the seating plan is broken into three: the middle tables' seats are positioned so people are looking straight at the stage; the tables to stage left have seats angled looking towards stage right; while the tables stage right have seats looking towards stage left. That means that wherever you are sitting, your view of the stage is unobstructed.

During the week when it is quiet, there is a jukebox, and people can choose music or allow the system to choose randomly. Weekends Jonestown is ram packed, so if you want to watch live music you have to book a table or you will need to stand at the back or by the bar. On busy nights there are five staff behind each bar, and another four walking around taking food orders, clearing glasses and dishes; they rotate turns throughout the shift, so that everyone gets a turn behind the bars or working the floor.

The area directly behind the stage houses two rooms for the musicians to relax before going on stage. Behind the stage rooms is the main kitchen that services all the

different areas of Jonestown. Outside the kitchen is a well-lit courtyard where the smokers are kept for smoking their ribs and other meats. The courtyard is surrounded by the different parts of Jonestown: to the left is the pool hall; centre is the main kitchen; to the right is the restaurant and nightclub; and lastly, the boundary wall.

Between stage left and the bar is a pool hall with nine tables. A red neon sign above the swinging doors reads "Break Your Balls", and inside the pool hall are three rows of three tables – some with blue felt and others with green. There is wooden shelving along the walls for people to place their drinks and snacks, and bar stools are evenly placed around the room. There is also a small bar in one corner of the room for people to buy drinks and snack, even order some BBQ, without going back and forth between the main area and the pool hall.

To the side of the small bar is a self-service station to dump your empty plates and wash your hands after eating BBQ. On the pool hall walls there is more music memorabilia – photos of Elvis Presley, Marvin Gaye, and many other famous artists. "Break Your Balls" is always busy, and sometimes you can wait up to an hour before getting to play. It is less busy during the week, compared to weekends, but is always a popular meeting place for friends to have a good time, great conversation, and a few drinks to while away the evening.

Opposite the small bar are the toilets – a rectangular structure divided in half by a wall, creating two sections, one for men and one for women, both with a swing door in the outer wall. The men's toilets have a cubicle and a urinal trough along the back wall, with the basin and hand dryer near the door. The only difference between the two is the women's toilets has three cubicles, and a bigger basin area decorated in soft peach throughout.

Opposite the swinging doors, on the other side of the room, is a door leading onto a well ventilated and sheltered outdoor smoking area with a few tables and chairs. Its back wall faces onto the street but has no access to it. There are large metal spikes embedded in the top of the wall to prevent anyone trying to climb over from either side; as an extra precaution, there is barbed wire, too.

Next to each table is a heating lamp for warmth. Motion sensor lighting is in use in the smoking area, so when no-one is outside the smoking area is in darkness, not wasting electricity unnecessarily. In the summer months it is nice to sit out in the warmth, having drinks in the dying light of the long days.

Between stage right and the second bar is an open-arched doorway, above which are two blue neon signs: one says "Smoking Jones" and the other "Toilets". Dead ahead is a short corridor leading to the toilets. To the left of the short

corridor is a longer one that leads to Smoking Jones – Jonestown's famous BBQ restaurant.

The main toilets are oddly designed, as they are accessible from both sides. There is a dividing wall down the centre separating the men's and women's toilets, but both have an entrance door on either side of the structure. Walking into the women's toilets, there are six cubicles – two rows of three, back-to-back – and on opposite walls are the basins and hand dryers, again decorated in a soft peach colour. The men's toilets are white in colour, with three cubicles in the centre of the structure and three urinal bowls on the other side. On either side are the hand basins and dryers, like the women's toilets, and there is another urinal trough on the wall between the basins.

Smoking Jones is known for their drop-off-the-bone succulent ribs. They smoke their ribs on a low heat for at least six to eight hours, and do baby back and long bone pork ribs, extra-long bone beef ribs, and short stack lamb ribs marinated in a rosemary and mint dry rub 24 hours before smoking. Even the lamb shanks are smoked for three hours, letting the fat render, making it fall off the bone. They do different types of burgers, too. There is beef, lamb, chicken/pork burgers, and you can have them as single, double, or even triple stack burgers. You can build a burger out of any combination of meat; chicken and pork go well together, or even a lamb and beef, maybe even lamb and chicken.

The usual add-ons are on offer: crispy bacon, fried onions, gherkins, and three different cheeses – smoky cheddar, sweet chilli gouda, and strong blue cheese, which is also made into a sauce for the hot wings. They have the best triple cooked, thick cut chips – golden, crispy, and crunchy.

There are two entrances to Smoking Jones: one from the live music side of Jonestown; the other in the far corner, opening onto the parking lot, where the door is part of a wall of glass windows. Opposite the wall of glass is the main kitchen. The wall by the door has a mural of Jimi Hendricks, and opposite the mural of Jimi is the entrance to the toilets.

Smoking Jones isn't a large restaurant – only 100 diners can be seated. The tables are made of pine and have a high gloss caramel stain, while the chairs are made from the same wood and stain, and they are covered with real cow hide. Hanging above each table is a light with a rose-coloured shade. To get a table in Smoking Jones you have to book two weeks ahead, if you are lucky. If not, it can be anywhere between one month to a month-and-a-half before getting a booking.

There is another hallway in the opposite corner to the glass front door to Smoking Jones. It is a well-lit hallway which leads to the back entrance to the nightclub, and above the back entrance is a flashing red neon sign with the words "Diablo's Den". Going through the back entrance to the

nightclub, you will be met by a doorman checking ultra violet stamps. If you don't have a stamp, you won't be allowed in.

There is a main entrance in the front, leading onto the parking lot. Above the front door is another flashing red neon sign with "Diablo's Den", and on either side of the sign are two braided pipes. Coming out of their tips are flames – the two becoming one larger flame, framing the sign in the shape of horns. Running along the wall, from front door to the back door, is a long, black leather couch, with tables spaced a metre apart. On the opposite wall by the front door is the cloakroom, and a long, thin bar runs along the wall between there and the DJ booth which is opposite the back entrance. In the centre is the dance floor, with three mirror balls evenly spaced over the ceiling and disco lights between them.

On the front door are two well-built doormen who take no shit from anyone. If you have done something wrong, you will be asked to leave the nightclub, but they are fair and will listen to both sides of the situation before making a judgement and asking the guilty party to leave. If you are just going to Smoking Jones and don't plan on using the other areas of Jonestown, you won't get a stamp; if you choose to stay for the evening into the wee hours, you will get a stamp when you pay your bill. You will also get a stamp at the main entrances to the live music

area and Diablo's Den. The stamp gives you all access to Jonestown.

Diablo's Den is the last area of Jonestown to close at 3am. The rest of Jonestown closes at 1am on the weekends and midnight the rest of the week; the main kitchen stops serving food by 11pm to give staff time to clean up before going home.

Sarah-Jane is singing along to *Sweet Emotion* while waiting to go into Jonestown. Amanda is talking to Patsy, while Jenny and Agnes are standing away from the queue, having a cigarette before they go inside. The queue is moving along slowly as the doorman has to check everyone for ID, making sure not to let in anyone under age. By the time Sarah-Jane and her friends get to the front of the queue, there is an announcement that "Shines the Monkey" will be on stage in five minutes.

The doorman recognises Sarah-Jane and her friends as they get to the front of the queue. "Hey, Sarah, you made it," he says. "Happy birthday. See you later inside, and I'll buy you a birthday drink."

"Hey, Dan," replies Sarah-Jane. "How's your mom? I haven't seen her since your sister moved out of town for her new job."

Dan Meeks is the younger brother of Sarah-Jane's best friend Susie, who left the area a month ago to start her new

law job. While they were growing up, Susie and Sarah-Jane were like two peas in a pod – inseparable. They even went to the same university.

Dan stamps the five ladies one by one as they pass him, then they pushed open the big red leather doors. Once inside, Sarah-Jane hands Patsy her dinner jacket. "Would you mind handing this in at the cloakroom with your jacket while I sort out our tables?"

"Sure, my love, no worries," Patsy replies.

Sarah-Jane leaves the four ladies at the cloakroom while she tries to locate Mike and find out where her tables are allocated. Spotting him standing by the stage talking to the stage crew as they finish setting up Shines the Monkey's equipment, she goes over and hugs Mike from behind, saying, "Guess who!"

As Mike spins around in her arms, he laughs, "Happy birthday, Sarah. Glad you made it. I was starting to think you weren't coming." He gives her a kiss on the cheek.

"Mike, which tables are ours?" asks Sarah-Jane.

Mike replies, "Those two tables over there." He points towards the last two open tables close to the entrance to Break Your Balls, then continues, "As requested, someone

will bring over the two champagne bottles you paid for when you booked."

They walk over to the tables and Mike signals to one of the bar staff who comes over to find out what he wants. Sarah-Jane looks towards the cloakroom where Patsy has just finished handing over their jackets. "I'll be back," she tells him, "I just want to get the girls."

By the time they get back to their tables, the champagne is waiting in two ice buckets, alongside five glasses. Mike is pouring champagne into the last glass.

"Won't you join us for a glass?" Sarah-Jane offers.

Mike replies, "That is kind of you to ask. I'll just get another glass." He walks over to the bar and returns shortly with another champagne glass, then pours himself a drink.

Sarah-Jane lifts her glass to make a toast, and the others follow. "I just want to say how happy I am to have friends here with me on this special day," she tells them. "You have all been there for me during the last year-and-a-half. I hold a special place in my heart for you amazing people."

They all clink their glasses, replying, "Here's to your health. May you have many more years to come."

As they sip their champagne, Mike taps Sarah-Jane on the shoulder. "I have to dash off, something needs my attention," he explains. "But I will pop by later."

Sarah-Jane replies, "See you in a bit" and gives him a kiss on the cheek.

Jenny comes over to Sarah-Jane and mutters, "Dan. Why haven't you gone there?"

"He is like a little brother to me, and I have never seen him in any other way," laughs Sarah-Jane.

They sit down to wait for the band to start. "If you don't mind, I would like a crack at him," Jenny tells her. "He looks like he can go all night. Those bulging arm muscles and that rock-hard ass."

"Be my guest, I don't mind," says Sarah-Jane.

There seems to be a technical problem as Shines the Monkey haven't started playing yet, and they should have started ten minutes ago. Sarah-Jane realises this must be what Mike left to sort out

The two tables are in the front row looking stage right. From left to right are Jenny, Sarah-Jane, Amanda, Patsy, and Agnes, with one open seat.

Amanda says, "What's taking so long? Weren't they meant to start playing already?"

Sarah-Jane replies, "I think that is what Mike left to deal with. Maybe they'll fix it soon. Look on the bright side, at least this way we didn't miss any of their set. We could have been late if traffic had been heavy coming from Giorgio's."

"Ah, let's hope so," replies Amanda.

Just then Mike walks onto the stage towards the microphone stand. He taps the microphone a few times, and the sound it makes gets everyone's attention.

"Sorry, everyone, for the delay. There seems to be an issue with the sound desk, and the sound engineer has to reboot the system. This is going to take about ten minutes more, I hope. To say sorry for this mishap, please accept on behalf of Jonestown a free basket of wings and ribs each."

Someone in the crowd shouts back, "How about a cold beer with those wings and ribs?"

Mike replies, "All right, all right. No need to shout! One free beer or medium glass of wine per person with the wings and ribs." He continues, "Thanks for understanding." Then he walks off stage.

Mike Sloan is Sarah-Janes cousin on her mother's side of the family. He is 5 foot 10 of average build, and has never been into sport. He is five years older than Sarah-Jane. Mike has long, straight blonde hair tied back in a ponytail. He was there for Sarah-Jane when her parents died.

His own parents moved out of town when he graduated from high school, but he decided to stay. Mike was never the greatest academically-minded person, and never went to university. He has been working at Jonestown since he finished school, first as a barman and then worked his way up to becoming one of three senior managers.

Both Patsy and Agnes look at each other. Agnes says, "I don't know about you, but if they haven't started in 20 minutes it might be best if we think about leaving, as the two of us have work in the morning."

Patsy replies, "I agree, it is going to take 45 minutes for me to get home from here. Maybe we should pre-order our taxis home, as we live in different directions."

"Good idea, Patsy. At least they will be here waiting for us, and I'm sure Sarah will understand as we have to work," replies Agnes.

"I'll go tell her that we will be leaving in 20 minutes whether or not Shines the Monkey have started playing, so can you

please organise the taxis?" says Patsy. She gets up from her seat and walks over to Sarah-Jane and Jenny. Standing in-between the two chairs, she leans over to speak to Sarah-Jane.

"Sorry to interrupt your conversation, ladies, but it's getting late, and the band haven't started yet. As Agnes and I are working tomorrow, we are organising taxis to fetch us in 20 minutes. I hope you don't mind us running out of the celebrations."

Sarah-Jane shakes her head and smiles. "Don't be silly, my love, I fully understand. Thanks again for changing weekend shifts with me, I owe you one. I'm not sure how I'm going to feel in the morning, let alone how I would have been able to work."

Patsy replies, "Anytime, my love. I know you would do the same for me. We will come and say goodbye just before we leave."

Sarah-Jane nods in agreement with Patsy before turning back to her conversation with Jenny.

When Patsy returns to her own seat, Agnes is finishing her call with the taxi company. She tells Patsy, "We have two taxis booked – one in your name and the other under my name. When they arrive, they will text me. I informed them

that we are in a loud environment, and I won't be able to hear my phone ringing so I've put my phone on vibrate and I will keep it in my hand awaiting their text."

"Good news. I'm going to get our coats in the meantime. I'd rather be ready, so that there's no need to keep the taxis waiting," replies Patsy.

Agnes nods in agreement. "Good idea. And when you get back from getting our coats, I will go to the toilet before leaving. Champagne makes me want to go to the toilet – something to do with the bubbles. Unless you need to go, too, then we might as well go together."

"Yeah, we can go together after I get back," replies Patsy then walks off towards the cloakroom.

Just then, Mike comes back on-stage and taps the microphone again for attention. "Good news, folks, the sound engineer has told me the reboot is working and we should be ready to go in another ten minutes. He needs to check that the sound desk is picking up all the instruments, so there will be a brief sound check. Please bear with us."

There are faint murmurings from the audience as people head towards the two bars to get drinks before the band starts.

At the cloakroom Patsy is talking to the assistant. "Here is the ticket for the five coats, though only two of us are leaving," she explains. Jonestown has a system where, if you are in a group, you only need one ticket. Although you can choose to get individual tickets, having a group ticket allows several people to get their coats quicker and reduces queuing time.

"No problem, I'll bring them out and you take the two you need, then I'll put the others back," replies the assistant.

While Patsy waits for their coats, David Bowie's *Space Oddity* is playing over the house sound system which is separate to the one used for live music. Patsy is tapping her left foot to the music when the assistant comes back with the coats.

"Here they are, please take the ones you need," she says.

Patsy retrieves her and Agnes's coats and thanks the girl for her help.

"Always glad to help," says the assistant. "Enjoy the rest of your evening, and safe travels. Just remember to give the ticket to one of your friends that is staying."

Back at the table, Agnes has moved up chairs and is chatting to Amanda and suddenly bursts into laughter. "Amanda,

that is one hilarious joke," she says, then looks up as Patsy approaches. "Let's go to the toilet before the taxis arrive, They should be here soon."

Turning back to Amanda, Agnes continues, "I wish we could stay longer but you know how it is, can't burn the candle at both ends."

Amanda replies, "I don't envy the two of you tomorrow. Sorry to say, I'm glad to be off this weekend."

With a smile on her face, Patsy says to Amanda jokingly, "Alright, don't rub it in."

Patsy and Agnes are walking towards the toilet when Agnes's phone vibrates in her hand; the taxis have arrived early. Agnes texts back, "Sorry, will be as quick as possible. Don't want to keep you waiting."

A reply text arrives: "Ok, we will be waiting."

They get back from the toilet, picking their coats up off the back of Patsy's chair then walk over to Sarah-Jane. Out the corner of her eye, Jenny sees the two ladies walking over and informs Sarah-Jane.

Sarah-Jane stands up to say goodbye to her two friends. "Thank you so much for coming along this evening, it

means the world to me. I love you both." She gives them a double hug.

Agnes says, "Wouldn't have missed this for anything."

Patsy adds, "Try not get up to too much mischief tonight. Get home safe." "Oh here's the ticket for the coats" handing Sarah-Jane the ticket.

Sarah-Jane replies, "Get home safe, too, both of you."

As Agnes and Patsy walk towards the front door, Mike comes back on stage to make another announcement. "Folks, we are all set. Give it up for Shines the Monkey!"

The crowd cheer and clap as the lights are dimmed and the two spotlights are focused on the stage. The volume of the cheers increases to a loud din as the members of Shines the Monkey walk on stage – first the drummer, then the guitarists and bass player, take up their positions. Lastly, the vocalist walks on stage, heading towards the microphone.

As the door closes behind Agnes and Patsy, the last thing they hear is Shines the Monkey's vocalist saying, "Very late evening, all. Sorry for the delay. Hopefully, there won't be any more mishaps tonight." The rest of what he says is lost to them as they walk towards the parking lot where their taxis are waiting.

Agnes texts her driver asking where the taxis are parked and immediately she receives a reply text, saying they are parked next to each other at the entrance to Diablo's Den.

Before climbing into their taxis, the two women hug each other. Agnes tells Patsy, "See you in the morning, hopefully not too worse for wear. Sleep well, my friend."

Patsy replies, "Yeah, hopefully neither of us feels too bad in the morning. Sleep well, too. I just hope it doesn't take too long to fall asleep when I get home."

Agnes's taxi leaves first, turning right on exiting the parking lot, with Patsy's turning left. Both ladies look out the back window and wave at each other as the distance between the cars stretches until they can no longer see each other.

Chapter 4

Inside Jonestown, Shines the Monkey's vocalist continues, "I will try to keep my talking down to a minimum as we have lost close to half an hour due to a technical fault. We unfortunately have to reduce our set as well."

Dan Meeks is 5 foot 10, with an Army-style haircut and a well-toned body. A personal trainer, he has a very down-to-earth personality and only works as a doorman at Jonestown on weekends to earn some extra money.

As the band starts playing, Dan no longer has to stand outside checking IDs. All the guests watching the band should already be inside, so he finishes putting away the metal poles and rope barriers then goes to find Mike, who is standing at the bar watching the band.

"I have packed away all the barriers," he tells Mike. "Would it be possible to get someone to watch the door? I would like to give Sarah her birthday drink."

Mike replies, "No worries, I'll do it. I can't shift anyone around; we are rammed tonight."

Dan gets two drinks from the bar – a double Woodford Reserve for Sarah-Jane and a double Southern Comfort on the rocks for himself. He tries not to drink too often as it makes him sluggish the next day, making it difficult to focus on his personal training, but as it is Sarah-Jane's birthday he has made an exception and has not booked any clients for the next two days.

When Dan gets to Sarah-Jane's tables, the ladies have now spread themselves over the two tables to keep space for either Dan or Mike to join them. He places Sarah-Jane's whiskey down in front of her.

"Here is your birthday drink, as promised. Unfortunately, I'm still working till the band finishes," he says.

Sarah-Jane replies, "Thanks for the drink. What whiskey did you get me?"

"It's Woodford Reserve." He smiles. "I know how much you like it. As soon as the band have finished, I'll come back and spend more time with you girls."

Sarah-Jane gives Dan a hug and a kiss on the cheek as a thanks for the drink, then he walks over to the front door

where Mike is checking the IDs of a group of guys who have arrived late.

"I'll take over," he tells Mike. "Thanks for covering."

"No problem, always happy to help. Got to make sure everything runs smoothly," replies Mike.

Dan takes over and checks the last three IDs in the group while Mike goes back to the bar and gets himself a soda water. He has a long night ahead and needs to keep his wits about him; it's his turn to close Jonestown tonight. Mike will have to cash out all areas, checking each till's end-of-day receipts, making sure the cash and card totals match. Mike will only leave Jonestown around half five in the morning to head home to sleep.

Shines the Monkey have played three songs already. The vocalist announces the title of their next offering. "This song is called 'Shame For My Neighbour'," and the drummer counts off one, two, three, four, tapping his drumsticks together, bringing in the bass player and lead guitar. The rhythm guitar joins in as the vocalist starts to sing. The vocalist sings the chorus, "We play at night, having fun, no serious intentions, morning comes, shame for my neighbour as I walk in the sun, smile on my face, no regrets to be had, only fun."

The crowd cheer and clap as the band finishes the song. "We've got three songs left," announces the vocalist.

"You all having fun?" he shouts out to the crowd. They roar back "YES" as they carry on clapping.

"It's been an amazing gig for us. If you want to ask any questions, buy music or merchandise, we will see you after the show," adds the vocalist.

Mike joins Sarah-Jane's table as Shines the Monkey start their third last song, sitting between her and Amanda. Earlier, the three friends had been plotting amongst themselves when Sarah-Jane and Jenny told Amanda that Jenny fancies Dan. Sarah-Jane told Amanda, "Let's see if we can bring a little happiness into the lives of our lovely sister Jenny and a friend I adore as a little brother." Amanda agreed to help in trying to get Dan and Jenny together.

Mike leans over to Amanda and says, "Have you seen the band before? It's my first time, but they are awesome."

Amanda nods her head in agreement as she replies, "Yes, this is my third time. I have seen them at a couple of other venues around town."

"Oh," replies Mike, "I'm definitely going to book them again. They pull in a crowd. I now see why Jonestown is extra busy tonight."

Shines the Monkey finish their last song just after quarter past twelve, giving them just over a 45-minute set. They

normally play for an hour or longer, depending on the crowd and whether the venue can extend their curfew for live music beyond midnight. Unfortunately, Jonestown can't extend their live music curfew longer than an extra 15 minutes, due to the extra late licence they have for Diablo's Den which covers loud music and alcohol.

Once the rest of Jonestown is closed down for the night, the entrance to the main area is locked off from Smoking Jones and a large metal gate is placed and locked in the archway, allowing the clubbers in Diablo's Den access to the toilets in Smoking Jones. Other than the tables and chairs, Smoking Jones is empty; everything gets locked in the kitchen, a metal gate is pulled down and locked, blocking the swinging doors between the kitchen and Smoking Jones. The doorman who monitors the back door to Diablo's Den then moves into Smoking Jones to make sure clubbers don't get into any fights with each other, and Smoking Jones's seating area becomes a quiet area for clubbers to sit and talk as the music is too loud to have a conversation inside Diablo's Den.

A large number of the crowd leave as soon as Shines the Monkey finish their set. Others stay, but go off to Break Your Balls, leaving 30 people in the main area – five of those people are Mike, Sarah-Jane, Amanda, Jenny, and Dan, who has now joined the group, slipping into the vacant seat between Jenny and Sarah-Jane. The rest of the people are

the staff, the members of Shines the Monkey, and some new fans buying music and merchandise.

As Sarah-Jane puts an arm over Dan's shoulder, she says, "Dan, you remember my friend Jenny from the library?" She leans into him, forcing his body to shift position until he is now facing Jenny.

"I remember Jenny. We've met before – more than once. The last time was when I bumped into you and the girls at the cinema two months ago," replies Dan as he shakes Jenny's hand. "I was going to see a new horror film called *Masked Man Madness*. It was the release of the year for horror fans. The movie is for gore hounds, a run-of-the-mill slasher film, with a high body count and loads of blood."

Dan then says to Jenny, "It's been a while. How are things with you? You are looking well. Sorry for rambling on about horror films, it's just that I'm a huge fan." He is noticing for the first time how hot Jenny is; there is something different about her this time compared to the other occasions he has met her.

Obviously, he notices how the gold and silver dress hugs her body, showing her curves off in all the right places. *But that's not it*, he thinks to himself. *There is definitely something different about Jenny tonight. There is this new energy emanating from her this evening, and I can feel it.*

The feeling Dan is getting from Jenny is more open and inviting; previously he had felt that she was friendly but more reserved. He always knew she was lively and had a sassy attitude, but Dan has never felt this type of energy from her before.

Jenny replies, "Things weren't going well for the last six months to a year. When you last saw me, it had been six months since I had broken up with my boyfriend, and the girls were taking me out to the cinema to cheer me up."

Sarah-Jane quietly gets up from her chair, leaving them to talk. *Job done*; she thinks to herself with a smile.

Mike and Amanda are talking to the vocalist of Shines the Monkey, so Sarah-Jane heads off towards Break Your Balls to see if there is a pool table available. She feels like playing. She returns to tell Jenny and Dan that there are three tables open and that she would like to play pool.

"Maybe ask Mike and Amanda if they want to play pool, as there is only half an hour before they close – enough time to get a game in, maybe two," she says. "Here is some cash. Can you please get the next round of drinks, if you don't mind? I'm going to the toilet first."

Dan replies, "Sure. Do you still want Woodford Reserve or are you changing drinks?"

"I'll stick with Woodford Reserve for now. I'll change drinks when we go to Diablo's Den," replies Sarah-Jane, as she heads towards the archway and the toilets beyond.

Dan leans over and taps Mike on the shoulder. "Sorry to interrupt, but Sarah wants to play pool when she gets back from the toilet. She asked if the two of you would like to play. What drinks do you want? She gave me cash to get the next round."

"I'd like a large dry white wine and the largest glass of water you can get me. No ice in the water, please," says Amanda, then adds, "I'd love to play pool. It's been a while."

Mike replies, "Nothing alcoholic for me, thanks. I'm closing up tonight, so have to be clear-headed, but you could bring me another soda water, please. I'm going to have to give playing pool a miss, though. Soon I have to start the cash-up for Smoking Jones, before starting the cash-ups for here and Break Your Balls."

"I don't envy you having to do the cash-ups," sympathises Dan. "Cool, I'll be back with the drinks shortly." He heads off to the bar and returns five minutes later with the drinks on a tray.

When Dan hands Jenny her vodka, lime, and soda, she replies, "Thanks, Dan, you sweetheart." He hands the drinks

to Mike and Amanda, and places Sarah-Jane's whiskey in front of her chair just as she returns from the toilet.

"Who's ready to play pool?" she says.

Jenny, Dan, and Amanda all raise a hand to signal they are going to play, but Mike stands up and heads over to where Sarah-Jane is standing. "I'm sorry, cousin, but I have to start cashing up soon," he tells her. "I'll see you before Diablo's Den closes, I hope."

"No worries," she tells him with a smile. "It was good to spend some time with you. Maybe come to the house for dinner next week when you aren't working," Sarah-Jane adds.

Mike turns to the rest of the group. "Enjoy the rest of the night. Sorry I can't join the rest of the celebrations, but I have responsibilities to take care of. Jenny, it was good to see you again; Amanda, I really enjoyed our conversation; and Sarah, yeah, let's do dinner. I'll phone you Monday to confirm. Hope to see you all later before Diablo's Den closes, if not enjoy your weekend." He heads off to his office, which is situated in the far corner of the kitchen, next to the courtyard.

Sarah-Jane picks up her whiskey, takes a sip, then thanks Dan for getting the drinks. "Right," she announces, "let's go

forth and play." She heads towards Break Your Balls, pushing the swinging doors open as she passes through, with the others following behind – Dan first, followed by Jenny and Amanda.

He holds open the one swinging door to let them pass through.

"It's very polite of you to let us through first," comments Jenny. "A lot of guys wouldn't think twice about holding a door open for a woman."

The music in Break Your Balls tends to be more rock than blues, and *November Rain* by Guns 'n' Roses is playing over the speakers. Sarah-Jane starts dancing, her eyes closed listening to the song, as she stands by an open table near the small bar. "Love this song," she says, opening her eyes to look at her friends. "Amanda and I versus the two of you," she says. "As there are four of us, we might as well play doubles. Unless you want to play singles, as there is another open table next to this one."

Dan replies, "I'm cool with that. Jenny and I versus Amanda and you."

More of the pool tables have opened up as people either head home or go off to Diablo's Den to dance the night away. Kickstart My Heart by Mötley Crüe comes on after Guns 'n' Roses.

Dan sets up the balls and Amanda breaks, sending two stripes and one solid down. She aims for a solid ball – the number five – in the top-right corner, and sinks it, then turns to number two, aiming for the middle pocket. The ball hits the edge of the pocket and bounces away.

Jenny goes next, shooting for the ten-ball, getting it close to the other middle pocket, then Sarah-Jane plays the four-ball towards the bottom-left corner, sinking it. Next, she hits the three-ball, missing the bottom-right pocket, as the nine ball is just blocking it.

Dan looks at the layout of the table before taking his shot. He shoots for the nine-ball, sinking it. One by one the balls fall, leaving only the three-ball and the black.

It is Sarah-Jane's turn to play. Bending her knees until her chin is on the pool cue, her eyes level with the table, she aims for the top-right pocket and sinks the three-ball, lining up the cue ball just behind the black.

"No pressure!" shouts Jenny, hoping to break Sarah-Jane's concentration.

She takes the shot, sinking the black ball in the middle-left pocket, then looks triumphantly up at Jenny. "Suck it, you're shit out of luck."

As they finish the game of pool, it is ten past one. The staff have been kind enough to wait for them to finish playing. This is only because it was Dan and Mike's cousin, Sarah-Jane; any other customer would have been told to finish before one.

The group of four head off towards Diablo's Den, leaving the staff to collect any remaining glasses, place protective covers over the tables, sweep and mop the floor, before switching off the lights to Break Your Balls. Another staff member is checking the smoking area, collecting empty glasses and ashtrays, dumping the cigarette butts in the trash bag she is carrying.

The friends decide to go to the toilet before heading into Diablo's Den. Once in the women's toilets, Amanda asks Jenny, "How are thing going with Dan? You two seemed close when we were playing pool, hanging on each other."

Jenny replies, "Dan is great, and we have some things in common. He loves his horror films, and you know I don't mind horror but it's not my go-to genre. Let's see where this goes."

Sarah-Jane adds, "The two of you look good together. I hope things work out for you both. Just don't rush too quickly into things; keep it light and fun to start."

Jenny nods in agreement. "A little fun never hurts anybody. It's been eight months since my relationship to Shaun ended. It would be nice to be with someone, feeling cared for again, but I don't want to feel suffocated either. Dan told me he hasn't had a girlfriend in five years – too busy getting his personal trainer qualification. But he also said he believes there is someone for everyone in the world. Maybe I'm the person for him."

Dan is waiting at one of the tables in Smoking Jones when the three women come out the toilets laughing at something Amanda has said.

He stands up. "We all ready for Diablo's Den?"

Jenny replies, "I'm ready for anything," and makes a growling noise at Dan.

The four head to the hallway at the back of Smoking Jones, passing two women deep in conversation. Sarah-Jane can only make out a bit of what the women are saying, as the music level increases the closer they get to the door. She hears something to do with one of the women's mother having gone for her first cancer treatment, having only been diagnosed the week before. The woman mentions that the cancer is quite aggressive and wishes they had caught it earlier, while the other woman is trying to be supportive in consoling her friend.

As they enter Diablo's Den, it takes a moment for their eyes to adjust to the change in light, from the well-lit hallway to the almost lack of light inside Diablos' Den. There must be around 100 people on the dance floor, dancing to Guns 'n' Roses' *Paradise City*. Sarah-Jane sees a sea of black in front of her. She feels a little over-dressed for Diablo's Den but doesn't really care.

Dan leans in towards Jenny to talk, as the music is too loud to hold a normal conversation. "I'm quickly going to the DJ booth to say hi to my friend Mitch, who is DJing tonight," he tells her. "I'll meet the three of you at the bar shortly."

Jenny nods. "Ok, I'll let Amanda and Sarah know."

As he walks away to the DJ booth, Jenny leans towards Amanda and Sarah-Jane, her head between theirs, and explains, "Dan's quickly going to say hi to his friend Mitch who's DJing, but he will meet us at the bar shortly." Both women nod in reply and all three head off towards the bar.

Diablos' Den hosts a variety of themed evenings, catering to all types of music lovers. On Mondays they have R 'n' B and Hip Hop; Wednesday is Jazz and Soul; Fridays is Blues and Classic Rock; Saturday is a mix from Rock, Goth, Heavy Metal, and Industrial dance music; Sunday is the wide spectrum of electronic music, from Techno, Drum 'n' Bass, Trance, and Psychedelic Trance. On Tuesdays and Thursdays

Diablo's Den is closed to give staff days off. Working in the night-time industries allows little time to yourself, so the staff of Jonestown on a whole are looked after, and in return are extremely loyal.

It's 20 past one and Diablo's Den is still full; they are now operating a one out, one in policy. If you are going to smoke, they will let you back in, but if you leave and want to come back, you will have to wait in the queue to get in.

Mitch Davidson has been friends with Dan since primary school. Sarah-Jane knows him quite well, as he was often at Susie and Dan's house when they were growing up. She never really hung out with him, as he and Dan were younger than Susie and Sarah-Jane, and had different interests. He has long hair past his shoulders, and is dressed all in black – the typical style of dress for a heavy metal fan.

Mitch isn't the athletic type, despite Dan trying to get his friend into the gym for years. Towering at six foot one, Mitch has never felt the need to exercise much. In high school they wanted him to join the basketball team, due to his height, but he turned it down in favour of music appreciation, learning the drums and guitar instead.

"Hey, Mitch!" Dan leans as close as possible to his friend's right ear. "What's been happening, dude? Haven't seen you

in three weeks. Thought something must have happened to you, I was starting to get worried. You never returned any of my calls or texts."

"Sorry, man, things have been hectic the past three weeks. Been out of town, had some DJ gigs and my phone died. Stupid me; I go and leave the charger at home. Halfway through this trip, my car gets broken into and they steal some clothes, money, and my phone. On the way home, my car breaks down and had to be towed," grumbles Mitch.

"Dude, that sucks big time. I hope the car doesn't cost too much to fix. Have the police been able to identify any suspects? Were any fingerprints taken?" Dan replies.

Mitch nods. "The police aren't very hopeful that they will catch anyone. There were two viable prints, but the rest they found were either smudged or mine.

Dan points towards the bar. "I can't stay long. You remember Susie's friend, Sarah-Jane? She is celebrating her birthday, and I'm with her and two of her friends. The one in the gold and silver dress, her name is Jenny – I quite fancy her. Who knows? It could turn into something great or just good friends, let's see. The other one is called Amanda."

Mitch looks over at the bar, seeing the three women. "Dude, I'm so glad for you, you deserve some good in your life," he

replies. "If I get a chance, I'll come and say hi. I have to play till two and then Steve is taking over for the last hour."

"Cool, maybe see you in 40 minutes," says Dan, then he heads towards the bar.

While Dan has been talking to Mitch, the three women are waiting at the bar to be served. Finally, a cute surfer-type barman takes their order. "Hi ladies, what can I get you this evening?" he asks in a raised voice.

Surprisingly, they can hear him perfectly – due to there being no speakers behind the bar. It is the only place inside Diablo's Den that you can be heard without screaming.

"Can we have four gold tequilas, a large dry white wine, two margaritas, and a double Southern Comfort on the rocks, please?" Sarah-Jane says to the barman.

"No problem, I'll get that for you. Shouldn't be more than five minutes," he says. He comes back with the white wine, double Southern Comfort, and the four gold tequilas. "Here you go. Just got to make the two margaritas." He picks up the cocktail shaker, pours in the ingredients over crushed ice, then shacks it up. Before pouring, he salts the rims of two margarita glasses, then slowly pours in the liquid and places them in front of Sarah-Jane. "Ok, that will be 40 for the drinks."

Sarah-Jane hands him some cash. "The rest is for you" she says.

He counts out 80 and looks up in surprise. "Are you sure? That's a lot of money," he says.

"I'm sure," replies Sarah-Jane with a smile.

"Thanks, it is much appreciated. My name is Tim. If there is anything else you need, just let me know."

"Hi Tim, what I need is your phone number," says Amanda, winking at the barman.

"Sorry, ladies, I'm off the market. Getting married next week."

Amanda replies, "What a shame. Your fiancée is a lucky woman."

"No, I'm the lucky man," he replies. "I found the woman of my dreams, my best friend and soulmate."

As Dan gets to the bar, Jenny hands him his Southern Comfort. "Thanks," he says, giving her a kiss on the cheek.

Amanda asks, "Why can we hear each other over here but nowhere else?"

"That is because there are no speakers behind the bar, and also the speakers above us are pointing towards the dance floor, kind of creating a barrier around the bar. It's weird, I know, but that's how it is. The music is still loud, but soft enough not to have to shout," explains Dan.

Sarah-Jane shouts out, "SHOTS!" She hands one to Amanda, then Jenny, and finally Dan, before taking hers in hand. "To life. May it be long and filled with love and adventures," she says, as they clink the four glasses together.

The others reply, "Cheers. To life."

Dan says, "Should we grab our table? Mike said he would reserve one for us."

They didn't see when they entered Diablo's Den, due to the light levels, but the table that Mike has reserved for them is the second last table before the door they came through. On the table was a plastic sign with the word "Reserved For" engraved into the plastic, and Sarah-Jane written in a non-permanent black marker pen.

The long black couch is divided into sections, each one with an armrest on either side, giving the impression that they are individual couches. Each section can fit three people comfortably, four at a squeeze. The other side of every

table has two round stools that can fit underneath when they aren't occupied.

Dan sits in one corner of the couch with Jenny next to him, Sarah-Jane in the other corner. Amanda sits on one of the stools; opposite Dan is the other empty stool. They are enjoying the music. Led Zeppelin's *Dazed and Confused* starts playing when they sit down. The group of four are resigned to the fact that they can't actually have a conversation, so they take large sips of their drinks. This is a ploy of many bars and nightclubs, who want you to spend less time talking and more time drinking, so spending more money at the bar. With the music being loud, all you can do is drink or dance if you can't talk.

Mama I'm Coming Home by Ozzy Osbourne comes on and Dan asks Jenny if she would like to dance. She nods and they get up and walk onto the dance floor. It isn't very fast for a rock song, so they slow dance to it in a hug. Jenny's head comes up to the bottom of Dan's chest, with his arms wrapped around her shoulders.

Sarah-Jane leans over to Amanda. "They look so cute together. Jenny looks so short compared to Dan."

Amanda replies, "It's so nice to see people happy." She takes a large sip of her wine and turns around to look at the couple dancing. The song ends and they come back to

the table. Mike and Sarah-Jane are talking to each other, and Amanda has almost finished her glass of wine.

She gets up and says to Jenny and Dan in a loud shout, "Do you want anything from the bar? I'm going. Mike said he has told Tim not to charge us for the rest of the night."

Dan says he would like two double Southern Comforts, in that case, but to put them in one large glass and fill it up with ice.

Jenny says, "Maybe we should get another bottle of champagne."

Amanda agrees and goes to the bar. Jenny sits down, and Dan goes to speak to Mike. "Just want to say thanks," he tells his boss. "That's really kind of you for the free drinks."

Mike replies, "My pleasure. Jonestown was really busy tonight. As manager, I can give some free drinks away." He smiles. "Just don't go completely mad."

Sarah-Jane adds, "Don't worry, cousin. It is almost home time and I'm already feeling the worse for wear. I'm definitely going to have a bad hangover tomorrow."

"That's why I try to stick to the same drink throughout the night. You have all been mixing your drinks," replies Dan.

Mike tells Dan, "Make sure Sarah gets into a taxi home. Actually, make sure the three of them get the same taxi home, as they all live in the same direction."

"No problem," replies Dan and goes back to sit next to Jenny, leaving Mike and Sarah-Jane to continue talking.

Amanda has returned from the bar with an ice bucket and a champagne bottle in one hand, and four champagne glasses in the other. She leans over to Dan and says in a loud voice, "I got you a glass just in case you want some champagne. Would you mind getting the rest of the drinks, as I can't carry them?"

Dan replies, "No worries, I'll get them." As he gets up, he gives Jenny a long kiss on the lips, feeling a warm tingling sensation in his crotch. He heads to the bar and picks up a tray filled with drinks then returns and hands out the glasses: Mike has soda water, Jenny and Sarah-Jane are each having another margarita, while Amanda is sticking with the champagne instead of having another large wine. There is also a large jug of water and a stack of four empty glasses, plus another four gold tequilas.

Mike thanks Dan, then tells Sarah-Jane, "I'm glad you are enjoying your birthday. I will call you at the beginning of the week and make plans for that dinner, but I have to go now. I've got to continue the cash-up." He gives her a

hug and kiss and says goodnight to everyone else before he leaves.

Dan looks at his watch; it is almost half two. He says to Jenny, "I'm going to the toilet and then I'll call a taxi for the three of you. Mike wants me to make sure you all leave together."

"Wait, I'll come with you," says Jenny. She leans over to Sarah-Jane and says, "We are going to the toilet, then Dan is going to organise a taxi for us."

"Ok, see you in a bit," replies Sarah-Jane.

They head to the toilets in Smoking Jones, blinking their eyes to adjust to the bright light of the hallway as they exit Diablo's Den. Dan is walking ahead of Jenny, holding her hand, when suddenly she yanks his arm. Dan stops and turns to face her. Jenny stands on her tiptoes, pulling Dan towards her and they share an open-mouth kiss, pulling each other closer, both feeling a warm, tingling rush through their bodies.

Jenny says to him, "You don't know how badly I want you to come home with me. I want to fuck your brains out."

Dan replies, "I would love to sleep with you, but we both know that if we want this to be more than a one-night stand, we should wait."

"I know," says Jenny, hugging him. "It's been such a long time since I last got laid, but you're right. There will be more than enough time for shenanigans."

They walk hand-in-hand towards the toilets. When Jenny comes back out, Dan has just finished talking to the taxi company. He tells her, "The taxi should be here in 15 minutes. Let's go tell the others."

Once back at the table, Jenny sees that Amanda and Sarah-Jane have got themselves ready to leave. Amanda has drunk half the bottle of champagne while they were away, so she and Sarah-Jane go to the toilet while Dan and Jenny finish their drinks. When they return, all four make their way to the front door to wait for the taxi in the parking lot. There is a light, low-hanging fog so all they can see is each other.

The taxi pulls up in front of Diablo's Den and Dan escorts them to the car. He gives Amanda and Sarah-Jane a hug goodnight, then kisses Jenny and says quietly, "I'll phone you in the afternoon. Guess we all need a long sleep."

Jenny replies, "Ok, hear from you then." She smiles, then whispers in his ear, "Still wish you were coming home with me," before climbing in the back.

Sarah-Jane lives the closest to Jonestown; she is only ten minutes away. Dan watches as the taxi drives off, Jenny

waving to him through the back window, and he waves back. He decides to walk home from Jonestown, as he feels the cold air will help him to sober up a bit. It will take 15 minutes to get back to the warmth of his apartment, unless he stops off to get some drunk-hungry food, which tends to be very unhealthy but ever so delicious. While he is walking, he thinks to himself, *I will have to work harder in the gym if I do get something to eat*. He is still in two minds whether or not to get food.

Chapter 5

Late the next morning, Sarah-Jane awakes with a really bad hangover, making her feel like her head is three times the size, a heavy pounding in her forehead. She remembers getting home, saying goodbye to Amanda and Jenny, walking up the path from the front gate, then nothing else. She wonders what carnage she caused when she got home, as she looks at the trail of clothes on the floor. Leading from the door to the bed, there is a long line starting with her shoes, dinner jacket, dress, and then the matching bra and panties.

Sarah-Jane lifts the duvet to find she is completely naked. *I must have been too drunk to even get my pyjamas on*, she thinks to herself, then realises she has actually said it out loud. Getting out of bed, she puts on her dressing gown and slippers.

Her mouth feels dry like sandpaper, so Sarah-Jane walks to the bathroom and brushes her teeth to get that stale taste out of her mouth. While brushing, more of what happened

last night when she got home starts to come back to her. She lets out a little burp, tasting tuna in the back of her throat. *That must have been what I ate last night*, she thinks to herself, realising she forgot to brush her teeth before bed. No wonder her mouth feels gross this morning.

Sarah-Jane opens one of the cabinets to get some headache tablets, and takes two from the box. They are in a liquid form, covered by a gelatine casing, which she prefers to the solid tablets, as they seem to be more fast acting. She cups her one hand to collect some water to swallow the tablets with, then does it again to ensure there is enough water for the tablets to go down.

She goes over to the shower, turns on the mixer tap and adjusts the temperature. Hanging up her dressing gown, Sarah-Jane climbs into the hot shower and lets the water soothe her. Leaning forward, she tilts her head under the flowing water, blowing out to make gargling noises. She stands there motionless, really feeling the pounding in her head and the stiffness in her shoulders. After a while, she picks up her shampoo bottle and looks at it through blurry eyes. *Not today,* she thinks. *I don't care if my hair is a mess, I'm not going anywhere*. Sarah-Jane replaces the bottle, picking up the soap instead, then soaps and rinses herself.

Climbing out the shower, she stands on the mat, towelling herself off in a lacklustre manner using what little energy

she can muster. She leans forward and hangs her hair down, then towels it as dry as she can before wrapping it up in the towel on her head. The pounding in her head is so heavy that she decides to lie down on the bed. She sits on the edge, her feet touching the floor, then leans back and closes her eyes.

Why do I do this to myself whenever I go out? I never learn. Dan is right: don't mix drinks. I think the saying is 'don't mix grain and grape', she thinks to herself. After what seems like ages, she opens her eyes and slowly sits up. Then, with a heavy sigh, she walks to the wardrobe and takes out underwear and comfy clothes – a plain grey t-shirt, black sweatpants, and a black woollen jumper. As the laundry she did yesterday is still in the tumble dryer, she doesn't have any matching socks. A quick rummage through the drawer produces two that could resemble a pair – the left sock a charcoal shade; the right one black.

She throws her dressing gown at the stool by the dressing table, but doesn't have much energy in her effort so it lands on the floor. Putting on her underwear, socks, and the rest of her clothes, all she can think about is the dark liquid medicine she is craving – some call it the nectar of the gods: coffee. Her slippers are the last thing Sarah-Jane puts on then heads downstairs to make coffee before tackling the mess she knows she left in the kitchen after craving toasted tuna mayonnaise sandwiches to quell the hunger she felt

when she got home. She knows that drunk eating so late at night isn't healthy for you, but in her mind Sarah-Jane justified it by convincing herself that it was healthier than takeaway fast food, which tends to be extremely tasty when your drunk but ever so greasy.

She gets to the top of the stairs and realises she has left her phone on the bedside table last night. She didn't even bother setting an alarm with it being her weekend off. Sarah-Jane picks up her phone, pushes the power button to see what time it is, and the phone reflects back 12:20pm. Placing her finger on the fingerprint scanner, her phone jumps to life, and she can see some notification badges on the status bar at the top of the phone. Sarah-Jane swipes her thumb downwards opening up the status bar.

There are a couple of notifications from her different social media apps, and a text message from Agnes. As she walks back to the staircase, she reads the text from Agnes: *"Hope you got home safely, thanks again for a great evening. Giorgio's was superb as usual. Hope you're not too badly hungover."*

Sarah-Jane decides coffee first, then breakfast and tidy up afterwards – no need to clean up twice, she doesn't have the energy or willpower to clean more than once. As she nears the downstairs hallway, she hears the post being dropped in the wooden post-box outside, but decides to collect it on the way back to her room later.

What awaits Sarah-Jane in the kitchen isn't the worst mess she has seen. In the past, when her parents were away, she has woken up to some disasters. Once, the kitchen looked like a bomb had gone off with pasta on the floor, tomato sauce dripping down the tiles, and an overturned pot dripping sauce all over the stove. Coffee granules and white sugar had been spread over the island away from the sink, as if it was the aftermath of an exploding volcano.

This time, however, she had almost succeeded in leaving a tidy kitchen, other than the can in the sink, sitting in a grey bowl on top of a small black side plate. Next to the bowl is a teaspoon and a butter knife. Sarah-Jane shouts out, "THANK FUCK!" before placing a hand over her forehead and grimacing. "Well, that was stupid," she continues in a much lower volume, trying not to aggravate her hangover any further.

She walks over to the island, opens a cupboard underneath, and takes out a coffee mug and a large plate. Placing them on the counter surface, she gets out the coffee and sugar, before placing them next to the mug, Sarah-Jane then opens a drawer and finds a knife and fork, plus a clean teaspoon. Behind the island, either side of the stove, are two custom-made, under-the-counter fridges, with a cabinet housing pots and pans in-between.

Sarah-Jane takes the milk, eggs, and sweet milk cheese from one fridge, then bacon, sausages, and mushrooms

from the second one. One fridge has a freezer section and the other has a vegetable drawer. The two chest freezers in the basement were emptied and switched off after her parents died. She's been meaning to get rid of them for a while now but keeps putting it off, just like clearing out her childhood bedroom and all the boxes in the basement.

The last ingredients Sarah-Jane needs to complete her fry-up are bread, tomatoes, and baked beans. The cupboards under the counter backing onto the dining room are where the canned foods are kept, and the bread box is on top of the counter. Next to the bread box is a long trough-like basket, divided into sections for fruits and vegetables that don't need to be kept in the fridge.

Sarah-Jane isn't bothered with expensive coffee blends; to her, there are some very good instant coffees out there that are close in taste to some of the more expensive connoisseur brands. She fills the kettle with fresh water and switches it on, then puts the coffee in the mug, adds the milk and stirs them together before adding the sugar while waiting for the kettle to boil. She gets a pan from the cupboard below the stove, placing it on one of the heating rings. When the kettle boils, she pours the hot water into the mug, stirs once more, then places the teaspoon in the sink.

Getting out a cutting board, she slices a tomato in half for frying with the bacon, sausage, eggs, and the two medium,

flatbed mushrooms. Before taking a sip of her coffee, she blows over the top of the mug to cool it a bit, then she takes a sip and sighs with a look of complete satisfaction on her face. Sarah-Jane cooks two rashers of bacon, one sausage, two eggs, one half of the tomato, and the two mushrooms. Realising she hasn't made any toast, she decides she is too hungry and can't wait, so picks up her knife and fork in one hand with the coffee mug, her fry-up plate in the other, and heads to the dining room table to eat her breakfast.

Once Sarah-Jane has eaten half her food and drunk almost all her coffee, she starts feeling a bit more human. She has been scrolling through social media on her phone while eating, not really concentrating on what she is reading. Finishing her food, she takes the last sip of her coffee, and texts Agnes back. *"Hi Aggie, just finished breakfast. Got home safely. I'm dying here, got such a bad hangover. Just going to lie in front of the tv, watch a film, and will try to have a nap later. Have a fabulous weekend when you finish work."* She then gets up to do the dishes and clean the kitchen.

When everything is tidied up, Sarah-Jane heads towards the lounge, collecting the post and her purse, which is sitting on the thin long table in the entrance hall. She is forced to shield her eyes as she enters the lounge, having not closed the curtains before leaving for Giorgio's the night before. This is one of those rare times Sarah-Jane would prefer not for the sun to be so bright.

She turns on and dims the lights before closing the curtains, props up one end of the couch with pillows, then sinks down on the couch and covers herself with the thick cream fleece blanket which hangs over the armrest. Scrolling through an app on her phone, she selects *Close Encounters of a Third Kind* – one of the digital copies in her online film collection. While she was growing up, Sarah-Jane watched this film between 50 and 100 times. It is one of those movies that gave Sarah-Jane her love of science fiction. Having seen the film so many times before is the exact reason she has chosen it now, as she knows that she will probably fall asleep, and can easily drift in and out of the film without having to concentrate.

Sarah-Jane thinks how lovely it is to have such wonderful technology, having been born in a time before the internet, online shopping, and being able to video call anyone anywhere in the world. She loves the ability to stream films and tv programmes on her television, as well as being able to cast content from her phone to the television.

Picking up the post, she looks through it. Even though it has been a year-and-a-half since her parents died, she is still receiving mail for them, and there are also a few bills amongst the bundle. She drops the letters on the carpet, picks up her purse, and takes out the birthday card she received from her friends at Giorgio's.

She had folded it up to fit it in her purse, and now unfolds it to read the lovely messages again that they had written for her. The emotional comments bring tears to her eyes. Inside the card is a piece of paper with the username and password she needs to login to her profile for We Play. She enters the URL into the open webpage on her phone.

As she waits for the page to load, Sarah-Jane thinks to herself, *What cheeky sods they are for doing this, but they only have my best interests at heart, and this comes from a place of love.* She logs into her profile and sees the photo they have used for her profile is from last Christmas's work party, with her dressed in her novelty Christmas jumper and fake reindeer horns on her head. She reads through her profile, looking at all the information they have written about her. *They are spot on!* she thinks. *They really do know me better than I know myself.*

What they didn't tell her last night was that her profile has been active for two weeks already, and it looks as though she is quite popular; in that short time she has attracted 100 winks, 58 likes, and 75 gifts. She goes to the messages section and is overwhelmed to find that she has a total of 153 messages from both guys and girls! There is no way she can concentrate at the moment with her hangover, so Sarah-Jane decides to leave reading the messages for later when she feels she can focus her attention properly on reading them. The film has been on for 20 minutes when

she puts down her phone, turns on her side to watch the tv half-heartedly, and eventually drifts off to sleep.

At five o'clock Sarah-Jane is roused from her sleep. The tv switched itself off when the film finished, due to being inactive for so long. She is feeling a lot better, and her headache has gone, though she still feels dehydrated from last night's drinking and her stomach is making grumbling sounds. *Coffee probably wasn't the right thing to drink this morning,* she thinks. *I should have drunk water instead. It would have helped me get over the hangover a lot faster, but coffee is so good!!!*

Throwing the fleece blanket over the back of the couch, Sarah-Jane gets off the couch, and bends down to pick up the post and her purse. Needing to pee, she heads for the guest toilet, leaving the post, her phone, and purse back on the long thin table before entering the toilet. *Knowing my luck, I would drop my phone in the toilet,* she thinks. When she is finished in the toilet, Sarah-Jane goes to the kitchen and turns on the lights. The sun at this time of year sets earlier and earlier as the days pass by, leaving less and less natural light.

She opens a cupboard under the sink and gets out a filter for the water jug; she didn't have the energy this morning to replace it. She replaces the filter, fills it up with water, then gets a glass from another cupboard under the island.

She knows she will have to throw out the first two batches of water and refill the jug a third time before the water is ready to drink. In the meantime, she decides to make a sandwich as she is hungry and can't be bothered to cook. She can order a takeaway later, as it is Saturday and she can lounge around.

Getting a butter knife and a sharp cutting knife from the drawer and the bread board from a cupboard, she places them on the counter, then gets out the butter, cheddar cheese, mustard, and mayonnaise from one fridge, then some ham slices, cucumber, spinach, and red pepper from the other one. Before she makes her sandwich, Sarah-Jane fills the water jug again, hoping it will have finished filtering by the time she has finished making her sandwich. Taking four slices from the bag, she places the bread on the board – two next to each other, and two below them. First, she butters all four slices, then adds some mayonnaise to two slices and mustard to the other two.

Realising she needs the board to cut the cucumber, red pepper, and tomato, Sarah-Jane gets a large plate and places the bread on it. Wiping the crumbs off the board to avoid them sticking to the vegetables, she first slices the cucumber, cutting six rounds and placing them in the top left corner of the board, then cuts and deseeds the red pepper and slices it into thin strips, placing them in the opposite top corner. Sarah-Jane slices four medium-thick

pieces of tomato last, as it creates a lot of juice from the seeds.

She places the spinach on the two slices of bread that have mustard, next she puts the pre-sliced cheddar over the spinach. On top of the cheese, Sarah-Jane places two pieces of ham per sandwich, folding them in half to cover the cheese end to end, not spilling over the edge of the bread. The cucumber is next, followed by the red pepper, and finally the tomato slices. She sprinkles some salt and black ground pepper over the tomatoes before placing the other slices of bread on top, closing the two sandwiches.

She pours herself a glass of water and takes it, along with the filter jug, to the table in the dining room then comes back for her sandwiches. Sarah-Jane gets herself two napkins before taking her food to the table.

Sitting down to eat, she looks at her phone and sees a message from Mike. Reading it, she takes a bite from her sandwich, and almost immediately as the food reaches her stomach the rumbling stops. The text says: *"I know I said I was going to phone you Monday, but just got my shifts for next week. I can come on Wednesday to you for dinner, is that ok with you?"*

Sarah-Jane has eaten half the first sandwich, but puts it down briefly to reply to Mike's text. *"Wednesday evening is*

fine. We can get pizza, have some drinks, and talk. Haven't been able to spend time with my favourite cousin recently," she replies to his text.

She has finished the second sandwich by the time Mike answers her text: *"Yeah, it has been mad at Jonestown since our competition down the road closed. People need a place to go out."*

"I understand," she texts back, *"sometimes life get busy and before you know it three months have passed."* She takes the empty plate and glass in one hand and the jug in the other, leaving her phone on the table, and goes to the kitchen to rinse the plate then place both items in the dishwasher.

Picking up her phone, she walks to the lounge to turn off the lights before picking up her purse, deciding she will deal with the post tomorrow when she is completely clear-headed. She heads upstairs to her room. It's now half-six and pitch-black outside. Sarah-Jane thinks to herself, *I'll have a shower, sit on the bed with my laptop, and order some takeaway. I can look at some of those messages on We Play while I wait for my food.*

Sarah-Jane has changed into her pyjamas after her shower, so can happily lounge around for the rest of the evening before bedtime. She sits on the bed, wrapping herself

within the caramel blanket like being inside a cocoon. The nights are starting to get colder, but it's not yet cold enough to put the heating on. Sarah-Jane has put on a pair of thick, warm hiking socks to stop her feet becoming cold. She used to go hiking with her parents when they were home from archaeological digs, giving seminars, or lecturing around the world. Since they died, she hasn't been hiking, so now the only use the socks get is keeping her warm in the colder months. They haven't seen the inside of a boot in two years.

Turning on her laptop, waiting for the system to boot up, Sarah-Jane brushes her hair to get the knots out. "I need a haircut; I'm starting to get split ends. I'll phone tomorrow and see if I can get an appointment for next week or for as soon possible," she mutters to herself.

Finally, the laptop has booted up and is ready to use. Sarah-Jane opens a webpage. *What do I feel like eating?* she wonders. *Should it be pizza or curry; maybe a burger and fries, or even Chinese would be good. What's best for a hangover? What comfort food do I crave?* She decides on ordering Chinese food, so searches for the nearest Chinese restaurant to her home and clicks on the "Lotus Flower" website. Scrolling through their menu, Sarah-Jane adds to her online basket a quarter crispy aromatic duck, which comes with six small pancakes, thin strips of spring onion and cucumber, and a small tub of plum sauce. Feeling ravenous,

as her body is craving lot of calories, she also orders the house special chow mein, which has prawns, beef, pork, and chicken plus loads of vegetables mixed in with the Chinese noodles. For dessert, she orders two bowties – sweet pastries shaped like bowties, covered in a runny golden syrup.

Sarah-Jane goes through the payment process and receives a confirmation that her payment has been taken and her order will be with her in 45 minutes. She opens her email app on the laptop and finds the receipt from Lotus Flower in her Junk folder. Sarah-Jane sends the email to her inbox to keep it as a reference in case anything is wrong with her order.

Closing her email app, Sarah-Jane goes back to the webpage, putting in the address bar www.weplay.com and clicks Enter. We Play's webpage loads, and she enters her details, saving them to the laptop for easier logins in the future. Sarah-Jane clicks on the message icon, the page loads. She is utterly shocked; her inbox is now close to 400 messages. "There is no way I am going to be able to read all these messages," she grumbles. "I will have to work out a system to whittle down the messages." She decides the only way to choose who she will contact is based on the message title and the opening paragraph of each message. There seem to be a lot of messages titled with either "Let's Fuck" or "Do You Want to Play?", but there are the occasional ones that aren't so forthright.

After 15 minutes she has only gone through 50 messages. None of them pique her interest, the vast majority being just too vulgar for her, so they have been deleted. The messages from the females on the site seem the most forthright and vulgar, but Sarah-Jane has never been with a woman before. She has only slept with three people: the first broke her virginity; the second was a guy she fancied in high school; and Connor was the third. Sarah-Jane wonders if she should maybe try being with a woman. She might be missing out; it could be the experience of her life. She decides she will be open-minded if the right woman comes along.

Sarah-Jane decides she is going to wait downstairs for her food and will eat it in the dining room, so she gets up from her bed, taking her laptop and phone with her as she heads downstairs. As the hallway lights are still on, she turns off her bedroom light and walks towards the stairs. As she does, her phone vibrates with a text from the delivery driver to say they are five minutes away. Sarah-Jane leaves her laptop on the dining room table and goes to the kitchen to get a plate and a set of chopsticks, which she places the on the table in front of her laptop. She goes back to the kitchen to get a glass and the rest of the bottle of wine she was drinking yesterday before going to Giorgio's.

There is a knock at the front door. Sarah-Jane places the bottle of wine and her glass on the table as she passes on

her way to answer the door and collect her food. Opening the front door, she is greeted by the delivery driver. "Here is your order. Hope you enjoy your dinner."

Sarah-Jane replies, "Thanks so much. Here is a tip for you." She hands the driver a couple of notes.

"Are you sure you want to tip me so much? That's a lot for a tip," replies the driver.

She nods her head. "Life is short, and you can't take it with you," she says.

With a smile, the delivery driver says, "Not everyone is as generous as you. My name is Samantha, but people call me Sam."

"Hi Sam, nice to meet you. My name is Sarah-Jane but please call me Sarah. Maybe you will deliver here one day again."

They chat a little before saying goodbye. Sarah-Jane watches Sam walk down the path to the front gate, closing the gate behind her as she walks to her car. Closing the door behind her, she thinks to herself, *What a lovely person.* Sam is 5 foot 6 inches, with curly brown hair to her waist and a slender, well-toned build from being a dancer. During their conversation, Sam explained she has only been in town a

couple of months and doesn't really know many people. She moved there to pursue an acting career, studying under the famous Von Burgan Institute of acting and dance. Sarah-Jane told Sam that she should keep in touch; having grown up in the area, she would make the perfect tour guide. Sam agreed to keep in contact, but she has a busy schedule at the moment with classes during the day and being a delivery driver in the evenings, so it doesn't leave much time for a social life. However, she explained, the end of her first semester is in a couple of weeks and then she will be free.

Sarah-Jane walks to the dining room, laying the bag of food on the table next to her plate. Sitting down, she takes out the different containers of food then opens the bottle of wine, pouring herself a large glass. She tears open the foil bag to expose the pancakes, the steam rising off them. Ripping open the other foil bag, she can see the duck. Using the chopsticks in her left hand, and holding the duck quarter by the protruding leg bone, she shreds the crispy aromatic duck. Sarah-Jane then opens the small tub of plum sauce followed by one of the large plastic containers with the spring onion and cucumber strips. She leaves the two remaining containers closed.

Placing a small pancake on her plate, Sarah-Jane pours some of the plum sauce on the pancake, then uses the chopsticks to pick up some of the cucumber and spring

onion strips to smear plum sauce around the pancake, before picking up the duck and placing it next to the sauce-covered strips of vegetables. Rolling the pancake with her right middle and index fingers, she picks it up and takes her first bite, a look of contentment on her face as she lets out a sigh of joy. In-between each pancake Sarah-Jane swigs some of her wine. She repeats this ritual until all that is left is some duck and plum sauce. Taking some of the remaining duck with her chopsticks, Sarah-Jane dips it into the plum sauce before putting the meat in her mouth. Chewing slowly so she can savour the flavour, she continues until there is no more duck.

Sarah-Jane opens one of the remaining thick foil containers which is shaped in a rectangle and closed with a white cardboard lid. Inside is her chow mein, the steam rising out of the container. Using her chopsticks, she empties out half of the contents onto her plate. "I think I'll leave half the chow mein for tomorrow. That is breakfast taken care of," she says to herself. Before taking the first mouthful of her chow mein, she sighs, "I was hungry, but my eyes were obviously bigger than my appetite. I will have one bowtie and leave the other for tomorrow as well."

Chewing her chow mein, the first thing she can distinguish is the prawn and mixed vegetables with some of the fried noodles. Taking a large swig of wine, Sarah-Jane empties her glass. Refilling the glass before eating more of her chow

mein, Sarah-Jane looks at her laptop still open on her profile page and decides that she will look at it when she gets into bed. Putting the laptop into sleep mode, she closes the lid and carries on eating. After eating the rest of the chow mein, Sarah-Jane places her chopsticks on the plate.

Picking up the last container with the bowties inside, she removes the plastic lid, realising she is going to need a side plate and dessert fork. Sarah-Jane rises from her chair and walks to the kitchen to retrieve the items she needs, along with a glass and the water jug, before heading back to the table and the delicious dessert awaiting her. Pouring herself a glass of water as she sits down, Sarah-Jane picks up the container with the bowties with her right hand and, using the dessert fork in her left hand, transfers one of the bowties onto the side plate. Tilting the container and holding the other bowtie in place with the desert fork, Sarah-Jane drizzles some of the golden syrup over her bowtie, making sure to leave enough of the syrup for tomorrow. She places the container back on the table before sliding her dessert fork through the crispy fried pastry, piercing the broken-off corner of the bowtie with the fork prongs.

Sarah-Jane twirls the pastry in the syrup before taking her first bite. The crunchiness of the pastry mixed with the sweet golden syrup sends shivers of delight up her spine,

triggering happy signals through her brain. Sarah-Jane slumps back in her chair with a warm cuddly feeling in her body and smiling from ear to ear. Sarah-Jane repeats this ritual again and again until the bowtie is gone, then uses her left index finger to mop up the last of the syrup and bowtie crumbs, sucking them off her finger. Placing the side plate and dessert fork on her plate with the chopsticks, she collects all the food packaging and takes it to the kitchen. She rinses off the plates, dessert fork, and chopsticks and places them in the dishwasher, then throws away the torn foil bags from the duck and pancakes.

Sarah-Jane puts the other half of her chow mein in a bowl with clingfilm over the top. She puts the bowtie and the bowl with the rest of the chow mein in the fridge, rinsing out the one plastic container that had the cucumber and spring onions strips, before putting it in the dishwasher. *I will run the dishwasher after I have finished my wine,* she thinks. She walks back to the table to fetch the water jug and her water and wine glasses. Downing the half full glass of wine, Sarah-Jane says to herself, "I'm going to regret doing that shortly," as the alcohol from the white wine rushes through her bloodstream, making her sway a bit.

Having had two large glasses of wine and finishing off the bottle, her hangover has gone, but may return later that evening or in the morning. She hopes that she won't get

one and, if she does, that it won't be as bad as today's hangover, but thankfully tomorrow is Sunday and she can take it easy. Sarah-Jane drains her water glass, refilling it and draining that glass, too. She fills the glass once again, only being able to fill quarter of the glass before the water jug is empty. "Hopefully drinking lots of water will lessen any hangover I get, flushing the wine toxins from my body and stopping me dehydrating causing the hangover in the first place," she says to herself.

Taking the water jug and the two glasses to the kitchen, Sarah-Jane fills the water jug in the sink, leaving it there while putting her wine glass in the dishwasher. She puts a washing tablet in the dishwasher before starting the cycle. By now the water has almost filtered through the jug. After filling the jug a second time, Sarah-Jane leaves the water jug on the counter top next to her glass, letting it filter. She refills her glass leaving enough space not to spill any water while she walks back to the table to get her laptop and phone then goes upstairs to her room.

Having drunk so much water, Sarah-Jane is now bursting at the seams. She leaves the glass of water on the table and runs to the guest toilet. After flushing the toilet and washing her hands, she fetches the laptop, her phone, and the glass of water, switches off the lights in the kitchen and dining room, and checks all the windows and front door are locked. Then she heads upstairs.

Turning on the lights in her room, she walks over to her bed and places the glass of water on the bedside table closest to the door, and the laptop on the bed. Lying under the caramel blanket and propped up by the pillows, she puts the laptop on her legs and wakes it up by opening the lid. Sarah-Jane looks at the clock on her laptop, it is now quarter-to-nine. She is starting to feel drowsy, though it is not yet her normal bedtime.

I'm sleepy, she thinks. *I will leave it to tomorrow to check more messages on We Play.* She closes the webpage before shutting down her laptop, placing it on the bedside table furthest from the door. Sarah-Jane gets up so she can brush her teeth before going to sleep and take one last pee. She works a large dollop of hand cream into her hands after she has washed them, and switches off the bathroom lights as she walks towards her room.

Sarah-Jane switches on the lamp that is on the bedside table then turns off the main bedroom lights. There is a warm light filling the area around the bed, as the light from the lamp pours out, fighting the darkness for dominance the further away from the bed the light gets. Sarah-Jane picks up a first edition of Bram Stocker's *Dracula* from the bookshelf. The book is a hardback and has the title engraved in bold gold-leaf on the front cover. Placing the book next to the lamp, Sarah-Jane folds the caramel blanket, before placing it on the stool, then climbs under the duvet and reads for half an hour.

At almost ten o'clock, Sarah-Jane leaves the book on top of the laptop, turning over to switch off the bedside lamp and check her phone one last time. There are no messages or notifications from her social media apps. Leaving the phone next to the lamp, she turns off the light and falls asleep almost immediately, but it is a restless sleep. Sarah-Jane has wild dreams. Waking up once through the night, at three o'clock to go to the toilet, she stumbles her way in the dark to the bathroom and back, climbing back into the warm bed and falling asleep as if she had not awakened.

Chapter 6

Sarah-Jane awakens early on Sunday morning. She hears the early morning singing of the birds, which happens before sunrise, and the eventual hustle and bustle of human activity. She looks at her mobile phone to check the time. The bright light from her phone bursts out of the darkness, casting light outwards and piercing the black around her. It is half-five. Lying in her warm bed, Sarah-Jane thinks to herself, *It is very early for a Sunday morning, as I fell asleep extra early last night. I've had my required amount of sleep. Maybe I should get up and go for a run.*

Turning on the lamp on the bedside table, Sarah-Jane half-heartedly drags herself out of bed, taking her running clothes from the wardrobe and gets dressed. Before putting on her running shoes, Sarah-Jane wipes the sleep from the inner corners of her eyes. As it is September, the mornings are a lot cooler but have not yet turned cold. She is a fair-weather runner; once the weather turns colder, she will most likely not go running till spring time when the mornings get brighter and warmer.

Putting her phone in her running waist bag, she clips it on as she finishes getting ready. She puts her wireless Bluetooth earphones in her ears and switches them on, syncing them to her phone. Now ready for her run, Sarah-Jane turns off the lamp and heads downstairs. At the bottom of the stairs, she spends ten minutes stretching her leg muscles to avoid getting a stitch or, worse, an injury. In her head she decides that she won't run too far; the hangover from yesterday has made her feel sluggish. Thankfully, the wine she drank with dinner last night didn't give her a second hangover, but she still doesn't feel one hundred percent.

She decides to run around the block twice, or until she feels tired and wants to stop. But to her surprise, she runs for 45 minutes – four times around the block – stopping just short of the front gate, with sweat dripping off her. Now out of breath, she switches off the earphones as she tries to slow her heavy breathing. Feeling much better for the run, Sarah-Jane has sweated out all the toxins from the last two evenings of drinking.

Walking up the path, she stops at the bottom of the stairs and places her water bottle down on the porch so she can stretch her muscles to avoid cramps later. Breathing normally again after her run, and having stretched out her legs and lower back muscles, Sarah-Jane goes inside the house and places her keys on the hook before going upstairs to take a

shower and get dressed. After her shower, she puts on a pair of black jeans, her long-sleeved t-shirt, and matching socks in dark navy blue. As she is most likely staying home again today, Sarah-Jane decides to wear her slippers.

Looking at the weather app on her phone, she mumbles in disappointment that she'd been hoping for a sunny day so she could spend the day in the backyard enjoying the last of the autumn sun. Alas, the app is showing heavy dark clouds with the possibility of showers for most of the day, only clearing in the evening. Sarah-Jane mutters to herself, "Typical! The day I'm all fucked up and hungover it's 'blindingly sunny', and the day I want it to be sunny, it's not. This sucks. Not much I can do about it. Guess I will spend my day the same way, indoors instead of outdoors."

She decides there is no point opening the curtains to let in the light if there is no sunlight, so she does a quick tidy-up of the bedroom then takes her laptop, power cable and phone and heads downstairs to the kitchen. She grabs the post before dropping all the items she is carrying on the dining room table, then she heads to the kitchen to get breakfast. "Maybe Chinese food for breakfast isn't the best idea. That was the wine talking last night," she says to herself. "Maybe something healthy will be the better option."

Settling on mixed nut muesli and plain yogurt, with fresh sliced strawberries, raspberries, and banana, she makes a

decaffeinated green tea to accompany the healthy breakfast. As she enjoys her breakfast, Sarah-Jane works her way through yesterday's post. Most of the letters addressed to her parents is junk mail, the rest are bills which she will take care of shortly. She is annoyed with companies still sending her paper bills when she has requested numerous times that she prefers them sent by email. In this day and age of the internet, Sarah-Jane believes their websites should have an online billing section added to the 'my account' section so that customers can view their bills before paying them and avoiding what she feels is an utter waste of paper.

Before paying the bills, Sarah-Jane clears up and gets herself another green tea then has a quick look at her social media. It is now half-eight and she feels like she has been awake for an age. The problem with social media is that once you start, you get sucked in and time flies by. The next thing Sarah-Jane knows, an hour has flown by, and her tea is now ice cold. "Silly me, that was a real waste of a good cup of tea," she says to herself, having not taken a sip. She decides to make herself another hot tea instead of reheating the cold one. Sarah-Jane believes that microwaving cold tea alters the taste for her and makes it very bitter; she prefers her tea plain, no milk or sugar, leaving the tea bag to brew in the mug while she drinks it. While waiting for the kettle to boil Sarah-Jane unpacks the dishwasher packing away its contents in their rightful places.

Starting her laptop and waiting for it to boot up, Sarah-Jane stares out of the patio doors thinking that it will soon be time to pick the apples from the tree; she will have to give Henry a call. Henry is the Morleys' gardener. Even before Sarah-Jane was born, Henry had a thriving landscaping business, but he'd decided to retire a year ago and only does Sarah-Jane a favour by tending to the gardens in the front and back yards. It was Henry who planted and sculptured the gardens, and he was adamant that he wasn't going to let anyone else look after his baby, his creation. His soul lives in these lush gardens. Besides, Sarah-Jane is useless, with not even a speck of green fingers in her.

By quarter past ten, with all the bills paid, she enters the We Play web details and goes to her profile. In the time since she last looked at her messages, at least another 200 have joined the already large count. Sarah-Jane uses the method of elimination she devised yesterday to whittle down the messages. Without realising that time has yet again escaped her, by quarter-to-one Sarah-Jane's tummy is grumbling and making strange hunger sounds, similar to the sound of water swirling down a drain. So far, she has eliminated 500 messages, though new ones keep coming in.

"I'll take a break and carry on after lunch," she says to herself. "Hopefully not too many more messages will be waiting for me. Glad I didn't have that Chinese food for

breakfast. That chow mein will hit the spot. Not to forget that sweet syrup bowtie." Turning the power on the microwave to a medium-low heat setting, Sarah-Jane places the bowl of chow mein into the microwave, having poked holes in the clingfilm to let the steam escape. Heating up the food over a longer time over a lower heat keeps the food from drying out.

She sets the microwave for five-and-a-half minutes, then takes the bowtie out the fridge, hoping it will be at room temperature by the time she finishes eating the chow mein. She goes back to her laptop and carries on going through messages until the beep of the microwave draws her attention away from We Play. Another 15 messages have been deleted.

The sound her stomach is making sounds like a loud deafening waterfall. Picking up her chopsticks and the chow mein, Sarah-Jane takes the time to enjoy her food, one mouthful at a time, leaning back in her chair with her legs outstretched, chopsticks in one hand, the other hand hovering just below her chin.

The bowtie is still too cold, and the syrup isn't runny enough, so Sarah-Jane turns the power on the microwave down to just before defrost, allowing the syrup to turn a warm liquid without destroying the firmness of the pastry. This time she eats the bowtie over a side plate seated at the

table. The container housing the bowtie is perfect to eat out of, and hopefully none of the syrup will be wasted on the side plate. Instead of a dessert fork, Sarah-Jane uses a teaspoon to mop up the last of the syrup after she finishes the bowtie, determined not to let any of that sticky goodness go to waste. The runny sweetness of the syrup again sends happy signals to her brain, like large explosions going off. Sarah-Jane can feel the goosebumps growing like a wave up her arms, over her shoulders and up her neck, sending shivers down her spine and ending at the tip of her toes.

She finishes her bowtie and notices the time on her laptop; it's five past two. She clears up, taking the items to the kitchen, rinses them, before placing them in the dishwasher. All of a sudden, the natural light fades and light rain starts, gradually becoming heavier as the seconds pass. "Glad I'm indoors," she says to herself. "I wouldn't want to get caught in this rain without an umbrella. I do feel sorry for anyone who has to be out in this weather."

She takes a frozen lasagne out of the freezer to have for dinner, leaving it on a plate to thaw before going back to her laptop. By half-past five, Sarah-Jane has deleted almost all of the messages. There are 23 left to go through, and she has whittled the messages down to seven profiles that have piqued her interest. Once she has gone through the rest of the messages, deleting the ones she

isn't going to consider, she will look properly at the remaining profiles before making a choice of whom to reply to.

Feeling thirsty, Sarah-Jane realises she hasn't had anything to drink since her last tea. She gets herself some water and checks on the lasagne. It has almost thawed completely, but she doesn't feel hungry yet so places the plate in the fridge. The lasagne is leftovers from two weeks ago, having made it for a dinner party she and the girls had. The recipe has been in her family for many generations, being passed from mother to daughter down the line until it was taught to Sarah-Jane by her mother. If she one day has children of her own, she will teach it to them, passing the knowledge onto future generations.

The lasagne always gives her a warm, hearty feeling when she eats it. Made up of layers of rich, full bodied, tomato sauce, minced beef, onion, peas, and mushrooms, a creamy white bechamel sauce made with full cream milk, butter, flower, salt, pepper, and a couple of pinches of grated parmesan cheese for depth of flavour, the fresh, soft pasta sheets easily tear away with a fork, and the grated cheese and breadcrumbs form a crust over the top layer of bechamel sauce. From your mouth to your stomach, it leaves a warm trail of wholesomeness on its journey, giving you a feeling of being at peace with the world. After you finish eating, you are always left with a feeling of wanting

more. Unfortunately, today there is only enough for one portion; no second helpings for Sarah-Jane even if she fancied more.

Feeling a bit dehydrated, she drains her glass in a matter of seconds, refills it, then goes back to the dining room table and her laptop. *I can see how people get sucked into social media as it happens to me very often*, she thinks, *but I never thought how you could get sucked in while on a website. Time has flown by today, and most of it has been occupied by one website. Just crazy!*

Her phone shudders on the table, sending out little waves of vibration that Sarah-Jane can feel, and she picks it up to see a message from Jenny. *"Hi sweetie, just wanted to say thanks again for getting Dan and I together. He phoned me today and we are going on our first date during the week. Also, how bad was your hangover yesterday?"*

Sarah-Jane hits reply and types, *"Hey, it's my pleasure, you two look good together. Yesterday was killer. I suffered the whole day with a monster hangover. See you at work tomorrow. Enjoy the rest of your evening ahead."*

Continuing her quest to weed through the final messages on We Play, she is almost done when her phone vibrates again. *"Thanks, I will. Enjoy your evening, too. See you tomorrow,"* replies Jenny.

Sarah-Jane has finally finished deleting messages. There are ten profiles that have piqued her interest, and she will have to look more closely at each one before deciding on the first three that she will reply to. Feeling hungry now, Sarah-Jane looks at the clock on the laptop, it is quarter past six. Getting up, she puts the lasagne in the microwave for five minutes on a medium temperature setting.

"While I wait for my lasagne, I will do some online shopping," she decides aloud. "I will need some new outfits to go on these dates."

The beeping sound signals her food is ready, and she uses the dishcloth to remove the plate from the microwave, then picks up the spatula and uses it to ease the lasagne from the plastic container and onto her dinner plate. Using the dishcloth she used to remove the plate from the microwave, Sarah-Jane picks up the plate in her left hand and a fork and knife in the right and heads for the table. While waiting for her lasagne to cool, Sarah-Jane carries on her search for some new clothes.

Feeling that the room is a bit too quiet, Sarah-Jane opens an extra tab, searching for internet radio. The search results yield hundreds of different radio stations. Feeling in a chilled mood, she picks a classical music station. A rendition of Mozart's Fifth Symphony by the Vienna State Orchestra is playing; this rendition is five years old, and Sarah-Jane

remembers watching the live performance with her parents. It was beamed around the world via satellite. The music brings back some lovely memories of her parents and she is a bit upset at having missed the first nine minutes of the symphony, which would have allowed her to enjoy the full experience.

She goes back to the first tab to carry on the search for new clothes, but after ten minutes have gone by, the smell of her lasagne wafts its way up her nostrils. The plate has cooled enough for Sarah-Jane to pick it up without the dishcloth. Sliding her laptop off to the side so she can eat, she cuts the lasagne up into cube-size chunks, allowing her to carry on looking for clothes while she eats. By the time Sarah-Jane has finished eating the lasagne, she has decided on a couple of items of clothing: a black, mid-thigh, shoulder-strap dress with streaks of silver and red entwined around the dress, which can be worn on its own or over a pair or trousers or jeans; a pair of trousers, grey with fine, black pinstripes, in a slim fit, hugging the legs of the wearer; and a long-sleeved, black blouse with gold buttons. All the items could be worn separately or together, creating a variety of different outfits.

As Sarah-Jane pays for her new clothes, she thinks, *Twenty years ago I would never have been able to buy clothes online. I would have had to drive to a store so I could look around before finding what I want and trying it on, seeing if*

it fits. The one drawback of online shopping is you can't judge clothing sizes and may end up with clothes either too big or too small. Not having to go to the store has its upsides, though – not having to wait in line for changing rooms, not having to fight with someone else over who gets the last item you both picked up at the same time, and queuing for ages to pay at a till when stores are busy.

Mozart's Fifth Symphony has just finished by the time Sarah-Jane pays for her clothes. She gets up to rinse her plate before the lasagne forms a hard, dry crust, making it harder to clean, then closes the lid of the laptop, putting it to sleep for the time being. Placing the plate, knife, and fork in the dishwasher after rinsing them, she-Jane drinks another glass of water before placing the glass in the dishwasher.

Collecting her laptop and phone from the table, Sarah-Jane switches off the lights before going upstairs to her bedroom, checking that the front door and windows are closed and locked. It is now quarter-to eight. The weather forecast had been accurate, with rain showers all day, clearing by nightfall. Turning on the lamp before laying her phone on the nightstand and her laptop on the bed, Sarah-Jane decides to have a shower before getting into bed; she will compare profiles after her shower.

Getting a clean pair of pyjamas from the closet and tying her hair up so not to get it wet, Sarah-Jane walks to the bathroom.

Twenty minutes later she emerges from the bathroom glowing a rosy colour from her hot shower. Steam bellows out into the hallway, as Sarah-Jane has again forgotten to open the window to vent the bathroom. Untying her hair as she walks towards the bedroom, she chastises herself, "Nice hot shower, but silly me for forgetting to open the window. Hope that doesn't cause any damp."

She sits down at the dressing table and picks up a flat paddle brush and brushes her hair. When she has finished, she turns off the hallway light and walks to the bed, taking the caramel blanket off and placing it on the stool. Sarah-Jane moves the laptop over to the other side of the bed before climbing in. Once she has made herself comfy, propped up with pillows between her and the headboard, she picks up the laptop and places it upon her outstretched legs.

Waking the laptop up as she opens the lid, she finds that all the web pages are still open as she left them. Schubert's Ninth Symphony is playing on the classical radio station Sarah-Jane was listening to while she was eating her dinner. No longer in the mood to listen to classical music, she pauses the music while searching for something livelier. She settles on an alternative rock station and the first song to play is Pearl Jam's *Alive*.

Sarah-Jane closes the tab she used for clothes shopping, leaving two open – internet radio and We Play. Clicking on

the We Play tab, Sarah-Jane checks her messages to find ten new ones. She goes through them quickly, deleting all ten, then begins studying the ten profiles that have piqued her interest. By half nine, Sarah-Jane has chosen the three profiles she is going to reply to.

The first is Ken Mansfield. He isn't extremely good looking, more on the average side, but the reason Sarah-Jane has chosen Ken is the glowing reviews he has received from other members. One person said, "Don't judge a book by its cover. Ken knows how to please, especially with that tongue of his." Ken is 5 foot 5 inches, not excessively overweight, but has some wobbly bits around the stomach. He keeps his head shaved, as he is balding, and he has a short, well-groomed, dark beard. He is 37.

Next, Charles De Witt. He is tall and lanky, edging on 6 feet, with long blond dreadlocks and a long beard. From his profile pictures Sarah-Jane gets the impression Charles is a fun-loving, hippy-cum-surfer, and is well-tanned. Charles is 40. Though his appearance says one thing about him, what Sarah-Jane has read in his profile leads her to believe there is more to Charles than meets the eye. He seems to be quite intellectual.

Lastly, Lance Rosemead. He is 5 foot 10 inches, with long, straight black hair. Lance has a well sculptured body – not the body builder type with oversized muscles, just well

proportioned. Lance is a rocker who rides a Harley Davidson, as she can see from pictures on his profile. Lance is 33 – the closest to Sarah-Jane's age. His profile is very intriguing to Sarah-Jane, as he seems out of the three to be the most adventurous sexually, being into light bondage – the more obscure end of sexual expression. Lance is the person Sarah-Jane is most looking forward to meeting.

Sarah-Jane writes a short hello to Ken, Charles, and Lance. She is looking for some brief, get-to-know-you conversations with each of them, before meeting them in person. By the time Sarah-Jane has finished writing the three messages, it is five to ten, Soundgarden's *Black Hole Sun* is playing in the background, and she is starting to feel drowsy. Obviously, her body can't process alcohol the same way it used to when she was 20, and it strikes her how much of a difference 11 years makes. The hangovers seem to last longer and are more severe than when she was 20, and it takes at least two – if not three – days to be completely over them.

She thinks how nice it is going to be seeing Mike on Wednesday, as it has been so long since they spent time together. Before Mike became one of the three head managers of Jonestown, they used to spend lots more time together, but she understands that unfortunately the more responsibility you get, the less time you can expect to have with loved ones when working in the night-time industry of hospitality.

Sarah-Jane closes both the tabs before shutting down her laptop and closing the lid. Rolling to her right, she places the laptop on the bedside table before she rolls back to her left to pick up her phone. She sets her alarm for quarter-to-seven, then gets out of bed to leave her phone on the dressing table to ensure she doesn't ignore the alarm. After one final trip to the toilet, she massages some cream into her hands then gets into bed, turns off the lamp, and goes to sleep.

* * *

It is half four on Wednesday afternoon. Sarah-Jane has just arrived home from work, parking her car in the driveway as the electric gates close behind her. She collects her belongings from the passenger seat before getting out of the car, then walks down the path to the porch steps. Before opening the front door, she checks to see if there is any post. Unlocking the front panel of the post-box, she swings it open to find no post has arrived. Sarah-Jane closes the panel and locks it, then opens the front door, placing her keys on their hook after closing the door behind her.

It is a warm September afternoon and Sarah-Jane decides that she is going to sit outside in the backyard to enjoy the last of the afternoon sun before Mike arrives for dinner. Leaving her backpack leaning against the leg of the long, thin table, Sarah-Jane goes upstairs to change out of her

work clothes. She puts on a pair of sweatpants, a hoodie, and her slippers, leaving her work clothes in the laundry basket under the bathroom sink before going back downstairs.

Picking up her backpack from the floor, she takes it with her to the kitchen. She takes out her empty lunchbox and rinses it out before placing it in the dishwasher. She had a fresh chopped salad with chunks of torn smoked salmon and cottage cheese for lunch, having prepared it in the morning before going to work. Luckily, there is a fridge at the library for the employees to keep their food in, as well as a microwave to heat up food in the cold winter months and a kettle for those all-important coffees and teas.

Opening the sliding doors, Sarah-Jane can feel a slight breeze greeting her before she steps out onto the patio. Leaving her backpack on the table, she gets herself a glass of water, putting in some ice and a slice of lime, before going to sit in the sun. Taking a sip of her water, she places the glass on the table and takes her phone out from the backpack along with her laptop. Placing the laptop on the table, she unlocks her phone and looks through her emails then decides to message Mike to find out what time he will be arriving for dinner.

Scrolling through her various social media apps to see if there are any new posts she has missed during the day, her phone

vibrates in her hand before a notification pops up. It is a text from Mike. *"I should be at your house by half seven."*

"Cool, see you then," she texts back before carrying on scrolling through her social media. Five minutes have passed before her phone vibrates again; it is another text from Mike.

"What would you like to drink with dinner? I'm going past Jonestown before I come to you. I've got a managers' meeting to go to first, as we are deciding on some new promotions to run for the next couple of months." Working at Jonestown Mike gets alcohol and food at cost price.

Sarah-Jane replies, *"I can't have too heavy an evening of drinking, as I have work in the morning. Please bring a couple of bottles of beer, thanks. Beer goes well with pizza, unless you would prefer something else to eat for dinner."*

While waiting for Mike to reply, Sarah-Jane switches on her laptop. It has almost finished loading when her phone vibrates again.

"Cool. I will bring some beers with me from Jonestown. I'm ok with pizza for dinner," Mike texts.

"We can decide what pizzas we will order when you get here. Thanks again for getting the beers. I totally forgot to get some for this evening," replies Sarah-Jane.

She opens the web browser and loads We Play. Having saved her login details previously, the homepage for We Play loads automatically. Sarah-Jane clicks on the mail icon which shows the number 13 in red. There are some new messages from other members which she glances through before deleting them.

There are three messages left, so she opens the first message which is from Ken. It says: "Thank you for replying to my message. If you have any questions you would like to ask, please feel free to ask. I will reply honestly as there is no need to lie on here. Lying on here gets you nowhere. Take care, hear from you soon."

Sarah-Jane clicks the return button on the webpage, waiting for the page to reload and take her back to her inbox. She clicks on the second message which is from Charles. It reads: "Welcome to our community of adventurous folk. There is a wide world of sexual expression to explore. Come explore with me. Hear back from you when you get the chance."

Clicking the return button once again, she waits for the inbox to load so she can read the last message which is from Lance. Lance's message is more to the point: "Hi, beautiful, glad you decided to reply. I want to take you to sexual heights you may not have experienced and give you mind-blowing orgasms. You won't regret it. You know you want to. You know you are going to reply."

By the time she has finished reading her messages, it is five to six. Sarah-Jane decides she will reply to the messages just before she goes to sleep. She closes the lid of the laptop, putting it to sleep, before placing it and her phone into her backpack. Picking up her glass of water, she goes back inside as the sun is setting; it is starting to get chilly, and the breeze has picked up, sending shivers up her spine.

Sarah-Jane closes and locks the patio door behind her and walks towards the entrance hall, leaving her backpack leaning against the long, thin table again. She will take it upstairs with her once Mike has gone home. Sarah-Jane decides to watch a bit of television while waiting for him to arrive. All of a sudden, her bladder is screaming to be emptied, so she quickly goes into the guest toilet to relieve herself.

While she is on the toilet, Sarah-Jane thinks it might be best to reply to the messages before Mike arrives. After all, he might leave quite late, and after a few beers she could feel too tired to reply when she gets into bed. After washing and drying her hands, she picks up her backpack and takes it with her to the lounge, switching on the lights before sitting down on the centre couch. Looking out the window, she can just see over the top of the great oak tree as the daylight fades from orange-red to purple-black with the dying of the light.

Taking out the laptop and her phone, she unlocks her phone to check for any messages. As there is nothing new, she lays her phone on the couch beside her. Placing the laptop on top of her legs, she opens the lid, waking it from its sleep. She refreshes the webpage, reloading the page with her inbox, and finds another five new messages awaiting her. She quickly looks over them before deleting them. All the messages are from women, none of them subtle. Sarah-Jane is still shocked by how forward women on this site are.

She clicks on Ken's message. Once it has loaded, she clicks on the reply icon, and writes: "Hi Ken, I'm new on this site and don't know what to expect. I would like to know a bit more about you before we meet in person. Tell me what you like and dislike sexually, so I know what to expect when we first meet. We can go for a drink or two first, have a conversation to feel each other out, and see if we want to take it further. Enjoy your week. Speak soon."

After she has finished writing her reply, she clicks on the send button, and a few seconds later a notification message confirms that her message has been sent.

Sarah-Jane clicks the message icon which loads her inbox page, she clicks on the message from Charles, repeating the process. She writes: "Hi Charles, thanks for the welcoming message. Can you tell me what are your favourite sexual

positions? What are the things that turn you on? We should meet in person before anything happens sexually. As I'm new to this site, I want to take precautions to assure my safety."

She repeats the process again before leaving Lance a message. "Hi Lance, I would like to meet in person to see if we will take this to the next step. I'm intrigued by your profile and just want to make sure I'm safe, as I'm new to this type of website and not to sure what to expect. Going for a drink beforehand will put me at ease."

Having replied to all three messages, she looks at the clock on her laptop. It is now quarter-to-seven. She decides to watch some music television until Mike arrives, so shuts down her laptop and puts it into her backpack. Picking up the remote, she turns on the television and scrolls through the channels, landing on a rock music channel. The first video that jumps on screen is Slipknot's *Duality*; it is halfway through the song. The next song to play is Red Hot Chili Peppers' *Under the Bridge*.

Sarah-Jane is enjoying the music while she scrolls through her social media on her phone. Just then, the phone vibrates with a message from Mike. *"I'm leaving Jonestown shortly. Should be at your house in ten to 15 minutes."*

She replies, *"Cool, see you then."*

Saliva is the next band to play, with their song *Click, Click, Boom.* By this time Sarah-Jane is up off the couch, dancing along to the music, her hair flailing in the air as she is head banging to the beat. System of a Down's *Chop Suey* bursts onto the screen, sending Sarah-Jane into a dance frenzy, bouncing up and down on the rug in the middle of the couches. The next song to play is Pantera's *Walk*, and by the time this song has finished, Sarah-Jane is almost out of breath and needing to sit down. She is glad that the next song is a slow one, Stone Sour's *Bother.* It is an emotional song, and she pants to regain her breath as she sits on the couch again.

Stone Temple Pilots' *Creep* is playing when Sarah-Jane hears the knocker banging against the front door. She gets up from the couch and goes to open the door to find Mike waiting, holding a plastic bag in his outstretched right hand.

"Hi, cousin. As promised, here's the beer."

"Thanks. Hope your meeting was productive. Come in. It is quite chilly out now that we are heading towards winter." She takes the bag with the beers then closes the door behind him. "Go sit in the lounge while I put the beers in the fridge. Would you like a coffee or tea before we order pizza?"

"Can I have a coffee, please?" Mike replies.

"Do you still take your coffee black and three sugars?" she asks.

"No, I have started taking my coffee without sugar nowadays."

"Ok, black it is. Switch off the television if you don't want to listen to music. I know working at Jonestown you probably get overloaded listening to music," she says before going to the kitchen.

"I'm ok at the moment," he replies, "but maybe something not so lively would be good."

"You will have to scroll through the channels to find something different. I won't be too long."

Once Sarah-Jane has made the coffee for Mike, she heads back to the lounge, his coffee in one hand and an herbal tea for herself in the other. Silence greets her as she reaches the entrance hall.

"You couldn't find anything to listen to?" she asks in surprise.

Mike replies, "Nothing I wanted to listen to. You were right, I get music overload while I'm at work. Hope you don't mind."

"Not at all. I was having quite the time before you arrived. Some silence doesn't hurt anyone," she tells him. "Here's your coffee."

Mike is sitting on the couch opposite the window, looking out at the clear night sky. Sarah-Jane sits back on the middle couch again. "What pizza do you feel like eating?" she asks. "Do you feel like sharing a pizza, or having one to yourself?"

Mike replies, "If you don't mind, I would like a pizza to myself. If there is any left, I can have it for tomorrow then I won't have to cook and can have it before I go to work."

"I don't mind. I will take my leftovers to work tomorrow, too, so there will be no need for me to prepare food in the morning."

While they are talking, they decide on two large pizzas, and place their order. Mike is having a pan-thick base with bacon, olives, mushrooms, and mixed peppers. Sarah-Jane has decided to have a thin crust base topped with ham, bacon, mushrooms, and pineapple. She loves the sweet taste of pineapple on pizza, even though she knows there are a lot of people who think fruit on pizza is wrong. She doesn't care; her pizza, her taste.

Half an hour later, their pizzas arrive, and Sarah-Jane tips the delivery driver before closing the front door. She calls to

Mike to join her in the dining room. "Do you want a plate for your pizza?" she asks. "I'm going to eat mine from the box."

Mike replies, "No thanks, I'll have it out the box, too. One less plate to clean."

Placing the boxes on the table, Sarah-Jane goes to the kitchen to get some serviettes, the salt and pepper grinders, and a bottle of hot chilli sauce. Mike has taken the seat with his back to the wall so he can look out towards the back yard. He has put Sarah-Jane's pizza in front of her chair at the head of the table and opened the lid of the boxes, so the steam is rising from them.

"Please start eating. I'm just going to get us a couple of bottles of beers," she says, placing the condiments and serviettes on the table between them before returning to the kitchen to get an ice bucket with ice. She puts four bottles of beer in the bucket then brings it and a bottle opener to the table. As she sits down, she takes out two beers, removes the caps and places one bottle in Mike's waiting hand, and they clink bottles. At the same time, they say, "Cheers. To good health."

They have a pleasant conversation while eating their pizza, and by quarter past nine they have each eaten half their pizzas and drunk two beers.

Sarah-Jane asks, "Do you want another beer, or some more coffee?"

"I'll have another beer if you're having another, but if you don't mind, I would like another coffee, too," replies Mike.

"I don't mind making you another coffee. I'll get the beers while I wait for the kettle to boil."

Mike says, "You can use the same mug I was using earlier."

"Are you sure you wouldn't prefer a fresh mug?" asks Sarah-Jane, getting up from her chair.

"I'm sure."

Sarah-Jane walks to the lounge to retrieve their mugs from earlier and returns to the kitchen, placing a fresh tea bag in her mug and instant coffee in Mike's. She switches on the kettle before getting the last two beers from the fridge and takes them to the table before going back to the kitchen to get the freshly-made coffee and tea. Mike is checking his phone while he waits for her to return.

It is half ten by the time they have finished their cold and hot drinks; time seems to have passed them by in a blink of an eye. Mike gets up from his chair. "Thanks for the wonderful evening and the great conversation. We need to

do this more often. We don't get to spend as much time together as we would like."

Sarah-Jane nods in agreement. "Yes, we should do this more often. We only have each other; you are the only family I have left here since my parents died and yours moved out of town."

Mike picks up his pizza box and they head towards the front door. As he leaves, he turns around and they share a warm embrace before Mike walks down the garden path.

"Drive home safe. Sleep well when you get home," she calls to him.

"Hope you sleep well, too," he replies.

Closing and locking the front door behind her, she walks to the dining room to tidy up before going upstairs. Sarah-Jane has a quick shower, and by the time she is ready to get into bed, it is eleven. Sarah-Jane has set the alarm on her phone for quarter-to-seven, once again leaving her phone on the dressing table before getting into bed.

Once in bed, she reads a couple more pages of Dracula then places the book on the bedside table, turns off the lamp, moves onto her side, and drifts off to sleep.

Chapter 7

Two weeks have passed, and the weather has changed for the worse; it hasn't stopped raining for five days straight. It is almost the end of September, and the days are shorter, the nights longer and colder. It seems autumn didn't hang around very long as winter is rearing its ugly head with the type of cold that seeps straight through to the bone.

Sarah-Jane and Ken have agreed to meet for coffee close to Ken's home. Being a little cautious, she didn't want to meet close to her home. She told Ken that as it was her first meeting off the We Play website, she wanted to meet him close to his home, and if they get along and take things further, she would rather it be at his home than hers. Agreeing, Ken admitted he'd had the same reservations on his first meet-up from the website.

They have chosen to meet at a coffee shop around the corner from his apartment. Cherry's is a small, friends-run coffee shop; it has a homely atmosphere compared to the big, mass-produced coffee shop chains. The inside of

Cherry's is dimly lit, giving it a warm atmosphere, and there are five two-seater tables and three four-seater tables available. They are evenly spread out, giving enough space not to feel cramped but allowing people to have a conversation without worrying that they will be overheard. Soft music is playing in the background for ambiance, not to be overbearing, so customers don't have to raise their voices to be heard over the music.

Each table has a different coloured tablecloth, upon which sits a jar with sugar sachets – there is a mixture of white sugar, brown sugar, and artificial sweeteners. Next to the jar of sugars is a thinner but taller jar, with teaspoons. Placed behind the two jars is a candle in a glass. The candles are fragranced and are changed once a week. This week they are lavender fragranced.

As you enter Cherry's, the tables run from the front of the shop towards the back. There is a counter that runs along the back, almost wall to wall, only giving space for a toilet to be used by both men and women. Between the toilet and the counter is a small walk space for the staff to come and go. The counter has a glass screen so you can see the freshly baked cakes, muffins, and other sweet treats like scones and an arrangement of donuts. There is a small kitchen behind the counter where the cakes and other pastries are baked each day, and where the staff wash up the cups, plates, and cutlery. On arrival, you are greeted by

the friendly staff, who lead you to your table where they will take your order. Being seated and having your order taken is what makes Cherry's stand out, compared to the big chain stores where you come in, order from the counter, and wait to be given what you ordered to eat and drink.

The walls are painted in a pale orange colour, with a variety of paintings hanging on the walls. Some are by local artists and others by artists from around the world. The local artists are given precedence over the international ones as Cherry's supports local people. If a customer wishes to purchase one of the paintings from local artists, Cherry's doesn't take a commission for the sale, preferring to give the full sale amount to the artist.

One of the owners of Cherry's used to be an artist but struggled for so long that when she sold some of her art and made enough money, she decided to channel her energy into something that would give her a lasting income and a stable future. She went into business with two of her friends ten years ago and has never looked back. Now her passion is baking all the delicious cakes, pastries, and sweet pies that are sold at Cherry's. Most of the time her two partners run front of house, making the coffees, teas, and other drinks, as well as taking customer orders.

Cherry's is open six days a week, from ten till seven. Their busiest times are over lunch and when people are finishing

work and want to meet friends before going home. Over the summer they get someone to help out for a month or two to allow each partner the chance to take a holiday. All three partners take turns baking and serving, so there are no gaps in the service or quality of food when someone is away on holiday.

Sarah-Jane and Ken have arranged to meet at Cherry's at six, giving her time to get home, have a shower and get ready. She chooses a pair of dark blue jeans with a black blouse and a navy-blue jumper to wear, plus her winter jacket. Cherry's is a 45-minute drive from Sarah-Jane's home, and luckily she is off tomorrow, as it is her turn to work the weekend shift.

Sarah-Jane and Ken have exchanged phone numbers just in case either of them has to get in contact for any reason. Trying to find a parking space leaves Sarah-Jane running about five minutes late, but the area around Cherry's is very busy and there are no spaces close by. She texts Ken: *"Sorry, I'm running a little late, can't find any parking outside Cherry's. Will be there as soon as possible, just having to find a place to park."*

Her phone vibrates and the screen lights up showing Ken's reply: *"Not to worry. I'm inside waiting for you. I should have warned you that it is very busy this time of the evening and you may find it hard to get a parking spot. See you shortly."*

She drives around the area and finally locates a spot to park four streets away from Cherry's. Picking up her handbag, she places its strap over her right shoulder, the handbag sitting on her left side, then picks up her umbrella. As she climbs out of the car, she quickly opens up the umbrella to avoid getting soaked by the heavy rain. The sky is a dark black with the heavy rain clouds, and there has not been a ray of sunlight since the rain started.

It takes Sarah-Jane five minutes to walk from her car to Cherry's. Before she opens the door, she vigorously opens and shuts her umbrella six times to shake off the excess water. She doesn't want to leave a trail of water drippings from the door to the table where Ken will be waiting.

Once inside, she sees Ken is seated at a table near the back. It isn't right against the wall, more middle of the coffee shop. He is wearing dark blue jeans and a plain, light green, long-sleeved jersey, and he stands up as Sarah-Jane approaches the table.

"Hi, nice to finally meet in person," he says to her.

They kiss each other on the cheek before Sarah-Jane replies, "Yes, nice to finally meet. Again, sorry for being late."

She hangs her coat on the back of her chair before sitting down, placing the wet umbrella on the floor next to the table.

"I didn't know what you wanted to drink, so I decided to wait until you arrived to order anything for myself," he explains.

"That is very thoughtful of you. Do we go to the counter to order our drinks?" Sarah-Jane asks.

"No, it is table service. This is why I chose Cherry's to meet; the service here is way better than the chain coffee shops," he replies.

They chat for about five minutes before Josie comes over to take their order. She is 5 foot 7 inches, slightly overweight, and has curly, black, shoulder-length hair. "Are you ready to order?" she asks them.

Ken addresses Sarah-Jane. "What would you like to drink?"

Looking at Josie, Sarah-Jane asks, "What herbal teas do you have?"

Josie replies, "We have red bush tea, which is an antioxidant and caffeine-free tea that only grows in one part of the world, which is South Africa. If you haven't tried it before, it's worth trying, though it is an acquired taste. We also have green tea, both regular and decaffeinated. The fruit teas we have are apple and cinnamon, lemon and ginger, or cherry and wild berries."

Sarah-Jane thinks for a moment then says, "I'll try the red bush tea, thanks. I have never tried it before. Do I need to add milk and sugar to it?"

"It's up to you if you want to add milk and sugar, but the proper way to drink it is allowing the tea to brew and build its flavour in the teapot, not adding milk and sugar, just letting its natural flavours come through. Milk only dilutes the tea, and sugar kills off the natural flavour," Josie explains. "Would you like anything to eat with your tea?"

"Can I have a slice of your carrot cake, please?" Sarah-Jane replies.

Josie turns her attention to Ken. "Would you like your usual triple expresso, Ken, with a slice of apple pie?"

He smiles and nods. "Yes please, Josie. Thanks,"

While they are waiting for Josie to bring their order, they carry on chatting. "What made you join We Play?" asks Ken.

"My friends clubbed together and bought me a six-month subscription as a birthday present," Sarah-Jane explains. "It was my birthday almost three weeks ago. How did you end up joining?"

"I had tried different online dating sites in the past, but to no avail. Whenever I would write to someone, I never got any replies and if I did get a response, it just felt that I was being strung along. To me it seemed that most of these sites employ people to respond to users' messages with the knowledge that they are never going to meet them in person." Ken went on, "Most dating sites or apps get you to purchase tokens. Each message you send costs one token, so you end up playing message ping-pong, never getting to meet in the real world. Newer apps only allow men to message women if they match with someone, but the women have to message first. I found that if I matched with someone, they messaged hi, I'd reply, then there was just silence from them. I got disillusioned by it all. One day a friend told me about We Play, so I joined, and the rest is history."

"That sucks that people can be so shitty," Sarah-Jane sympathises. "Don't you ever long to be in a relationship?"

Just before Ken gets the chance to answer, Josie arrives with their order. She places Sarah-Jane's teapot and cup, plus the carrot cake, in front of her, then Ken's coffee and apple pie in front of him. It is half six as Josie brings their order.

"Enjoy your drinks and food. If you need anything else, please don't hesitate to ask," she tells them.

Ken replies, "Thanks, Josie, will do. Will you be closing on time today?"

"Yeah, we are still closing at seven," she tells him, "but you can stay a little longer."

Now that Josie has left them to enjoy their hot drinks and sweet, wholesome cake and pie, Ken replies to Sarah-Jane's last question. "Yes, I do miss being in a relationship, but I haven't met anyone yet. I don't pine to be in a relationship, though if one day I meet someone and there is a spark, a strong energy between us and we would like to see if that develops into a relationship, then yes, I would like to see where that leads. But until that time, I'm quite happy having fun on We Play. How about you?"

"It has been a long time since I was in a relationship," Sarah-Jane admits. "I was still at university when my last relationship ended. Like you, I'm not looking for a relationship. If one happens to develop from meeting someone on We Play, then I would see where that goes. But I'm new to this and want to explore what We Play has to offer before even thinking about a relationship. Life is too short not to have fun and be happy."

Sarah-Jane takes a bite of her cake, then continues, "This carrot cake is so moist and light. I haven't had carrot cake like this before. Would you like to try some?" she asks Ken.

Taking a sip of his expresso, Ken replies, "Don't mind if I do. I haven't had it before, as I usually go for the same thing every time. You're welcome to try my apple pie. They put a little cinnamon and nutmeg in the apple pie, which gives it a nice, spiced flavour, warms you up on the inside. Makes you feel like you are eating your grandmother's home cooking."

They both lean forward to try a little of each other's dessert on their forks, taking it into their mouths. There is a brief silence as they enjoy each other's choice of desserts.

"I may have to have this next time I come here, which will shock the staff," Ken laughs. "In the five years I have lived around the corner and been coming here, I have never tried anything else."

Sarah-Jane replies, "I see what you mean. I have had lots of different apple pies, but nothing compares to this. Reminds me of when I was a child, visiting my grandparents. My grandmother would take fresh apple pie out of the over. It warms your insides, giving you a feeling of safety and love."

At ten past seven, Josie approaches their table. "Sorry to bother you, but we are closing now."

Ken replies, "Thanks, Josie, for letting us stay a little longer than usual." Looking at Sarah-Jane, he asks, "Shall we go back to mine?"

Sarah-Jane nods. "Yes, let's go back to yours."

They get up from their seats and put on their jackets, ready to go back out into the rain. Ken holds open the door for Sarah-Jane. She has already partially pre-opened her umbrella before stepping outside, so she can quickly open it fully and avoid getting wet. Ken exits Cherry's right behind her, and she holds the umbrella so they can share it.

"Which way to yours, left or right?" she asks.

Ken replies, "As it has quietened down now, there is going to be a lot more parking available. Would you like to fetch your car and move it closer to where I live, so you won't have to walk as far when you leave?"

"Yes, that is a great idea. Thanks for mentioning it."

They walk back to her car, talking as they walk. As they approach her car, Sarah-Jane walks to the passenger side with Ken, unlocking the door for him, still holding the umbrella over his head until he gets in. She then walks to the driver's side. He has leant over and unlocked the door for her, she gets in still holding the umbrella outside, and shakes the excess water off before she places it on the floor behind Ken's seat.

Sarah-Jane starts the car and asks Ken which way to go. They are very lucky, as there is an available parking spot

right outside Ken's apartment block. They decide to leave the umbrella in the car and make a mad dash for the front door to avoid getting wet.

The apartment block is loft-style apartments, two to each floor. Ken is on the third floor; the building is only six floors high. There are two elevators in the lobby and Ken pushes the button. While waiting for the elevator to arrive, Sarah-Jane asks, "Do you enjoy living in the hustle and bustle of downtown city living? Doesn't it get too noisy?"

He shrugs. "At first it took me about four months to get used to living the city life, but before I knew it the noise faded away and it becomes ambient background noise. Besides, I don't have to travel very far to get anywhere, as everything is at my fingertips. I don't even own a car as there is no need; public transport is good and there are buses going in every direction. Sometimes I may have to wait ten to 15 minutes for a bus if the traffic is heavy. I have grown to love it over the past five years."

They exit the elevator on Ken's floor, and find two brown varnished doors in front of them. Ken walks to the one on the right, unlocks it, and walks inside, holding the door open for Sarah-Jane. As she enters Ken's loft apartment, she is greeted by a bank of windows along the right-hand side of the large, dimly lit apartment. Unfortunately, the sun is no longer visible in the dying light of the day; the

street lights have awoken, throwing their light out over the streets below. Some light manages to escape upwards, clawing at the windows below.

Ken turns on the apartment lights, which aren't ceiling hanging as the ceiling is high-vaulted. Hanging down from the ceiling is a network of pipes and metal, giving the apartment an industrial feel. There are three rows of large metal lightshades hanging from the framework, and in each row are four sets of lights. As Sarah-Jane's eyes become accustomed to the light, the layout of Ken's apartment comes into view. There are six sections before her, all in an open-plan layout. To her right is the kitchen; to the left is the lounge area; the dinner table next on the right; the bed to the left; in the corner, opposite the windows, is the bathroom which is the only part of the apartment that is walled off; lastly is a work station, between the bathroom and the dining area. Spread out, hanging on available wall space, is a variety of different-sized, painted canvases.

"Sarah, would you like something to drink? Please have a seat on the couch," Ken says.

Taking off her jacket, she replies, "What are you offering?" She hangs her jacket on the coat stand that sits next to the front door.

"I've got hot drinks, soft drinks, or hard drinks," he replies. "Which would you like?"

"I would like a hard drink, please. What's on offer?" she shoots back.

"I've got white or red wine, or some single malt whiskey. What tickles your tastebuds?"

"A glass of red would be lovely, thanks," she replies, sitting on the couch with her back towards the bed so she is able to see the kitchen.

The lounge is oddly-shaped. Next to the coat stand, running along the wall to the corner and then out along the back wall towards the bed, is a handmade, rich brown coloured, oak shelving, with books, films, and CDs. Built into the shelving unit in the corner is a curved front television stand, resembling a wedge of cheese, with a large, flat screen television and soundbar on top of it. The couch is a two-piece set made from rich, warm, brown leather with three cushions to each piece of the set. One end almost meets the coat stand, with a gap so people can pass; it's straight, with a small, square table joining it to the other half of the set. The other end almost meets the back wall, completing one of the six areas.

The other side of the front door is the kitchen, where there are two L-shaped counters opposite each other, forming a broken square, hollowed out in the middle, with a walk-through at either end. One L section runs along the wall,

the longer leg of the L running in line with the windows. A double kitchen sink is in the corner of the unit, with an area for a dry rack next to it. The other side has a large counter surface for preparation of meals, with a gas stove housed in the counter top. Below the stove is an oven unit. Under the sink area is a built-in washing machine, and next to the oven is a stainless-steel fridge freezer unit with three doors. The opposite L-shape is all storage for dry foods, teas and coffees, and Ken's crockery and cutlery, wine glasses, and coffee mugs. On top of the counter is the toaster, kettle, and microwave.

Ken retrieves two wine glasses from under the counter, along with a bottle from the wine rack also housed under the counter. While he is opening the bottle of wine, she gets up to survey the apartment. The bed seems to be larger than a double, due to the heavy pine frame. Deep red and black silk bedding shimmers in the light, with tall, black metal candle holders close to each corner of the bed. Opposite the bed is the dining table. It's a four-seater, burnt oak table, and there are books, paints, and sketch pads filled with illustrations strewn on top of it.

The bathroom is in the far back corner of the apartment. It isn't a square-shaped bathroom; it is curved, with the door in the middle of the curve. In the far corner opposite the door is a large shower cubicle, with a toilet to the left of the door and the basin on the right. A shower

mat lies outside the shower cubicle, there is a large towel rack for three towels between the shower and the toilet, and a hand towel hangs between the shower and the basin. The bathroom has a heated floor for those cold winter nights.

The last part of the apartment is Ken's work area. Sarah-Jane admires the canvas on an easel in the corner by the window. A piece in progress, only the beginning touches can be seen. On the counter surface are tubes of paints, some almost empty, squeezed of their contents; others plump, unopened, eager to share their hue with the canvas. Two palettes sit on the counter – one a cascade of bright colours, the other filled with the warmer, darker tones. Both palettes show signs of work fatigue, thick caked stains of paint, bits of wood that have chipped off, paint seeping into the uneven surfaces of the missing chips from many years of use.

"Here is your glass of red. I hope you enjoy it." Ken hands her a large glass of wine. "Sorry to say it wasn't my best purchase. I've been working my way through a case of it."

"Thanks, I'm sure it will be fine. We all make mistakes from time to time," replies Sarah-Jane. They clink glasses and say cheers before taking a sip. "I can see what you mean about the wine. It's quite a harsh aftertaste, a very heavy wooden taste. So, you are an artist?" she asks.

"Yes, found a passion for it when I was six. As the years have passed, I have sold a few paintings," Ken tells her.

"Are some of the paintings hanging up in Cherry's yours?" she replies.

"Yes, there are three of mine in Cherry's," he admits. "Two are sold, and I'm in discussions for the third. Cherry's loves to support local artists. They have given me an avenue to showcase and sell my paintings. As they support me, I support Cherry's." Ken takes another sip of his wine.

He is holding a remote control for the apartment and as he pushes a button, the curtains start moving from both sides of the bank of windows, meeting in the middle to shut out the outside world. Ken dims the lights by pushing another button.

"Shall we make ourselves more comfortable?" he gestures towards the couch closest to the bed, and they sip their wine as they walk over and sit down.

Sarah-Jane takes a large gulp of her wine before handing her glass to Ken. "May I use your bathroom? I just want to freshen up," she enquires.

"Feel free. Make yourself at home. The bathroom is the curved section at the back," he replies, then asks, "What music would you like to listen to?"

"Do you have some classical, blues, or light jazz?"

Ken unfortunately doesn't have many CDs, but he loads internet radio on his flatscreen television with the sound coming out from the soundbar.

Sarah-Jane recognises the piece of music as she returns from of the bathroom. It is Mozart's Fifth Symphony. "I love this piece," she tells him as she sits back down on the couch.

"I don't know much classical music," Ken admits. "I just chose the first internet radio station playing classical music. I think I will also freshen up. Won't be long."

When he returns from the bathroom, he sits back down beside her on the couch. Sarah-Jane has taken off her navy-blue jumper, having hung it over the back of the couch.

"Are you feeling a little nervous?" he asks. "Are you sure you want to go through with this? I know how it felt when I was in your position, it being my first-time meeting someone just for the purpose of sex. It was quite unnerving at the time."

Sarah-Jane replies, "I'm a little nervous, but I'm not going to let that stop me. Life is short, and there are many experiences to be had. As you have been through this many

times before, will you take the lead and open me up to new experiences?"

"Ok, we will go slowly, and at any time if you want to stop, just say so and we will stop," Ken assures her, moving closer.

"I will say stop if I'm uncomfortable at any time with what we are doing," replies Sarah-Jane, as Ken puts his left arm under her legs while his right arm supports her back.

He pulls her closer to him, draping Sarah-Jane's legs over his knees, the curve of her bottom firmly against his upper right leg. He places his left arm on her thigh, with his right arm slowly moving her towards him, and they kiss. Closing their eyes, they open their mouths, their lips gently locking together, their tongues swirling around each other's like dolphins swirling in the open ocean. A warm feeling starts in Sarah-Jane's stomach and moves throughout her body in waves. The longer they kiss, the faster Sarah-Jane's nervousness fades away, the more relaxed she becomes, and the more into the experience she is willing to take herself.

They have been kissing for ten minutes, their mouths briefly breaking away from each other only to breathe more freely.

Ken speaks first. "Would you like to stay on the couch a while longer, or should we move to the bed?"

"Let's move to the bed. I think we will be more comfortable there," she replies. She stands up and takes Ken's right hand and leads him towards the bed.

Ken turns on the electric heating, pushing a button on a panel on the wall next to the bed to dispel the slight chill that's starting to creep in. They sit facing each other, one leg on the bed, the other on the floor. Ken opens one button at a time, removing the black blouse Sarah-Jane is wearing, folding and placing it on the bed, then he unclasps her lace bra, folding it and placing it on top of the blouse, tossing them at the couch hoping they will land on top of Sarah-Janes navy jumper. He then removes his own jumper and t-shirt as one item, flinging them in the direction of Sarah-Jane's clothes.

Sarah-Jane removes her shoes, leaving them at the base of the bed then lies back waiting for Ken to move closer.

Their lips find each other again, their kiss more intense than the first; it is deeper, slower, their bodies pressed firmly against each other. Sarah-Jane can feel the growing throbbing of Ken's cock brushing against her, making her push her body closer to his.

Ken rolls Sarah-Jane on her back, leaning in to kiss her again. His kisses are slow and gentle as his mouth moves from her lips to her right ear, planting light kisses along the

way, lightly nibbling her earlobe, making Sarah-Jane emit a small sigh of pleasure. His tongue snakes its way from her ear to her breasts, making her shiver, goosebumps appearing on her skin, the little hairs on her arms standing to attention. His tongue dances around her inviting nipple, which becomes firm and large. He teases it before taking her breast deep inside his mouth, making Sarah-Jane's lower back slightly arch off the bed.

Ken's mouth makes its way to Sarah-Jane's left breast, his tongue teasing the nipple as it travels anticlockwise with less effort than the first. It's excited, waiting, almost standing at attention, firm and hard. Sarah-Jane's breathing is slow and deep as Ken continues to tease her nipples, moving from left to right and back again. She lets out a longer, deeper sigh of pleasure and Ken moves back up to kiss her inviting mouth.

She pulls Ken in closer to her, as her body is awash with tiny explosions of desire. It is building up inside her, waiting to explode, and all she wants now is Ken's large, throbbing cock inside her. Just thinking about it makes Sarah-Jane wet between her legs. He unbuckles her belt, loosens the button on her jeans, then slowly releases the zipper, prolonging the anticipation of her being free from her clothes.

Ken's fingers caress her legs as he peels the jeans from her and tosses them onto the floor, just short of the couch. His

attention is firmly on Sarah-Jane, watching as she rubs her fingers over her panties, making the wet stain larger as she rubs up and down in a straight line.

They look deep into each other's eyes, and Ken can read an unspoken look of 'fuck me now'. He quickly removes his own his jeans, throwing them towards the couch and not caring where they land. Kissing her waiting mouth again, his tongue then snakes its way down between her breasts, her nipples still rock-hard waiting to be teased again. He carries on past Sarah-Jane's belly, making his way towards her panties, which he bites softly, clasping the material between his teeth as he pulls them down to her knees. Using his hands, he removes them the rest of the way and tosses them in the direction of the pile of clothes on the floor.

Sarah-Jane opens her legs, waiting for Ken's touch. He plants light kisses on her right leg as he makes his way to her warm, inviting pussy. Lying on his stomach with his mouth on her wet pussy, he licks her labia, opening her lips to spread her pussy juices, the tip of his tongue finding her throbbing, swollen clit and licking in a clockwise direction. She pushes her pelvis towards his waiting tongue and open mouth, and he sucks in her clit gently but deeply, driving Sarah-Jane wild, squeezing her legs together as she has an intense orgasm.

Ken's hands are fondling her breast while he is going down on her, her nipples rock hard. His tongue is a machine. He

has been teasing and licking Sarah-Jane's pussy for 20 minutes, giving her five incredible orgasms – the last one so intense that Sarah-Jane arches her back off the bed, gripping the bedsheets in both hands as she lets out a loud moan, coming hard and releasing a flood of pussy juices onto the bed below her. Her breathing is faster with each orgasm she is having.

Ken inserts his middle finger inside Sarah-Jane, moving it in and out, in and out, while he rubs her clit with the thumb of his other hand, bringing on a further two orgasms.

"Fuck me now! I need to feel you deep inside me," she pleads.

Taking off his underwear, Ken stands next to the bed, his fully erect, hard cock in full view. Sarah-Jane makes her way to the edge of the bed and takes his cock in her left hand, stroking it up and down a few times before taking it deep in her mouth, moving her head back and forth, back and forth, leaving his cock moist, glistening in the light.

Ken puts on a condom and Sarah-Jane lies back on the bed. Gently, he shifts her body so that she is lying on her side, her left leg between his, bent at the knee, holding her right leg straight up against his body. He rubs his cock up and down her labia, the head of his cock separating her pussy lips as her juices lather his cock, then slowly it disappears inside her, inch by inch, until he is balls deep inside her.

Moving his pelvis back and forth, his cock in and out, her juices are thick and creamy, coating Ken's throbbing hard cock. As he is fucking Sarah-Jane, at first Ken's body is doing all the work, until their bodies become in tune with each other, moving together as one, the motion of their bodies getting faster and faster. Sarah-Jane pushes her body into Ken's, and he holds her leg tight as he pushes his pelvis deep into hers.

Turning Sarah-Jane onto her stomach, her legs spread wide, Ken takes Sarah-Jane from behind, inserting his hard cock inside her pussy, leaning forward with his arms outstretched on either side of her. Ken thrusts long and deep, slow at first, getting faster and faster the closer they are to coming, letting out a loud moan as they come together, their breathing fast and laboured. Ken slows his strokes after he comes, staying inside Sarah-Jane until the sensitivity subsides.

Ken's once rock-hard cock slips out of Sarah-Jane's wet creamy pussy and they lie on the bed next to each other, trying to get their breath.

Sarah-Jane says, "Wow, just wow! You sure know how to use that tongue of yours.

"Thanks, I said you wouldn't be disappointed. If we give it a while, we can go again if you like," Ken replies.

"Oh definitely, I want more," she tells him.

They lie next to each other motionless as they wait to get their energy back, dripping wet from sweat. After a few minutes, Ken goes to the bathroom to get them towels to wipe themselves down with. "I'm going to have to wash the bedcovers after tonight, we have made a sweaty mess of them," he says.

"Sorry for making a mess. I haven't had such an intense orgasm in a really long time, and I have never gushed so much pussy juices before," she admits.

"Don't worry about it. I like when a woman is so into the experience that her body releases its juices," replies Ken.

They are so worn out from their session that they both fall asleep. When they waken, Ken says, "You are more than welcome to spend the night. It's too cold and wet outside, and driving home could be quite dangerous."

"Are you sure? I don't want to be a bother."

"Yes, I'm sure. At least that way we get to fool around again in the morning," he says, smiling. They climb under the covers and fall asleep straight away, still drained of their energy.

Waking in the early morning to the noise of traffic ferrying people to work, Sarah-Jane is scrolling through her social

media when Ken opens his eyes. "Would you like a coffee or tea?" he asks.

"Coffee, please. That hot brown nectar of the gods is a must-have first thing in the morning. But first, you have some work to do."

Ken is about to get out of bed to make the coffee, but pauses at her comment and gets back under the covers. He rubs his hands together, warming them up, then lies facing Sarah-Jane. Ken rubs his index finger up and down, back and forth over her clit, spreading the moistness from her pussy between her lips, massaging her clit in a circular motion, slow at first, getting faster as his fingers lightly squeeze her clit between them.

Sarah-Jane's legs close tightly over Ken's hand as she has a full body orgasm, sending shivers around her body. He lies back as Sarah-Jane takes his cock in her mouth, giving him a wet, sloppy blowjob, then he moves her so that she is on top of him, her pussy now in front of his face. He licks her pussy while she is giving him a blowjob, which makes Sarah-Jane really wet again.

Ken stretches for the box of condoms, passing it to Sarah-Jane. She opens one and rolls it over his throbbing, hard cock, then moves forward to slide it inside her. Leaning forward, Sarah-Jane holds onto Ken's ankles as she rocks her pelvis back and forth, back and forth, grinding her body

in a clockwise motion, slow and steady, building, getting faster and faster. She leans backwards, her arms behind her, and their hands clasp together as she gets closer to orgasm. Sarah-Jane squeezes her pussy muscles as she comes, making Ken explode inside the condom.

"Do you still want that coffee?" Ken asks Sarah-Jane eventually.

"That would be lovely," she replies. "Do you mind if I have a shower? After such an energetic night and morning, it would be nice to go home feeling refreshed."

"For sure you can have a shower and freshen up before going home. I'll get you a fresh towel, as the ones from last night are sweaty and smelly." Ken gets a fresh towel from the closet that is between the bed and bathroom, handing it to Sarah-Jane.

Fifteen minutes later, Sarah-Jane emerges from the bathroom feeling fresh, her hair wrapped in the towel. "I wasn't expecting to stay over last night so I didn't bring fresh panties with me, I will go home without, feeling free, letting it all hang out," she tells Ken as he hands her the mug of strong coffee.

"Nothing to be ashamed of. I have had to do the same from time to time. Enjoy your coffee," replies Ken.

After finishing her coffee and towel drying her hair, Sarah-Jane gets ready to leave. Ken walks her to the door. "Thanks for the great night. We should do this again sometime."

Sarah-Jane replies, "Yes, we will. Next time you will come to my home."

She pushes the button to call the elevator and they chat as they wait for it to arrive. When it does, they kiss each other goodbye. This time it is a lingering kiss on the lips.

As Sarah-Jane enters the elevator she says, "Have a lovely day. I will text you to organise our next encounter."

"Thanks, I'll look forward to it. Enjoy your day, too." He closes his front door once the elevator door has closed.

Once Sarah-Jane is back at her car, she realises that it has stopped raining and the sun is trying to peek through the clouds. She takes a few minutes to text Amanda before she leaves, as her friend has used We Play. *"Just had the most amazing night of sex."* Then she starts the engine and drives away with a smile on her face from ear to ear.

Five minutes have passed, and Sarah-Jane's smile is still as big as it was since she drove off from Ken's apartment bloc. When her phone vibrates, Sarah-Jane knows that it's a text from Amanda, probably wanting to know all the juicy details from last night. Sarah-Jane thinks to herself, *I'll text her back when I get home.*

Chapter 8

It's been just over a week-and-a-half since Sarah-Jane's encounter with Ken. She is looking forward to meeting Charles this evening, as they have been chatting for the last three days, organising where they will meet. It has been raining on and off for the last 10 days but thankfully this evening is a clear night with not a cloud in the sky. There is, though, a definite chill in the air.

Sarah-Jane is feeling a lot more confident since her time with Ken, and she has chosen to meet Charles at Giorgio's. It has been just over a month since she was there for her birthday dinner with the girls. They have arranged to meet there at eight for a light dinner and drinks, and Sarah-Jane has asked for a table in the back so they can be in the quieter area of the restaurant.

It's a Friday evening and Giorgio's is packed, the front of house buzzing with people when Sarah-Jane arrives. Knowing she will be drinking this evening, she has taken a taxi to the restaurant. She has also agreed that Charles is

going to drive them back to her house so there is no need for two cars or for one of them to leave their car at Giorgio's.

Sarah-Jane enters Giorgio's to a warm greeting from Sergio, "Hello, Sarah, so nice of you to join us again. Your guest is wating for you. We have a booth table in the back, as you requested."

"Thank you, Sergio, so nice to be back," she replies as he leads the way to her table.

Charles rises from the booth to greet her. "Hi, Sarah, so nice to finally meet in person," he says, as he leans in for a warm, friendly kiss on the cheek.

Sarah-Jane replies, "Yes, it is. We have chatted so much in the last three days that it feels like we have known each other for a long time." She removes her dinner jacket, placing it on the booth's seat next to Charles's black cotton one. She is wearing her new grey trousers with fine, black pinstripes, and the long-sleeved, black blouse with gold buttons.

Charles is dressed in a collarless, pearl white shirt, with the top button undone, a casual pair of black, slim fit trousers, and black suede shoes.

"I'll be back in a little while, giving you some time to look at the menu," Sergio tells them as they get comfy in the booth.

Sarah-Jane is a bit surprised. In Charles's profile pictures he had long dreadlocks and an unruly, long beard – both of which are missing now. "Wow, I'm a bit shocked," she says. "What happened? From your profile pictures, you looked more the hippy/surfer type."

"Those photos were taken two years ago," he admits. "I need to update the photos on my profile. I was on a research sabbatical going around the world, which turned into a two-and-a-half-year holiday mixed in among the research. It was easier to dread the hair and have a long beard. But unfortunately, everything has to come to an end when reality sets in and the holiday is over."

Charles takes a sip of his water before continuing, "Sorry, I should have warned you that my appearance has changed."

"It is just a shock, I wasn't expecting it," she replies. "You look great, it suits you."

Charles has had half the length of his hair cut off, so that it is now touching just below his shoulders, and the dreadlocks are gone. He explains that it took almost the entire day at a hair salon for the hairstylist and three other staff members, taking it in turns and adding more and more conditioner to the dreadlocks, to be able to comb them out. He has also shaved off his long beard.

"What research were you doing?" asks Sarah-Jane.

"I was doing my doctorate on the migration of sea turtles and the impact that climate change is having on their mating habits, due to the warming of the oceans, the rise of new turtle colonies in areas of the world that never had a turtle population before, and the steady decline of turtle populations where they had always been before," says Charles in reply.

"That sounds very interesting. I would love to hear more about the plight of the sea turtles," Sarah-Jane tells him, taking a sip of the water Charles had poured for her.

Sergio comes back to their table. "Are you ready to order, or do you need some more time?" he asks.

"Sorry, Sergio, we will need some more time. We haven't even looked at the menu yet," Sarah-Jane admits.

"I'll come back in five minutes," he says, "or will you need more time?"

"Five minutes should be fine, thanks," Sarah-Jane assures him. Turning to Charles, she says, "Let's decide on what we are having to eat, then we can carry on talking after Sergio has taken our order."

They look at the drinks menu and decide to have wine with their food, but they will order by the glass, as Charles is driving. By the time they have decided what they are going to eat, Sergio is back to take their order.

Sarah-Jane goes first. "Can I have a large glass of red wine, some mixed olives in oil as a starter, and a kids' portion of spaghetti bolognaise?"

"And for you, sir?" asks Sergio, looking at Charles.

"I will have a small white wine, the calamari to start with, and the seafood spaghetti as my main," says Charles.

"Thank you. Your drinks won't be a moment," Sergio assures them and heads off. Two minutes later, Mario places their glasses of wine on the table.

While waiting for their starters to arrive, they carry on talking. When their olives and calamari are served, Maria places the two dishes on the table with two clean side plates. They have chosen to share the calamari and olives. Charles holds the dish of calamari over Sarah-Jane's plate while she scoops some of the dish onto her plate. Then she picks up the bowl with tartar sauce, adding some onto the plate next to the calamari. Charles dishes the rest of the calamari onto his plate, and Sarah-Jane spoons the rest of the tartar sauce onto his plate.

Picking up the bowl of mixed olives, she first gives Charles some, before taking some for herself. A silence falls over the table as they enjoy their starters.

"Great calamari. Got to say that's maybe the best I have eaten in a long time. The olives are more on the sweeter side, at least they aren't bitter," Charles says as he finishes the last bite of the starters. "This must be a favourite restaurant of yours, as you seem very friendly with the staff."

Sarah-Jane nods. "The food here is so amazing, I have never had a bad meal here. Yes, I've been coming here for years. My friends and I come at least once a month, sometimes twice if we get the chance. Giorgio's is a family-run restaurant. Even though there are now nine branches, they are all run by different family members. They put so much love into their cooking, and it comes out in the flavour of each dish."

Sergio has come back to the table. "How is everything?" he asks. "If you need anything else, please don't hesitate to ask." He removes the empty dishes from the table.

"That is the best calamari I have eaten in a long time," Charles tells him.

"We only cook the freshest ingredients, and we get our seafood fresh every day," replies Sergio, smiling. "I'm glad

you are enjoying it. Your main courses won't be much longer." He takes the empty plates to the kitchen.

It is quarter-to-nine when their main courses arrive. Mario is holding a tray with his right hand, placing Sarah-Jane's spaghetti in front of her, then putting the seafood spaghetti in front of Charles. "Enjoy your food, I hope it is to your pleasing," he says to them. "Would you like some freshly ground pepper, parsley and garlic oil, or some parmesan cheese for your pastas?"

Charles replies, "Can I get some of the parsley and garlic oil, please?"

"I'd like the parmesan cheese, please," adds Sarah-Jane.

Mario places two small bowls on the table – one with the parmesan cheese, the other with the parsley and garlic oil – before he leaves them to enjoy their meal. A second silence has fallen over their table, except for the occasional sounds of "mmm" as they enjoy their spaghetti.

They are halfway through the main course when Sergio reappears. "Would you like to order any desserts, coffee or tea?" he asks them.

"Can we decide after we have finished our main course?" replies Sarah-Jane.

"No problem, I just wanted to know because the kitchen is very busy tonight, and it may take longer than expected. Hope you don't mind the wait," Sergio explains.

"We don't mind the wait," Charles assures him. It is ten past nine by the time they finish eating their main courses. "Do you want any dessert, coffee or tea?" he asks Sarah-Jane.

"Normally I would have a dessert after my meal, but today I don't want to feel like I've over-eaten as we have a very energetic night ahead of us," she replies. "I think I will just have a coffee instead."

"Are you sure? We can share one, if you like. Maybe some sorbet; it will be light," suggests Charles.

She smiles. "Oh well, twist my rubber arm, why don't you? Yes, maybe some sorbet with coffee."

Five minutes later, Sergio comes to take their order. "Have you decided yet if you will have dessert?" he asks.

"Can we please have two coffees, one black and the other with milk, thanks? And what flavour sorbet do you have?" asks Charles.

"We have three flavours which are prepared daily: a strawberry flavoured sorbet with pieces of strawberry;

fresh vanilla, made with rich vanilla seeds squeezed from fresh vanilla pods; and a lemon and lime sorbet, made with the zest from fresh lemons and limes," Sergio explains.

"Can we have one scoop of each to share? Thanks," replies Charles.

"So, two coffees, one black, one with milk, and a bowl of sorbet to share," Sergio repeats the order back to them.

"Yes, please," replies Sarah-Jane. "And can you bring the bill in the meantime, please Sergio?"

He returns shortly with the bill, placing it on the table.

"I will pay this time, you get dinner next time," she tells Charles.

"Are you sure I can't contribute towards dinner?" he asks.

"I'm sure. But, if you want, you can leave a tip for the staff."

Maria brings them their coffees and sorbet. "Who is having the black coffee?" she asks, and Sarah-Jane lifts her hand.

She places the black coffee in front of Sarah-Jane and the coffee with milk in front of Charles, then puts the bowl of

sorbet in-between them, placing a spoon wrapped in a servette on either side of the bowl.

"Thanks, Maria, and can you please bring the card machine? I would like to settle the bill," says Sarah-Jane

Maria nods. "Won't be a minute," she says and comes back a few minutes later with the card machine.

Sarah-Jane hands over her bank card, which Maria inserts in the reader then enters the amount in the machine. She hands the reader to Sarah-Jane who enters her pin. Finally, Maria tears off the customer receipt copy and hands it and the card back to Sarah-Jane.

After she has left the table, Charles asks, "Where should I leave the tip?"

"There is a jar at the front door, you can leave the tip there," Sarah-Jane tells him.

"That is the freshest flavoured sorbet I have eaten," Charles comments as they finish their dessert. "The only other place I have eaten sorbet that flavoursome and fresh was when I was in Italy during my research sabbatical."

Sarah-Jane suggests that they use the toilet before they leave. While she is at the toilet, Charles goes to the front

desk and puts some cash in the tip jar. On her return, he explains, "I have been to the front and left a tip." Then he heads to the toilet while she puts her coat on and gets ready to leave.

When Charles gets back, he says, "Ready? Sorry, I had to park three streets away, as there wasn't any parking close by."

"Not to worry, the walk won't hurt us." She goes on, "I should have told you that it would be difficult to find a parking spot close by."

They say goodbye to the staff as they leave, and thank them for a delicious meal. Sergio wishes them a good evening as he holds the door open for them.

Outside it is a lot colder than when Sarah-Jane arrived. There is a light mist hanging in the air and the temperature has dropped by about six degrees.

"Which way to your car?" she asks.

Charles points to his left and before she knows it, they have reached his car. The cold is starting to bite through, chilling her to the bone.

Opening the door for Sarah-Jane, Charles says, "You're shivering. I'll put the heating on for you."

"Thanks, I didn't expect it to be this cold. The weather has just crept up on us," she replies, climbing into the passenger's seat.

Charles walks around to the driver's side and gets in, switching on the power to the car and switching the heating on. They sit for a while to allow the windows to demist before he drives off.

Starting to warm up, Sarah-Jane gives Charles her address, which he enters into the satnav to calculate the best route back to her home. It takes them 45 minutes to reach her house, due to the traffic being so heavy on a Friday night, and just managing to avoid two traffic jams along the way. The satnav re-routed them both times, allowing them to avoid the congestion, but it makes the journey longer than it would normally have been.

Sarah-Jane has parked her car in the garage, allowing Charles to park in the driveway instead of on the street. They walk up the path to the porch and Sarah-Jane opens the front door, letting Charles enter before she does. Closing the door behind her, she puts her keys on the hook and her purse on the long, thin table.

"As we aren't going anywhere and you won't need to drive, unless you will be going home later, would you like some more wine? Unfortunately, I only have red," she tells him.

Charles replies unexpectedly, "Would you mind terribly if I said no to the wine? And would it be too much of an imposition if I smoked some weed before we have sex?"

She shrugs. "It won't be a problem. Why do you smoke weed before sex?" Sarah-Jane has never smoked cannabis before, even though she was around people who did when she was at university.

"I find alcohol makes me horny while I'm drunk, but the problem is the more alcohol I drink the less likely I will be to get or even maintain an erection. The trials and tribulations of being 40; the body doesn't work like it used to when I was in my twenties. On the other hand, for me, when I smoke weed it brings a calming sense of euphoria, my senses are heightened, and I'm a lot more focused. During sex your senses are sharpened even more, you feel every sensation threefold. Do you partake?" he asks Sarah-Jane.

"No, I have never partaken before. Whenever in the past I have asked people who smoke, why they do it, no-one has been able to explain why. Usually, the answer I get is 'I don't know, I just enjoy it.' You are the first person to give me an answer that makes sense to me. Shall we go to the backyard? You can smoke there." Sarah-Jane points towards the dining room and kitchen.

Charles follows Sarah-Jane through the dining room towards the kitchen. "That is a lovely canvas painting of an African watering hole," Charles comments before he continues, "I come prepared, usually I have a joint or two pre-rolled. It saves time when you aren't at home and feel like a smoke. As you have never smoked before, would you like to try with me? You may experience something new and like it. As you are in your own home and with someone experienced in the finer art of smoking, I can guide you through it."

"Are you sure I won't have a panic attack and freak out?" Sarah-Jane asks nervously. "If I do smoke with you, can you guarantee that you can calm me down if anything were to happen?"

"Just take it slow, there is no need to overdo it. You have two or three drags of the joint, see how you feel, and if you would like more then have another two or three drags. People only become overwhelmed if they have too much to start with, not knowing how to control the high," Charles assures her.

Feeling more at ease with the situation Sarah-Jane decides she is going to try smoking weed for the first time. If she doesn't enjoy the experience, she will never try it again. "Sure, I will try smoking weed with you," she tells him. "Life is short. There are many things in life we just don't do

because we are afraid to, then we regret having not done them when we had the chance because we are too old, and it is too late."

As Sarah-Jane opens the sliding door, a rush of icy cold air greets them. "Let's make this quick, it is bitterly cold out there," Charles says. Pulling out a lighter and a metal tube from his left inside jacket pocket, he unscrews the lid of the metal tube, takes a rolled joint from it, then screws the lid back on and puts the tube back where he had taken it from.

Putting the joint between his lips, Charles flicks the lid of the lighter open. A green light appears in the space for a person's finger. Once the light is broken, it ignites the electric lighter, and two blue bolts of electricity arch between the four metal probes protruding from the top of the lighter. Charles lowers his head towards the arch of blue electricity, and the tip of the joint starts smouldering. He takes a drag of the joint as it ignites, and an orange red flame appears. Charles blows some smoke towards the tip of the joint, extinguishing the flame, leaving a red glowing coal at the top. He inhales deeply for a second time, blowing out a large plume of smoke.

"Here, don't inhale as deeply as I did for your first drag," he advises, passing her the joint.

Sarah-Jane puts it to her lips and takes a small drag, not inhaling as deeply as Charles did. She blows out the smoke and starts coughing. "Is that normal to cough like that?" she asks.

Taking the joint from Sarah-Jane, he takes another drag and blows out the smoke. "Yes, it is very normal to cough like that," he replies. "The smoke hits the back of your throat, and you get a tickling sensation in your throat which makes you cough. You get used to it, and coughing becomes less after the third of fourth drag. I still cough occasionally." He takes another drag of the joint before passing it to Sarah-Jane.

This time, when she tries another drag, it's a little bit longer and a little bit deeper, but she still coughs as she exhales. Sarah-Jane is starting to feel lightheaded; she notices that her breathing seems easier, like her lungs can take in twice the amount of air as normal. Her mouth feels dry like a desert, and she feels like she needs to drink lot of water. A warm, comforting feeling starts to wash over her, and she thinks, *Wow, I'm feeling light, like I'm floating. I'm so comfortable right now.*

There is a tingling feeling inside Sarah-Jane's head, in the forehead region, in the middle just above the eyes. It sends a shiver of joy down the whole of her back to her stomach and along her arms, giving her goosebumps, Sarah-Jane

passes the joint back to Charles, telling him how she is feeling.

"Maybe one more drag of the joint for you," he says. "For your first time, you are in the perfect place. Any more and you may become too overwhelmed."

The joint has now been half-smoked. Charles takes another two drags before passing it to a very focused looking Sarah-Jane. Her eyes look like half slits as she peers off into the distance, as though she is lost in thought and gazing out into the mists of nothingness, not looking at anything in particular.

Before she can take the joint from Charles, he says, "I think two drags is enough for you. I'll put it out and we can finish it later." He lets the joint die out on its own, tapping it lightly against the metal tube to knock off any ash, then puts the unfinished joint back in the metal tube.

Leaving the patio, they go back inside to the inviting warmth and away from the biting cold. Sarah-Jane gets the water jug and two glasses, "Do you want some water?" she asks. "My mouth is so dry; it feels like a desert. Is that normal?"

"Thanks. Yeah, dry mouth is totally normal," he assures her, taking the glass of water. "I noticed some African spears on the wall in the dining room. Where did you get them?"

"There are more of them in the lounge if you want to see. They belonged to my parents. They were archaeologists, and these are some of their private artifacts they found while out on expeditions; there are different masks, shields and spears from different tribes from around the world. Unfortunately, just over a year-and-a-half ago they died in a freak accident," she explains quietly. "There was a flash flood that washed out the road they were driving on and their car was taken by the raging river current, quickly dragging the vehicle underwater. It all happened so quickly, they didn't have time to escape, and they drowned. This is our family home, the house I grew up in."

Charles is a little shocked by this revelation. "Wow, this is weird," he tells her. "When I started studying at university, I was undecided what field I wanted to study, it was only in my last year I decided what I was going to major in. I went to a few different lectures to get a feel for what I wanted to study, and a few of those lectures were held by your father. I found them very interesting and informative. Your father's work, though brilliant, wasn't connected to the field of study I chose, so I stopped going to his lectures. I had heard that he had died. I'm sorry to open old wounds."

Sarah-Jane shakes her head. "Enough sad talk. Let's make our way to being more comfortable upstairs."

She takes Charles by the hand, switching off the lights in the kitchen and dining room, as they head up the stairs. *Good thing I went to get a box of condoms on the way home from work,* she thinks to herself, leading Charles to the den of delight.

"I'm going to change quickly," she tells him. "Why don't you get comfortable on the bed? You can hang your clothes over the leather stool in front of the dressing table."

Sarah-Jane was well prepared; she had left a knee-length, red silk nightie in the bathroom, which she quickly changes into. She can feel the smooth fabric sliding over her breast as she pulls it over her head, and the sensation makes her nipples tingle and start to harden. Charles was right; she is feeling things at a heightened level. She decides not to wear any panties under the nightie, as she wants to feel the silk rubbing up against her pussy while she walks back to the bedroom.

When she gets there, Charles is already under the duvet, and is completely naked. Sarah-Jane lights the vanilla scented candles on either side of the bed and on the dressing table before turning off the lights in the hallway and bedroom. A soft warm glow lights up the room as she joins Charles on the bed.

She gently pulls back the duvet, exposing Charles's naked body and his large but flaccid cock.

"Sex can be a lot more intimate and sensual when you are high," he tells her.

Sarah-Jane leans forward, opening her mouth to kiss Charles as their lips meet. Their tongues swirl, their saliva mixing as they share a long deep passionate kiss, sending a warm tingle between Sarah-Jane's legs. The longer the kiss, the wetter Sarah-Jane becomes. She takes Charles's cock in her hand, moving it up and down as she feels it harden.

Leaning over, Sarah-Jane takes a condom from the box on the bedside table, opens it, and rolls it over Charles's now hard, pulsating cock, then she straddles him, still stroking. Charles is massaging Sarah-Jane's breast while they are still kissing. He takes off her silk nightie, breaking their kiss briefly to remove it. Charles takes her left breast into his mouth, sucking it in deeply, and goosebumps appear on Sarah-Jane's body as the feeling triggers little explosions of lustful joy.

Charles's tongue twirls around Sarah-Jane's nipple, making it bullet hard, then he takes her right breast in his hand and does the same to her right nipple. She has never felt this type of heightened senses during sex before, and she is loving it. She thinks to herself, *Have I been missing out all this time? I should have tried weed a long time ago.*

Sarah-Jane's pussy is so wet that she slides Charles's cock inside her with ease. His legs are straight out in front of

him, and he is seated with his back up against the headboard. Sarah-Jane is holding the headboard with both hands, either side of Charles's head, while he sucks and teases her breasts. As Sarah-Jane begins moving her pelvis up and down, Charles's left arm supports her back and his right hand holds her bottom. He moves both his hands to Sarah-Jane's waist as she keeps grinding her body into his, the pair kissing very deeply as though they were one, this deep feeling joining them on a sensual, spiritual level.

Sarah-Jane grinds her pelvis back and forth, her rhythm becoming faster and more urgent, then clenches her pussy muscles as she comes. Charles's cock explodes into the condom as he feels the pressure when she orgasms. Locked in an embrace, they wait for the intense feelings to subside, Sarah-Jane's body shaking from the orgasm, both waiting for their breath to return.

After a while, Sarah-Jane climbs off Charles and falls backwards on the bed with her legs open, her juices dripping onto the sheet. "That is the most intimate sex I have ever had," she admits. "Weed definitely enhances the experience."

"Like I said earlier, I prefer to smoke than drink, so now you know why," he replies.

Charles leans forward and slides his hand up her leg. It glides over the top of her pussy, and he rubs his finger up

and down over her lips, her juices moistening his fingers, making her clit swell. Sliding his middle finger inside Sarah-Jane, he moves it in and out, back and forth. Her eyes are closed, her breathing deep and slow, and as Charles's finger moves inside her, the wetter she gets, and the faster and more heightened her breath becomes.

"Let's try this position. I lie back on my elbows, my legs on the outside, you move in as close to me as you can between my legs. Your legs then go over mine, so they are on either side of my hips, then you slide my cock inside you, and you lean back on your elbows and move your pelvis back and forth," Charles suggests.

"I have never tried that before. Sounds like it could be really good," Sarah-Jane replies. She struggles to get the words out, as Charles is still fingering her now creamy pussy, his hand covered in the white creamy fluid of her juices.

They move themselves into position and Charles replaces the spent condom for a fresh one. His cock slips out twice, as Sarah-Jane is so wet and he isn't fully hard yet, but on the third try his cock stays in. Sarah-Jane rocks her pelvis back and forth, letting out a loud moan as she bites her lower lip, the feeling of euphoria building inside her. Their pelvises bang into each other the faster they move together, their breathing becoming fast and shallow as they find their rhythm. Sarah-Jane's moans get louder and louder as she

comes, her orgasm so powerful that the force of her juices pushes Charles's cock out and she falls onto her back panting. As Charles hasn't come yet, he takes off the condom and moves closer to Sarah-Jane's head, kneeling in front of her.

"Could you suck me off till I come?" he asks.

Sarah-Jane takes his hard cock in her hand and starts sucking him off. She is so into this blowjob that her eyes are closed as her mouth bobs up and down the length of Charles's cock. He clenches his butt cheeks and lets out a loud moan as he shoots his load into Sarah-Jane's mouth. As he comes, Sarah-Jane sucks his cock so deep inside her mouth that she lets his cum slip down her throat, the sensation so intense it makes Charles's body quiver. They finally collapse on the bed exhausted.

"What is the time?" Sarah-Jane asks Charles.

He picks up his watch from the bedside table. "It is now quarter-to-one. I think I will take you up on the offer of sleeping over as it is too late to drive home, if that's okay," he says.

They take turns going to the bathroom before they go to sleep. Charles puts some toothpaste on his index finger and uses it like a makeshift toothbrush. Sarah-Jane has blown

out the candles and is waiting in bed. Charles climbs in beside her and switches off the lamp, and they drift off to sleep after a bit of chatting, their bodies buzzing from endorphins.

In the morning, Charles is wakened by the smell of hot coffee – and a smile. "What time is it?" he ask Sarah-Jane.

"It's half seven," she replies, handing him the coffee. "The weed has made me feel groggy this morning, but thanks for the wonderful experience last night. We need to do this again soon. I would like to smoke again with you before we have sex, as I have never felt like that during sex before."

"Yes, we can do this again soon," he replies.

By quarter past eight Charles has finished his coffee and gotten dressed. Sarah-Jane kisses him goodbye and uses the remote control to open the electric gate to let Charles out from the driveway. She waves as he reverses his car out of the drive. Once his car is out of sight, Sarah-Jane walks inside, closing the front door behind her.

Chapter 9

It is the last day of October, Halloween. Sarah-Jane and Lance are meeting at Jonestown this evening, where there is a Halloween theme throughout the entire complex. Sarah-Jane is glad it has fallen on a Saturday this year; it is a long weekend for her. It was her turn to work the Saturday shift at the library, giving her the Monday off as well.

She and Lance have been texting each other all day, deciding what time to meet at Jonestown; neither of them are driving to Jonestown. Being Halloween, they have to dress up in costume to enter Jonestown. Sarah-Jane is going as a witch, Lance as a vampire. They have agreed to go to Smoking Jones for dinner first, then maybe watch some live music or play a bit of pool. They haven't made any firm plans on what they will do while at Jonestown. Dinner is a definite, the rest is up in the air.

Sarah-Jane asked Mike to book a table for two at Smoking Jones for half eight. If he wasn't her cousin, she would never have been able to get a table, but luckily for her

someone had cancelled their reservation. He said he would try to come by and say hi, but they both know Jonestown is going to be ram packed for Halloween, and even with hiring extra staff over Halloween to make sure everything runs smoothly, Mike will be busy.

Since Sarah-Jane's encounters with Ken and Charles, she has grown as a person and is grateful to have met two great guys who gave her the best sex she has had, letting her be free to express herself as much as she was willing to. She hadn't felt like she was being pressured into doing anything beyond her limits. Though she'd had a great time with them and looks forward to seeing them again, she knows that there wouldn't be anything more than great sex between them.

The taxi pulls up eight twenty-five, stopping outside the parking lot of Jonestown. "Sorry, I'm going to have to let you out here, I can't go any further. There is no access to the parking lot tonight, only guests get access," the driver explains to Sarah-Jane.

"Thanks. Not to worry, I'm early anyway," she replies. "How much do I owe you?"

"That will be 35 for the ride," the driver replies.

Sarah-Jane opens her door and stretches over to hand him the cash. "Here is 50. Hope you have a great evening."

Before she has a chance to close the door, the taxi driver says, "Just started my shift. You are my first ride for the evening, so I've got many hours ahead yet."

"In that case, do you have a card with your name and number? We will be needing a ride back to where you collected me, much later, if you don't mind?"

"Here's my card, miss, and my name is Jonny," he tells her.

"Thanks, Jonny. Would you like to agree on a time to collect us now, or should I text you half an hour before we want to leave?"

"Let's agree on a time now, and if you want to stay later than that time, you can text and let me know. How does that sound to you?" replies Jonny.

"Is one o'clock ok for you?" Sarah-Jane asks. "We may want to leave earlier than one, but I will let you know as early as possible to give you time. If you are busy with another ride, just let me know how long you will be, and we can wait for you. Otherwise, one in the morning."

"Yes, please let me know as soon as possible if you want to leave either earlier or later than one. Otherwise I will be waiting either here, or hopefully by that time they will allow taxis back in the parking lot. Enjoy your evening, miss."

"Thanks, Jonny, and you can call me Sarah," she replies with a smile.

"Ok, Sarah. See you later."

Sarah-Jane closes the taxi door and fixes her witch's hat into place before walking to the main entrance to Smoking Jones, which is in the parking lot. Opening the door, she walks inside and is immediately greeted by one of the staff.

"Good evening, my name is Kattie, welcome to Smoking Jones. Do you have a reservation?"

"Hi Kattie. Yes, I have a table booked under Sarah-Jane," she replies.

Kattie has only been working at Smoking Jones for two weeks, so Sarah-Jane hasn't seen her before. The girl looks through the reservation list on the tablet she is carrying. "Ah yes, table for two. Your guest is already here. Follow me, please.

Sarah-Jane is impressed at the décor as she follows Kattie to the table. Each year Jonestown puts on a great Halloween, and there are cobwebs and small statues of witches on broomsticks hanging from the lights above each table. Scattered around the restaurant are carved pumpkins,

each lit up by a candle inside. One table has been set up as two zombies sitting eating a meal of human brains. Sarah-Jane is curious as to how the rest of Jonestown has been decorated, as each area usually has a different Halloween theme.

She follows Kattie to the last table in the row, close to the kitchen and the corridor leading into Jonestown's live music area. She can hear Deep Purple's *Smoke on the Water* coming from that direction.

Lance immediately stands up and gives Sarah-Jane a hug and a kiss on the cheek. There is an instant chemistry between them as they embrace, like a lightning bolt of energy rushing through their bodies. The energy is so strong it's like two magnets stuck together, very difficult to pull them apart. Sarah-Jane didn't feel this strong energy pull with either Ken or Charles.

Lance is a bit taken a back, as this is the first time he has ever had this type of feeling before. He has had many girlfriends and met quite a few women from the We Play website, but this feeling is something new to him. It is as if the two of them have known each other before, maybe in a past life, yet they have never met until now.

Lance has already ordered two draught beers. "I arrived ten minutes ago," he explains. "I didn't know what you wanted

to drink, so I ordered two draughts while I waited for you. If you don't want the beer, that's cool, we can get you something else and I'll drink the second one as well. They brought the beers two minutes before you arrived so they're still nice and cold."

His hair is slicked back, and he has heavy makeup around his eyes, fake blood painted on his chin and running down his neck, and the vampire fangs have drops of blood painted on the tips.

Sitting down, Sarah-Jane replies, "The beer is perfect, I love a good draught. Did it take you long to get here? You said you've never been to Jonestown before."

"No, not too long. The taxi driver knew where she was going. I have heard from friends over the years about Jonestown but haven't had the opportunity till now to come see for myself. I'm always busy, and out of town quite a lot for work," he explains. "Being a professional photographer, I have to go where the work takes me."

Sarah-Jane takes a large gulp of her beer. "God, I'm thirsty. That hit the spot."

Kattie comes by to tell them the specials of the day and leaves the menus with them, saying she will be back in a bit to take their order.

"What would you recommend, as someone who has been here before?" asks Lance.

"If you like ribs, you should get some, they are drop-off-the-bone delicious," replies Sarah-Jane. "You can get one rack of pork ribs or ask for them to bring a platter of ribs, but whichever you choose you won't be disappointed. And you definitely want a portion of their triple fried, thick cut fries."

They are still looking at the menu when Kattie returns to their table. "Have you decided what you want to order?" she asks.

Looking at Lance, Sarah-Jane says, "You go first. I'm still deciding."

"Can I have a portion of your hot wings with blue cheese sauce, and a rack of your baby back ribs with the triple cooked fries, please?" Lance asks.

Kattie enters Lance's order on the tablet, then looks at Sarah-Jane. "Are you ready, or do you need more time?"

Sarah-Jane smiles. "No, I'm ready to order, thanks. Can I have the chicken and pork burger with the triple cooked fries? And could I please have some blue cheese sauce on the side? Also, could you find out if Mike is available and tell him his cousin is here? He said he would try swing by if he wasn't too busy."

Entering Sarah-Jane's order into the tablet, Kattie replies, "I'll get your order to you as soon as possible, and I'll go see if Mike is available to come say hi."

At ten to nine, Kattie comes by with Lance's chicken wings. "Here's your hot wings, I hope you enjoy them," she says to Lance with a smile. Looking at Sarah-Jane, she adds, "Mike is really busy at the moment, but he will try to say hi if he gets a chance. He said when you finish eating you can find him in the live music area if he hasn't seen you first." She goes on, "Your burger and ribs will be another ten to 15 minutes. Would you like two more draught beers, or would you like something else to drink?"

Sarah-Jane replies, "Thanks for letting Mike know I'm here." She glances at the two almost empty beers and adds, "Two more draughts, please, and two shots of silver tequila, thanks."

Kattie is off in a flash to get their drinks.

"You have a cousin who works here? No wonder you come here a lot," Lance comments.

"Yeah, Mike has worked here for many years. He worked his way up to being one of the three head managers. Mike's parents moved out of town once he finished high school, so we are the only family each other has here since my parents died just over a year-and-a-half ago," Sarah-Jane explains.

Kattie is back with their beers and tequilas, placing one tequila in front of Sarah-Jane and the other in front of Lance. "Enjoy the drinks, your food is almost ready. I'll have it to you shortly. Mike said all drinks are on him this evening," she adds.

The tequila has a slice of lemon on top of the shot glass. Sarah-Jane pours a little salt on her hand, then picks up the slice of lemon with the same hand, and the shot of tequila in the other hand. Lance takes the slice of lemon from the top of his shot glass, placing it on the edge of his plate of wings, then lifts the shot glass with the other hand. They look at each other and say, "Cheers!" before knocking the tequila back. Sarah-Jane first licks the salt, downs her shot of tequila, then sucks the lemon. Lance just downs the tequila, having not taken any salt, and discarding the lemon.

"How are you enjoying your wings?" she asks him.

"These are the juiciest wings I have eaten in a long time. They have a nice smoky hotness to them," Lance replies.

When Katie comes back with their food, it is ten past nine and Smoking Jones is buzzing with people. Some are dressed up for Halloween, other guests are dressed normally as they have only come for dinner and aren't staying to party afterwards. There is a queue starting to form outside as people arrive to have dinner.

"Sorry for the extra wait. I hope you enjoy your burger and ribs," Kattie apologises as she places the burger in front of Sarah-Jane and serves the ribs to Lance.

Lance has only eaten half his wings. He asks Sarah-Jane, "Would you like a wing or two? They are really hot."

"I'll have one, thanks," she replies "You're going to love those ribs. She takes a wing off his plate and dips it into the blue cheese sauce before taking a bite. "Ooh, that's smoky. The after taste is quite hot and spicy, but thankfully that blue cheese sauce cools it down a bit. I tend to eat the milder BBQ wings and I don't really go for hot wings, but these are tasty."

"Thanks, I'm sure I'm going to enjoy the ribs, they look so juicy. Enjoy your burger. I can't say I have heard of burgers like this before. I'll swop you some ribs for some of your burger," he suggests.

Sarah-Jane pours the blue cheese sauce over her burger before she cuts it into quarters, the sauce dripping down the sides of the meat. "Take whichever piece you want," she says, "and I'll have two ribs. Thanks."

Lance cuts off two of his ribs, placing them on Sarah-Jane's plate before removing some of the burger. He takes a bite of the burger and his face lights up in surprise. "Wow, that

tastes amazing! I never thought of mixing chicken and pork meats together. It gives you a completely new taste sensation, and that blue cheese sauce takes it to another level."

He finishes the piece of Sarah-Jane's burger before he cuts his baby back ribs into sections. Biting into his first rib, Lance has a look of complete satisfaction on his face. The meat slides off the bone, melting in his mouth as he chews. "That is the best fucking ribs I have ever eaten," he tells her. "Why has it taken me so long to come to Jonestown? All my friends were right. I'm an idiot! I should have listened to them and come here a lot sooner; my mistake. This is going to become my new favourite hangout,"

For the next while, all that can be heard at their table are noises of contentment as they enjoy their food in silence.

Kattie appears out of nowhere. "Is everything ok? Do you need anything else? Some more drinks maybe?"

"I think we are all good for now. Please could you bring the bill?" asks Sarah-Jane. "I think we will have our next drinks with Mike."

When Kattie leaves, Sarah-Jane asks Lance, "What you think of those fries?"

"I thought triple fried, thick cut fries would have been dripping in oil, having seeped straight through to the centre,

being fried so many times," he admitted. "But I've got to say I'm surprised. The centre is light, fluffy, and soft, and the outside crispy, crunchy, giving you a dark, golden slice of potato heaven."

It's five to ten when they finish eating dinner. Kattie has brought the bill and the portable card machine with her. Lance leans forward to take the bill when Sarah-Jane says, "This one is on me. You get the next one."

Lance replies, "Are you sure? I'm more than happy to pay."

Sarah-Jane gives Kattie a cash tip and pays the rest by card. "Next time you can pay," she tells Lance with a cheeky smile.

Kattie hands back the card and receipt. "Thanks so much for visiting Smoking Jones, see you again soon. I hope you enjoy the rest of Halloween at Jonestown."

"I need to go to the toilet after those two draughts," Lance says.

"Great idea. I think I'll go, too," Sarah-Jane replies.

They get up from their table, Sarah-Jane leading the way. "There you are; here I am." She points to the separate ladies and gents toilets. "You can walk out the door on the other side of the toilet; it has a double entrance."

"See you on the other side then," laughs Lance, and they swing through their respective doors.

Lance is waiting for her when Sarah-Jane swings through at the other end. "I didn't realise how busy this place is," he says as they enter the live music area. "It's crazy. Is it always this busy?"

"It is busy throughout the week, but on weekends the numbers double. Smoking Jones, though, is always busy," Sarah explains. "It can take you up to a month sometimes to get a table, and you can see why: the food is to die for."

As she speaks, Sarah-Jane is scanning Jonestown to see where Mike is. She spots him standing at the entrance to the bar opposite to them, talking to one of the staff. There are large spiders hanging from the lightshades, spiders on the walls, cobwebs over the front door, and on the stage are two coffins with plastic skeletons that have flashing red eyes leaning against the back wall.

"Follow me, I see my cousin over there." Sarah-Jane points in the direction of where Mike is standing and takes Lance's hand as she starts snaking her way through the crowd. She has to push her way through, holding on tight to Lance in the worry that they will be separated trying to get to the other side of the venue. Alice Cooper's *Poison* is playing over the house sound system.

"Phew, that sucked, but we made it," she says to Lance when they finally reach their destination.

"Glad to be on the other side of that. Let's not try to do that too often tonight," Lance replies.

"Not to worry," Sarah-Jane assures him, "there are toilets in the pool hall through there." She points to the swinging doors with the red flashing neon sign above them.

Lance sniggers. "Break Your Balls, that's so cool. Maybe we could play a little pool later?"

"Yeah, great name," she agrees. "Yes, we can play later if a table is available. Being the weekend, we could wait up to an hour, maybe an hour-and-a-half, though. Let's see how things go. The taxi driver will be here at one, so we have time."

The staff member Mike is talking to recognises Sarah-Jane and informs him she is standing behind him. "Good god, Sarah, you should have tapped me on the shoulder," Mike tells her.

"Hell, cousin, didn't want to disturb you, I can see how busy you are tonight. I can wait. Waiting never hurts anybody, does it?" Sarah-Jane spouts back at him, then they both burst out laughing before hugging each other.

"Mike, this is Lance. Lance, this is my cousin, Mike," Sarah-Jane introduces the two men. They both say 'hi' and shake hands.

"Nice to meet you, Mike. You've got such an awesome place here," Lance tells him. "It's my first time to Jonestown."

"Welcome and thanks. I hope you enjoy yourself. What would the two of you like to drink?" Mike asks them.

Sarah-Jane looks at Lance and suggests, "Should we stick to the beer and tequila?"

Lance replies, "Yeah, let's stick with the beer. Not too many tequilas, please. Too many of those and I get violently sick."

"I swear, just a couple more tequilas. We still want to be able to function later," she tells him quietly. Then she turns to Mike. "Can we have two draught beers and two tequilas, please? Thanks, Mike. Are there any live bands on tonight?"

Before Mike replies to Sarah-Jane's question, he leans over to the other member of staff and asks him to organise the drinks. Mike turns back to Sarah-Jane. "No bands tonight, only DJs. Had to put all the table and chairs into storage to make space for a dance floor but, as you can see, we are ram packed. Too full, in fact, with nowhere to dance. It will

empty out a bit in an hour or two, as some people will go off to other Halloween parties."

Joseph returns with their drinks, handing a draught to Sarah-Jane who passes it on to Lance before taking her own. He leaves the two shots of tequila on the bar counter with a salt shaker and a plate with some lemon slices.

"Sorry I can't spend more time with you and Lance this evening, but unfortunately I'm really busy tonight and have to get back to work," Mike apologises. He hands Sarah-Jane a plastic card. "Whenever you order drinks tonight, show this card and you won't be charged. When you decide to go home, just hand the card back to one of the staff and say you are returning Mike's comp card," he explains.

"Thanks a lot, Mike, that's very kind of you," she replies. The cousins hug again, then Mike shakes Lance's hand. "Nice to meet you, Lance. Hope to see more of you in the future." Before he turns away, he tells them both, "The two of you make a cute couple. You look perfect together."

Both Lance and Sarah-Jane start to blush, a sudden rush of blood to their cheeks giving them a warm, rosy glow. "Shush, you don't want to embarrass me," Sarah-Jane laughs, letting out a little giggle and sticking her tongue out at him.

"Nice to have met you, too, Mike. I love Jonestown, and will definitely be back," Lance tells him, trying not to make too big a deal out of Mike's comments about the pair of them. Though the more time he spends with her, the more he likes her. Lance thinks to himself, *Mike is right, though. We do look good together and we like the same music, and a similar taste in films. Maybe this can develop into something more meaningful.*

Sarah-Jane hands Lance his shot of tequila after putting her draught down. "No lemon or salt, right?" she says, pouring salt on her hand. Holding a piece of lemon with her fingers, she picks up her tequila with her free hand. "Here's to whatever the future brings to us," she toasts, then clinks her glass with his.

"Cheers to that," replies Lance.

They down their tequila and Lance puts his shot glass back on the bar, taking a large gulp of his draught he was holding in his other hand.

"What is the reason you don't have lemon and salt with your tequila?" she asks.

"When I was in my early twenties, I used to have lemon and salt with my tequila, but one day someone I met at a party invited me to have a spot of tequila with him. I was about to pour salt on my hand when he told me not to. He said

I should down the shot, breathe in slowly through my mouth, savouring the after effect of the tequila, then take a large sip of an alcoholic drink of choice. I tried it and haven't drunk tequila any other way since."

Lance looks around the room then continues, "I'm not complaining but I find it really odd that the music doesn't seem too loud in here. At least it allows us to talk at a reasonable volume, so we don't have to shout at each other."

"Maybe the music is soft in volume because there are too many people and no-one can dance," Sarah-Jane offers. "Might as well be able to listen to great tunes and still have a conversation. I'm taking a wild stab in the dark here; it's just a guess. Do you want to go see if there is a free table and we could play some pool?"

"Cool with me," he replies. "I would like to see what the rest of Jonestown looks like."

Sarah-Jane picks up her draught as they walk off hand-in-hand towards Break Your Balls. Queen's *We Will Rock You* is playing when they emerge through the swinging doors from Jonestown, and at first glance they can see that there aren't any free tables to play on. They walk around the outer tables to see how long the wait is going to be to get a game of pool. By the time they have walked around the

outer tables, they can see there is at least an hour-and-a-half wait to get a game in.

"Would you like some fresh air? I could do with some," Sarah-Jane says with a cheeky smile on her face.

Still holding hands, Sarah-Jane leads Lance towards the outside smoking area, the lights flicking on as they walk in. There isn't anyone outside, though a few of the heating lamps are still glowing and there is the smell from a freshly extinguished cigarette hanging in the air.

Sarah-Jane places her draught on one of the tables then turns and takes Lance's drink from him, placing it next to hers. Turning back towards him, she pulls on his Dracula cape, making him bend towards her. Lance leans closer, putting his arm around her back and pulling her towards him. There is a heated energy flowing between them as they kiss for the first time. Time seems to melt away while they kiss, pulling away only to breathe before going in again, their tongues swirling around each other. Pulling away slowly, the tips of their tongues dance around each other before their mouths join again.

Sarah-Jane feels Lance's cock hardening as their bodies are so close. It is throbbing, as she feels his cock against her, making her wet, she rubs her legs together as the tingling in her pussy grows making her panties damp in the process.

Breaking away, Sarah-Jane says, "Fuck, you're a good kisser. I'm horny now. I'm going to text the taxi driver and tell him to pick us up. I want you so bad right now, if we weren't in public, my god I'd have that throbbing cock of your in my mouth."

Lance looks a little shocked by her comment, but replies, "Cool, we will come back to Jonestown again soon, I hope. You drive me wild. I want you so bad right now, too. I haven't felt like this in a long time. There is this electrifying chemistry between us."

There is a huge smile on Sarah-Jane's face as she takes out her phone to text Jonny. It is quarter past eleven as she sends her message: *"Hi Jonny, could you let me know when you would be able to fetch us, please?"* She makes sure her phone has sound and the vibrate is on, so she won't miss his text reply.

"In the meantime, while we wait, kiss me!" Sarah-Jane pulls Lance close, rubbing his cock with her hand. *I can't wait to have him inside me*, she thinks. Just before they kiss, Sarah-Jane's phone buzzes like the sound R2D2 makes. She looks at her phone.

Jonny's message reads: *"I can be there in 20 minutes. Just dropping a ride off first, then I can collect you."*

"That's fine, text when you arrive so we can come out. And please also let me know where you will be parked. Thanks," she replies.

"Should we go back inside?" she asks Lance. "I'm starting to feel cold, plus we still need to finish our draughts, and I know I will need the toilet before we leave."

"Great idea. Me, too. Yeah, I'm starting to feel cold as well." Lance replies.

They pick up their beers and go back inside, walking towards the toilets. Sarah-Jane passes Lance her beer and says, "Hang on to this while I go first."

Drinking his draught while waiting for Sarah-Jane to come back, Lance notices that Break Your Balls has two zombies sitting at a table as if they were watching people play pool and waiting for their turn. Lance thinks to himself, *They really go all out here for Halloween. Why have I been such a dumb cunt? I could have been coming here for ages. But at least I have found myself a new home; the atmosphere is great, and that BBQ is mind blowing. Need to come here soon.*

Sarah-Jane comes back, taking her draught and Lance's from him. "Your turn." Taking a gulp of her beer, she watches his arse as he walks away, thinking to herself, *Can't wait to get home and get that throbbing cock in my mouth.*

"You ready?" she asks him on his return. "The taxi driver will be here soon."

Lance takes his draught and downs what's left. "Now I'm ready," he replies.

They walk over to the small bar and hand over their glasses and Mike's comp car. Sarah-Jane tells the lady there, "I'm returning Mike's comp card. Could I know your name, please, just in case he asks me who I gave it to?"

"My name is Helena. Sure, I'll give Mike his card. Enjoy the rest of your evening," the woman replies.

"Thanks, Helena, we will definitely be enjoying the rest of our evening, I guarantee it. Enjoy your evening, too," replies Sarah-Jane.

Helena calls, "Enjoy" with a look of understanding on her face. She recognises the look of two people who are going home to fuck their brains out.

As they are walking towards the swinging doors, Sarah-Jane's phone makes its R2D2 noise, and she sees it is a text from Jonny: *"Unfortunately the parking lot is still closed to taxis. I'm waiting more or less in the same spot. No more than 15 metres away."*

Sarah-Jane texts back: *"Thanks, Jonny, we will be out shortly."*

Placing her phone back in her purse, she whispers in Lance's ear, "Hope you're ready, tiger?" as she grabs his arse. "That cock is mine tonight."

Jonestown is still ram packed and they have to snake their way through the crowd to get to the front door. Just as they do, Sarah-Jane's phone vibrates again with another text: *"Head towards the car with the flashing emergency lights. A fog is settling, so you may not be able to see my car."*

Sarah-Jane texts back: *"Thanks, Jonny, we will be with you in a minute or two. We are just heading out the front door."*

She tells Lance, "That was the taxi driver; he says fog has started to settle and it is getting hard to see. We have to look for the car with flashing emergency lights."

As they head out into the cold night air, their costumes don't offer much warmth and they both start to shiver.

"I hope the taxi driver has the heat in his car turned on full, it is freezing out here," Lance comments through jittering teeth.

They pick up their speed – not quite a run, but not a slow walk either – and see the flashing lights up ahead.

"Fuck, yes," Sarah-Jane says through gritted teeth.

They quickly climb into the back of the car.

"Sorry again, Sarah, I wish I could have parked closer for you," Jonny apologises immediately.

"Not to worry, Jonny, it couldn't be helped. They were so busy inside, there's hardly a place to stand," replies Sarah-Jane.

"Ah, warmth," Lance says with a sigh.

They are huddled together on the back seat trying to warm up, but thankfully Jonny's heater is working, and the inside of the car feels warm and cosy.

Jonny tells them, "I was five minutes away from Jonestown and it was so surreal how this fog descended before me. A light mist appeared first, and you could see five metres in front of you no problem. But by the time I parked the car, the fog was so thick and heavy you couldn't even see your hand in front of your face. That's why I text you; better to be cautious in this type of weather, that's how accidents happen. I hope you don't mind but I'm going to be driving slower to try and avoid having any accidents tonight."

"No rush is good with us. As you said, rather avoid accidents tonight," Sarah-Jane replies. Her witch's hat is now on the

floor between her feet and the back of the driver's seat, its tip bent over.

Jonny accelerates slowly, using the side mirror to try and see if there are any bright headlights shining through the fog. Thankfully, there are no cars approaching so they get on their way. Lance extends his vampire cape around Sarah-Jane, pulling her to snuggle up against him as the cape and his arm settle around her shoulder. What should take them ten minutes to drive is taking twice as long, and the warmth of the car plus the beer and tequila have made Sarah-Jane and Lance a little drowsy. They nod in and out of sleep.

As the car slows to a stop outside Sarah-Jane's home, Jonny announces, "All right, folks, we're here."

Waking at the sound of his voice, Sarah-Jane mumbles, "Sorry, we must have fallen asleep. Thank you for getting us home safely. How much do I owe you for the ride?"

"It's 40 for the ride. Unfortunately, due to the weather I had to drive slower, which pushes up the price," replies Jonny.

"Not to worry. Here is 70. Have an enjoyable end to your shift," says Sarah-Jane.

Taking the money from her, Jonny replies, "With the fog this heavy, I think I might call it a night. Drive safe, drive another

day; take a chance, might end up dead. I know which one I prefer."

They get out the car and quickly make their way up the winding path and inside the safety of her home. As the door closes, Jonny's car drives off into the unknown, as the fog thickens with every passing minute.

Chapter 10

Once they are behind closed doors and out of the cold, Sarah-Jane says to Lance, "The warmth of the car made me so drowsy. What about you?" She leaves her purse and keys on the long, thin table. "I never expected it to be that cold. I'm going to check the heating; it feels a little chilly in here."

"I was drowsy in the car, but as soon as you step back out into the cold you are wide awake again," Lance replies.

Sarah-Jane is straightening the tip of her hat before she hangs it on one of the hooks on the coat rack. "Pass me your cape and I'll hang it up," she tells him. "Through the arch doors is the lounge. Why don't you make yourself comfortable in there, while I get us a bottle of red wine? Please be a dear and put on some music tv; at least we can have some tunes."

"Where's the toilet?" Lance asks. "I'm bursting for a piss."

"Here it is." Sarah-Jane opens the door to the guest toilet and turns on the light. "When you're finished and go to the

lounge, the light switch is just behind the door. Could you dim them a bit, too, please?"

She walks off towards the kitchen to fetch the wine and glasses. She opens the wine before leaving the kitchen, something to do with the oxygen mixing with the aromatics in the wine to bolster the flavour; Sarah-Jane read that in a magazine somewhere years ago. Holding the wine glasses in one hand, the stem of the glasses dangling between her fingers and the wine bottle in the other hand, she switches off the kitchen and dining room lights and makes her way to the lounge. She can hear Poison's *Every Rose Has Its Thorn* as she enters.

Lance is sitting on the three-seater couch with his head back and his arms stretched over the back of the couch. "Great song," he comments. "I've never seen them live, but maybe one day."

Sarah-Jane pours half a glass of the wine and hands it to Lance, who has moved over a bit to make space for Sarah-Jane, then pours half a glass for herself. She places the bottle on the right-hand corner table, and they clink their glasses and say "Cheers."

She notices a slight look of nervousness on Lance's face, as though he is trying to say something but stops as he doesn't know if he should.

Meanwhile, he is thinking to himself, *Don't be a pussy. Ask her. She can only say yes or no. Fuck it, here goes.* Taking a large sip of his wine, Lance finally plucks up the courage to speak. "I've had a really great evening so far," he pauses then carries on. "Sarah, I know we have only been speaking for a month, and the time I have spent with you this evening I have enjoyed every second with you. There is this electrifying energy between us, and I haven't felt like this with anyone before. What I'm trying to say is, I really like you and would like to see if this feeling between us grows into something more than just sex."

Sarah-Jane lets out a little laugh. "You should have seen the look on your face; you looked so nervous. When I started this journey of experimenting sexually on We Play, I said to myself that I was here to have fun first and foremost, but if I met someone who gave me butterflies in my stomach then I would want to pursue a relationship with that person. I do feel the same as you. There is this extremely strong energy between us, like two magnets, hard to pull apart." She pauses to smile reassuringly at him. "Yes, is my answer to you. I would like to see if this grows into a relationship. I'm sure the sex is going to be mind-blowing, and we will find out shortly how mind-blowing it is."

Taking a gulp of her wine, Sarah-Jane puts her glass on the table and takes Lance's glass from him, placing it next to hers. He is sitting with his back against the armrest, one leg

on the floor, the other outstretched on the couch. Sarah-Jane leans forward on her hands, moving along the couch, then unbuckles his belt, unbuttons his trousers, and pulls down the zip. Lance lifts his bottom as she pulls his trousers off, dropping them on the floor.

She rubs up and down with her one hand on top of his underwear and Lance's cock becomes larger the more she rubs, until it is engorged and throbbing. Sarah-Jane slowly pulls down his underwear until his large, throbbing cock breaks free, swinging back and forth at its release, then she pulls his underwear the rest of the way and drops them on top of the trousers.

"Lie back and enjoy," she tells him.

He lies back with his arms up and his head resting in his hands as he closes his eyes. Sarah-Jane lies on her stomach with her legs bent at the knee, feet in the air, one hand holding the base of his hard cock. She licks her lips, wetting them, before taking him into her awaiting mouth. Her tongue twirls around the head of his cock, sending shivers of joy over his body, then slowly her mouth moves down the shaft of his cock till her mouth meets the top of her hand, then moves her head back up. She continues to move her head up and down, getting a little faster with every stroke, each time taking his cock deep in her mouth. Lance lets out a sigh of pleasure, and the more he sighs the more

Sarah-Jane enjoys giving him the blowjob. Her eyes are closed, her head bobbing up and down, and the wetter his cock is becoming. She lets out a muffled moan as her saliva drips down the shaft of his cock and onto his balls.

"I'm going to come," Lance moans between shallow breaths, arching his back then letting out a loud groan. As he comes, she takes the full length of his cock down her throat, his cum dripping down her throat.

"Wow, no-one has ever deep throated me before," he admits shakily. "That sent shivers up my spine."

She slowly releases his cock from her throat, her mouth moving up the shaft until his cock pops out her mouth. Sarah-Jane gets off the couch, takes off her witch's dress and unclips her bra, dropping them on the ever-growing pile of clothes on the floor.

While she is standing, Lance pulls off her panties, which are soaked through, and drops them on the pile. Having removed the last of his clothes, he puts his hand on her waist, pulling her closer to him, and kisses her belly.

"Your turn," he says. He lies on the couch, his head in the middle raised by a cushion, his legs over the armrest. Sarah-Jane climbs on top of him with her legs either side of his shoulders. Leaning forward with her arms straight, holding

the other armrest with open hands, her pussy is hovering over his face. Lance has one hand on her left thigh and the other on her right, pulling her towards him. His tongue moves along her pussy lips, slowly parting them as she gets wetter. She pushes her pelvis towards him, moving her body position to expose her swelling clit to his adventurous tongue.

She lets out a little moan as he sucks her clit in deep, sending waves of pleasure up her spine. His tongue teases her clit as it twirls, making her moan louder. Sucking her deeply again, Lance inserts his middle finger inside her pussy, moving in and out, back and forth. He can feel her pussy juices dripping down his hand each time he moves in and out. Slowly, Lance inserts his index finger as well. Now he can feel her pussy muscles contracting around his fingers and Sarah-Jane's breathing gets faster with every stroke. Before she can warn him that she is going to come, she arches her body backwards, grabbing her breast with both hands and twisting her nipples, then she squeezes her legs together, having a full body orgasm as she quivers in ecstasy. Her juices shoot out of her pussy onto his chest as he removes his fingers.

Out of breath, Sarah-Jane lies next to Lance with his arm around her as they cuddle. She feels completely at peace lying in his arms, and closes her eyes. She thinks to herself. *I have never felt this energy connection with anyone before,*

including previous boyfriends. I hope we can make this work; Lance is a great guy. I haven't been open to a relationship since my parents died, but maybe it is time. The saying goes, you meet everyone in your life for a reason.

Opening her eyes, Sarah-Jane tells Lance, "Come on, we're going upstairs. You're not off the hook yet. I'm waiting for your large friend to wake again, as you still owe me a good fucking."

Sarah-Jane gets off the couch, switches off the television, then picks up the pile of clothes from the carpet.

"I almost fell asleep. It felt so nice having you lying in my arms, it was like the rest of the world didn't exist," Lance replies as he gets off the couch, stretching his arms out and backwards to take a deep breath.

"Switch off the lights behind you," she says as she walks through the lounge door.

Lance's cock swings side to side as he follows Sarah-Jane upstairs, along the lit corridor and into the bedroom. He lies down on the bed while Sarah-Jane neatly folds and leaves their clothes on the dresser stool. She lights the candles in the room before turning off the light.

He is lying back with his head resting on his hands, his flat, toned stomach muscles glistening in the light of the candles.

Sarah-Jane climbs on the bed to lie next to him and immediately takes his cock in her hand, stroking it up and down. After the third stroke, his cock has swollen and doubled in size. Lance slides his hand between Sarah-Jane's legs, rubbing his fingers up and down along her pussy lips, feeling the moisture of her juices covering his fingers. She widens her legs, letting his fingers spread her pussy lips as her clit swells under his fingers.

Lance gets off the bed. Standing against the side, he pulls Sarah-Jane towards the edge of the bed. She is still on her back, with her arse touching the edge of the bed and her legs dangling down. Taking a condom from the box Sarah-Jane had left on the bedside table, he sheaths his engorged cock. Holding each of Sarah-Jane's legs by the ankles, he spreads her legs apart, then he bends his knees until he's at the perfect angle and his cock slides inside her pussy with ease. As Sarah-Jane's wet, creamy juices cover the condom, he moves his pelvis back and forth, his cock in and out.

Changing position, Lance pulls Sarah-Jane slightly further off the bed, placing his hands on the back of her thighs just above her arse cheeks and pushes her outstretched legs towards her stomach, lifting her pelvis towards his throbbing cock, eager to be inside her again. He inserts his throbbing cock slowly inch by inch, making Sarah-Jane moan with desire. Moving his body back and forth, slowly at first, Lance leans slightly forward using the front of his

feet to push with, varying the pace of his strokes as he fucks her. Using Sarah-Jane's legs for support, he leans forward even further with his hands flat on the bed for extra support, then he pulls back slowly as his cock slides out, before ramming it hard and deep inside her.

Sarah-Jane lets out a loud moan each time his cock rams deep inside her, picking up pace with each thrust of his cock, until eventually their bodies are moving as one. Lance's cock is deep inside her as she comes, gripping the duvet in both hands and biting her bottom lip, her legs shaking as he pulls his cock out.

Lance helps Sarah-Jane back on the bed. He climbs on the bed, sitting with his feet and knees on the duvet, his legs slightly apart, with a straight back. He pulls Sarah-Jane towards him, lifting her pelvis as his throbbing cock penetrates her creamy pussy, his hands on her thighs, her legs bent under his arms, slowly moving back and forth. Each time his cock goes in and out, Lance builds up speed until a loud slapping noise can be heard as their bodies slam into each other over and over again. Both Sarah-Jane and Lance let out deep sighs as their breathing grows faster and faster with each stroke.

He lets out a loud moan as he comes, slowing briefly before fucking her harder and faster until Sarah-Jane comes. He can feel the pressure of her cum pushing him

out, her juices running down her arse cheeks to leave a puddle on the bed.

Out of breath and panting, they collapse back on the bed, Sarah-Jane snuggling up against his body.

"I'm going to have to change my bedding every time you sleep over," she whispers. "We are going to soil clean bedding every time. You make me come so hard, I will leave puddles on the bed."

"Unfortunately, that is a good side effect of our sex," he replies. "I don't mind your juices; the wetter the better."

"What time is it?" Sarah-Jane asks.

Looking at his watch Lance tells her it's quarter-to-one. "Why, do you want to sleep?"

"No. When we get our breath back, we've got more fucking to do," replies Sarah-Jane.

They lie motionless, out of energy, as their breathing slows to a normal pace. After half an hour, they have almost all their energy back.

"You're ready for round three?" Lance asks.

"Give me five more minutes and we can go again," says Sarah-Jane.

"Have you ever heard of autoerotic asphyxiation?"

"Yes, I've heard of it," Sarah-Jane tells him, "but never tried it before. Why do you ask?"

Lance replies, "Would you like to try? It intensifies your orgasm threefold. I have tried it twice, three years ago."

Sarah-Jane looks doubtful. "I'm not sure. Is it safe? What happens if something goes wrong?"

"As long as we follow certain guidelines it is safe," Lance reassures her, taking her hand in his. "We have to agree a safe word or gesture before starting, and that way we know when to stop."

"I'm a little nervous," she admits. "Are you sure you want to do this when we have been drinking?"

"I'm sure I want to do this with you. I trust you."

"Ok, if you're sure. What will the safe word or gesture be?" Sarah-Jane asks, still wary.

"Let's make the safe word 'banana' and the gesture is that I'll slap your right thigh three times. Do you have a long scarf?" he asks with a devilish smile on his face.

Sarah-Jane gets off the bed, walks to the right side of the wardrobe and slides open the door. Shuffling some things around inside, she retrieves a long, thin, black silk scarf that her mother gave her for Christmas five years ago. "Will this do?" she asks. She has a naughty look on her face as she waves the scarf back and forth in front of her. The silk brushes against her nipples as they grow and harden.

"Perfect," Lance replies. "Silk is soft. It glides and doesn't leave friction marks like other fabrics do." He takes it from Sarah-Jane's outstretched hand then lies back with his head on the pillows and wraps the scarf around his neck in a loop, evening out the ends, laying them on the bed either side of him. "You climb on top, facing me, and ride me until you are close to coming. Then pick up the ends of the scarf, lean back and grind against me until you come, using the scarf to support yourself. That's all you have to do."

Sarah-Jane still looks nervous as she listens to his instruction, but slides up the bed until she is at Lance's side. "Pass me a condom, please," she says, taking his flaccid cock in her hand. She strokes it up and down waiting for it to harden, taking the condom from Lance and placing it on the bed beside her. "Thanks. A little treat first before the main advent. Close your eyes and enjoy."

She leans over Lance's now rock-hard cock and takes the full length deep into her throat as she sucks him off. With her

free hand, she rubs her pussy, feeling the moisture covering her fingers. She rubs in pace with every stroke her mouth makes along Lance's throbbing cock, slow at first, going a little faster every third stroke, stopping before he can come. She stops and quickly sheaths his cock with the condom then straddles Lance edging the tip of his cock slowly inside her. White, creamy pussy juices cover the condom as she lowers herself till his balls are pushing up against her pussy. She can see the shadow of their bodies dancing around the room in the flickering light of the candles.

Sarah-Jane leans forward, placing her hands on Lance's chest for support as she moves her pelvis up and down, while he massages her breasts, teasing her nipples till they are bullet hard. With every up and down motion, Sarah-Jane's pelvis makes, white creamy juices drip onto and run down Lance's swollen balls. She straightens her back into a seated position, placing her hands on her hips, grinding her pelvis back and forth. Her breathing is slow and deep, becoming faster and shallower with every back-and-forth motion of her pelvis.

Lance moans, "I'm close to coming. You?"

"Me too," says Sarah-Jane in between moans.

Picking up the ends of the silk scarf, she leans back until there isn't any slack and the scarf is now supporting her

body weight. Closing her eyes, Sarah-Jane grinds her pelvis back and forth, back and forth, with more urgency as each passing stroke intensifies the euphoric feeling she is having. She feels the swelling of Lance's cock inside her as her pussy muscles contract around his cock, making him explode inside her, then his body quivers and shakes beneath her. She lets out an extra loud moan as she comes, squeezing her legs together as the full body-shaking orgasm hits her.

Slowing to a stop so she can get her breath back, Sarah-Jane gasps, "My god, Lance, that is the most intense orgasm I have ever had."

There is an eerie silence in the room. Her eyes remaining closed, Sarah-Jane can feel Lance's still body beneath her. She calls out his name, "Lance! Lance!"

Dead silence hangs in the air. Sarah-Jane opens her eyes to the sight of Lance's lifeless body, his bloodshot eyes staring back at her, his swollen tongue hanging out his open mouth, saliva running down his chin, his hands still holding the silk scarf, trying to loosen it to get air into his lungs.

As shock hits her like a hammer blow, Sarah-Jane vomits over herself and Lance's limp dead body. She lets out a howling scream, bursting into an uncontrollable fit of crying, then jumps off him. Tears streaming down her face, she can barely see through soaked, blurry eyes. Shaking

him, she screams, "WAKE UP! WAKE UP!" But he won't wake. Lance is dead.

Sarah-Jane's body is shaking uncontrollably as she sobs in shock. She collapses on the floor in the corner of the room, next to the dressing table. Still naked, she rocks back and forth with her arms wrapped around her knees, mumbling over and over again, "What have I done?"

Hours pass as she sits rocking on the floor, unaware of the time, tears rolling down her face and onto her breasts. Sarah-Jane can't move; she is paralysed with fear. She can faintly hear the morning bird song through the haze in her brain, but she is numb.

As the feeling of cold seeps through her body, she shivers and slowly crawls across the carpet to reach the caramel blanket that had been thrown on the floor before their sex marathon started, then ended in tragedy. She doesn't want to see Lance's dead body, so wraps herself in the blanket and stays on the floor, curled in the foetal position, rocking back and forth as she sobs.

A faint gleam of light peeks through the gap between the curtains and the wall. Not aware of the time, Sarah-Jane crawls to the door and out of the bedroom. Her phone is still in her purse, which is on the thin, long table downstairs.

Once out of the bedroom, Sarah-Jane struggles to her feet and repositions the caramel blanket around herself, and makes her way downstairs to retrieve her purse. She walks to the lounge and gets the bottle of wine and a glass. First, she pours the rest of the wine from Lance's glass into hers, then fills her glass just below the brim. Sarah-Jane gulps the wine, draining the glass. All she wants to feel is numbness. Emptying the bottle on her next pour, she drains her glass again, thinking to herself that this is all a bad dream. But she knows the reality: she killed Lance.

"I need more wine, I can't cope with this sober," she says out loud. Feeling lightheaded from the alcohol, she stumbles her way to the kitchen and leaves her purse on the island counter while she gets another bottle of wine from the cupboard and opens it. Not bothering with a glass this time, she puts the bottle to her lips and drains half its contents. Not having eaten since last night at Smoking Jones, the wine goes straight to Sarah-Jane's head.

Just as she starts to feel queasy, she projectile vomits into the basin, leaving a vile taste in her mouth and the back of her throat. Not caring about vomiting, Sarah-Jane downs the rest of the bottle and is immediately sick again as the alcohol takes its hold on her body. She grabs onto the island to steady herself, but Sarah-Jane is now almost blind drunk.

She needs to get to the lounge so she can lie down and pass out. Clutching her purse under one arm, Sarah-Jane uses her hands to steady herself against the sliding doors till she is at the entrance hall, finding any surface that she can hold onto for support till she reaches the lounge. The last steps from the door to the couch are heavily unstable as she stumbles, almost twisting her right foot.

She has just enough energy to flop over the back of the couch. As she lands on the soft cushions, she takes her phone from her purse, unlocks it, and registers blearily that it is quarter-to-eight in the morning. Then she loses her grip and the phone falls to the floor as she passes out from the exhaustion of the morning's events and the wine.

Sarah-Jane is in the midst of an alcohol-fuelled fever dream, her sleep restless, mumbling in her sleep. But it isn't in fact a dream at all. Due to the traumatic experience that she has just gone through, this dream is a repressed childhood memory.

"No, no, I want my mummy," she groans, before mumbling something incoherent again. In the fever dream she is about five years old and on an expedition with her mom and dad. They are in the Amazon rainforest, cataloguing an archaeological find left behind by a lost generation of South American jungle tribes. Their campsite is set up with the main exhibit tent at the centre and the sleeping tents in a

circle around it. On the right side of the camp enclosure are the toilet facilities; on the opposite side is the dining hall; at the top of the enclosure is the communications tent; the security tent is at the bottom.

A wire fence encases the campsite with the only entrance/ exit gate in front of the security tent. Sarah-Jane's parents are out at the dig site, which is three miles away, and she has been left in the care of Jemma, one of the archaeologists who is cataloguing the artifacts. Sarah-Jane is helping Jemma to clean the artifacts with a special brush and cloth, removing any dirt before they are wrapped in white cotton cloth and placed in shipping crates.

Sarah-Jane tell Jemma, "I'm tired. Can you take me back to my tent? I want to sleep."

"Sorry, Sarah, I'm really busy. Can you wait another half hour? I promise I'll take you to your tent then, ok?" replies Jemma.

"I'm tired, I want to go now," whines Sarah-Jane moodily.

"I'll take her," says Tom, one of the new interns on his first expedition.

"If you don't mind, it would really be of help," Jenna says gratefully. "I'm bogged down as there is so much here to

232

Sarah-Jane's parents have spoken to her before about adults wanting to touch her or asking her to touch them, and they have taught her to scream if she feels uncomfortable in any situation. She is about to scream when Tom puts his hand over her mouth.

"Shoosh, don't scream," he warns with an angry look on his face. "You will do what I say."

"No, no, I don't want to. I want my mummy!" screams Sarah-Jane in a loud voice. She carries on screaming as tears roll down her cheeks, drawing the attention of one of the cooks in the dining hall. He runs into the tent and sees Sarah-Jane naked and Tom with his cock in his hand.

Peter screams, "What the fuck are you doing!" And before Tom can say anything, Peter punches him to the ground. "Stay down or I'll put you down again," he tells Tom. Turning to Sarah-Jane, he says, "Sarah sweetheart, put your clothes on. It's going to be all right now, the bad man can't hurt you any more."

Sarah-Jane puts on her clothes. All the shouting has brought the campsite to a standstill and Jemma runs into the tent to see Peter tying Tom's hands behind his back. Tom is on his knees with his head on the ground.

"What was all the screaming about?" Jemma asks Peter.

"This piece of shit was trying to have his way with our Sarah. When I burst in, he had his dick in his hand and he had undressed her," Peter explains.

"Take him to security. the Morleys will want a word with him when they get back," Jemma replies.

Peter yanks on the rope tied around Tom's hands, forcing him to his feet. "Move!" he orders, as he kicks Tom in the arse.

"I'm so, so sorry. I should have taken you to your tent," Jemma tells Sarah-Jane. "Can you ever forgive me?" Sarah-Jane nods in reply to Jemma's question, her crying now just a sob. "I'll stay right here with you," Jemma assures her. "Why don't you lie down, try and get some sleep? You'll feel better once you've had a nap."

She helps Sarah-Jane onto her bunk and places a blanket over her then strokes her hair until Sarah-Jane finally drifts off to sleep. Jemma doesn't leave her side until the Morleys return back from the dig. That was the last time Sarah-Jane had gone on an expedition with her parents.

As the fever dream nears its end during her alcohol-induced sleep, Sarah-Jane bolts upright, letting out a gut-curdling scream. She is now wide awake, sweating and shaking from her sleep, those memories no longer repressed. She now

understands why her parents stopped taking her on expeditions and always ensured one of them stayed at home with her until Sarah-Jane finished high school.

That memory of her being molested as a child slowly fades as the reality of the dead body upstairs in her room hits her like a ton of bricks. Sarah-Jane has a blinding headache from downing almost two bottles of wine this morning, and her mind is a jumble of thoughts. "What am I going to do?" she says out loud. "I can't tell the police; they will arrest me for murder."

She picks her phone up off the floor, unlocks it, and the time staring back at her is half nine. She has been asleep for almost two hours. Still feeling queasy from the wine, Sarah-Jane unsteadily gets off the couch, almost falling into one of the tables as she stands. Her bladder is screaming to be emptied. She drops the caramel blanket on the floor and uneasily walks naked to the guest toilet. Sitting peeing, all of a sudden Sarah-Jane needs to vomit again. She quickly flushes the toilet before she is on the floor with her head in the bowl heaving up the last of the wine. Nothing but a purply red liquid looks back at her.

Not sure what to do, Sarah-Jane decides to have a shower to try to clear her head and make a plan what to do next. She goes upstairs to shower. She turns on the shower, setting the temperature so not to scald herself, then gets

under the hot water. As she closes the cubicle door behind her, she collapses on the shower floor and bursts into tears. Just the thought of having to go back into her bedroom is filling her with dread.

Sarah-Jane doesn't want to look at Lance's dead body, she would sooner forget that he is even there, but she needs to get clothes from her wardrobe. Lifting herself off the shower floor, she goes through the motions of washing her hair and body in a blur. She feels completely numb to the bone. She can't imagine she will ever be happy again. She just killed the one man who could've made her happy, who could've brought an end to all the tragedy in her life. Tragedy seems to follow her nowadays: first, her parents dying over a year-and-a-half ago; and now Lance, dead on her bed.

Having finished her shower, Sarah-Jane wrings the excess water from her hair, dries off her body before wrapping the towel around her throbbing head, then puts on her dressing gown. Still unable to pluck up the courage to go to her room, she decides to go to her childhood bedroom, climbing under the duvet and staring off into the distance, deep in thought, curled in the foetal position, biting her fingernails.

After what seems like an eternity, Sarah-Jane falls into a deep, restful sleep and it is dark when she finally awakes. When she opens her eyes, she feels quite refreshed, hoping

the nightmare that was Halloween was just a bad dream. But the reality keeps kicking her in the face: she has a dead body in her room, and she doesn't know what to do about it and this whole situation.

Feeling completely void of emotion, having come to the stark realisation of her actions, Sarah-Jane has an aching hollow in her stomach; she is starving. Getting out of bed, still in her dressing gown, she walks to her room. There is no getting around the situation, she is going to have to see Lance lying there motionless.

What awaits her senses first as she enters her room is the strong, putrid smell of vomit. Next is the lifeless body on her bed. It no longer represents Lance; it is just a hunk of dead flesh. His body has taken on a purple tinge as rigor mortis sets in, his hands still gripping at the silk scarf, his tongue still hanging out, the saliva on his chin long dried up, his eyes bloodshot and bulging. All the candles have long burned out.

Sarah-Jane walks to her wardrobe and takes out a pair of sweatpants, a hoodie, socks, and a t-shirt. She doesn't see the point of wearing any underwear. She won't be going anywhere for the foreseeable future – not until she has taken care of the body lying on her bed.

Once dressed, she goes down to the kitchen. Her hunger pains have returned, and all she can feel is this hollow in the

pit of her stomach. Sarah-Jane heads to the lounge to fetch her phone. She left it there when she dropped the caramel blanket on her way to the toilet earlier.

I need to message Agnes to tell her I won't be coming to work next week, she thinks. *I'm not looking forward to that conversation.* Sarah-Jane unlocks her phone to check the time. It's seven o'clock and she realises that the whole day has passed her by.

Back in the kitchen she consider what to eat. She doesn't feel like cooking, so it will have to be something simple. Sarah-Jane opens the fridge, looks inside, but doesn't see anything she wants. Knowing she needs some food, she makes a ham and cheese sandwich, but that doesn't fill her up. Sarah-Jane is still hungry, but it will tide her over until the pizza she is ordering arrives. It's easier to order takeaway, as she doesn't have to think too hard.

Sarah-Jane orders an extra-large, deep dish Hawaiian pizza, with added bacon and mushrooms, adding to the delivery note: *Driver must knock on the front door, leaving the pizza on the white wicker bench.* She doesn't want any human contact and has already paid online. Her confirmation email says her pizza will be there in 40 minutes.

She makes herself another ham and cheese sandwich as she has underestimated how hungry she is. It has been

almost 24 hours since she last ate. Not bothering to clean up after making her sandwiches, Sarah-Jane takes another bottle of wine, opens it, and thinks to herself, *Fuck it, I'll drink from the bottle!* She takes her first swig from the bottle before heading back to the lounge to wait for her pizza.

Turning off the lights in the lounge so she can sit in the dark, Sarah-Jane scrolls through her social media without actually taking note of anything. There is a knock at the front door; it's almost eight o'clock. "Your pizza is here," she hears the delivery driver say.

Sarah-Jane waits five minutes before peeking through the curtains to see that no-one is outside, then opens the door and retrieves her pizza. She goes back to the lounge, using the light from her phone to navigate her way around the furniture, and places the box on the couch while she switches on the television. She watches a rerun of the original *Ghostbusters* while eating her pizza and drinking wine.

Feeling stuffed after eating most of the pizza – there are only three slices left – Sarah-Jane closes the lid and puts the box on the table next to her. Retrieving the caramel blanket, she sits on the couch with her arm leaning on the armrest and her legs tucked up on the couch. After another swig of the wine, she writes a text to Agnes: *"Hi Aggie, hope you*

had a lovely weekend. Sorry to drop this on you with such short notice, but I think I may have food poisoning or coming down with the flu. I've been up all night and most of the day vomiting, so unfortunately I won't be coming to work this coming week. I'll let you know if I will come the following week. Enjoy the rest of your evening. Love S."

As she sends the text, Sarah-Jane thinks to herself, *I have just lied to one of my best friends! Oh well, fuck it. Life sucks, she will get over it.*

Next, she writes a text to Henry, who is due for his monthly grooming of the front and backyard. *"Hi Henry, hope you are well. I have unfortunately come down with the flu and don't want to pass it on to you. There is no need for you to come this month, but you will still get your fee regardless. I will text you when I'm feeling better. Love Sarah."*

Her concentration on the film is half-hearted as the wine dulls her concentration, but she doesn't mind. She has seen *Ghostbusters* over 50 times. Sarah-Jane looks at the almost empty bottle of wine, lifts it to her lips and drains the last of it. As she tries to get up, she stumbles and has to steady herself on the armrest. "I need more wine," she says out loud. "I need to feel numb. I don't want to feel any more."

Stumbling out of the lounge, Sarah-Jane goes to pee before she heads to the kitchen to get another bottle of wine.

While her parents were alive, they collected lots of different wines and now Sarah-Jane is drinking her way through their collection. Most of the wines are red; there were a few whites, but she finished them ages ago.

Sarah-Jane uncorks the bottle and takes a long, deep swig before walking unsteadily back to the lounge. Feeling drunk hungry, she finishes the last three slices of pizza. There is half a bottle of wine left by the time *Ghostbusters* finishes, but Sarah-Jane is feeling dizzy and knows she is going to pass out soon. She switches off the television, finding it harder to get off the couch.

She knows she should go to sleep in her old room, but isn't going to make it up the stairs. Squinting at her phone, she can barely make out what time it is, but it looks, blearily, like half nine. She sees there are message notifications, but is too drunk to read them.

Sarah-Jane tries to make herself as comfy as possible on the couch, covering herself with the caramel blanket before she passes out.

Chapter 11

Sarah-Jane is awakened by the loud banging of the door knocker. Her head feels like it is seven sizes too big, and the thumping in the front of her head is like a jackhammer pounding the street. She looks for her phone while the knocking continues, and unlocks it to see nine o'clock staring back at her.

Wishing the knocking would stop, Sarah-Jane gets off the couch. Her mouth tastes like stale wine as she hasn't brushed her teeth. She unlocks the front door, the chain latch still in place, and opens the door as far as the chain will allow. Outside, it is a bright, cold, sunny November morning, and it takes a little time for her eyes to adjust to the light.

"Can I help you?" she says in a raspy voice to the two ladies standing on the porch.

"Morning. Didn't mean to wake you. I'm Detective Simons, this is my partner Detective Brown," one of the women

explains. "Would you mind if we came in and asked you some questions?"

"Sorry, I do mind if you come in. I seem to have come down with a virus. I spent most of yesterday spewing from both ends; it wasn't a pretty sight. I would prefer not to give it to anyone else, I hope you understand," replies Sarah-Jane as she peers through the slightly open door.

"Do you know a Lance Rosemead?" Detective Simons asks.

Sarah-Jane nods slightly. "Yes, I met him off a sex site and we spent Halloween together. We went to Jonestown for a party, then we came back here and had sex. In the morning, I woke and he was gone."

"His flatmate reported him missing yesterday," the detective continues. "He says it is unlike Lance not to reply to his messages. It's been over 24 hours since he last spoke to Lance, who said he was meeting you. Yesterday evening, the flatmate officially reported Lance as a missing person, which is why we are now standing at your front door."

"Sorry," Sarah-Jane shrugs, "like I said, yesterday morning I woke up and Lance was gone. Can't help you with any further information, as I have none to offer. Will that be all? I really do need to get back to bed."

"No, that will be all for now, but we may be back to ask you some follow-up questions," Detective Simons responds. "You get some rest. Hope you feel better.

Sarah-Jane closes the front door, leaving the two detectives standing on the porch.

"There is a strange smell coming from inside the house, did you smell it?" Detective Brown says quietly to her partner as they walk down the path back to their car.

"Yeah, it smelt like stale vomit, but there was a stronger smell of something rotting. She certainly looked worse for wear. There is something fishy going on, and I don't fully trust what she was telling us." Simons frowns. "I've got this feeling she knows more than she let on. We're going to have to dig a little deeper."

"Where do you want to start looking?" asks Brown, getting into the car.

Simons replies, "I'm going to see the flatmate to ask more questions. You can get hold of Lance's mobile phone provider and ask for his last location, using the last mobile tower he would have passed. You might get a bit of resistance from them, as they may tell you to get a warrant to access that information."

* * *

Sarah-Jane slightly cracks the curtains, peeking out to see if the detectives have left. She knows they will be back, and next time they might have a warrant to enter the house. *I need to collect Lance's clothes, phone, and any other items he may have, and I will have to destroy his phone*, she thinks. *They can locate him with it. And I have to figure out what to do with his body.*

Closing the curtains as the police car drives off, Sarah-Jane is desperate to start drinking again but knows she has too much to do. Only once she has destroyed his phone, got rid of his belongings, and taken care of his body, then and only then can she drink. She knows she has to go back to the master bedroom and deal with what awaits her.

Sarah-Jane decides to have a cup of coffee first to help kick-start her brain and get her moving, so heads for the kitchen, switches on the kettle, prepares her coffee while waiting for the water to boil. Sipping her coffee, she sits at the dinner table, unlocks her phone, and reads her messages.

The first message is from Henry: *"Hi Sarah, thanks for letting me know. Hope you feel better soon. Let me know when you want me to come and do the front and backyard. Take care, Henry."*

She clicks on the next text; this one is from Agnes. *"So sorry you got food poisoning or flu. Hope you feel better soon. Let*

me know if I, or any of the girls, can do anything for you. I await your message about next week. Speak soon, love Aggie."

Sarah-Jane looks over some emails before she scrolls through her social media. It's quarter past ten when she finishes her coffee, and she decides to clean the kitchen and lounge, getting rid of the empty wine bottles. There is still the half bottle she didn't finish the night before.

Taking the empty bottles and her wine glass to the kitchen, she rinses her and Lance's glasses, placing them in the dishwasher along with the knife, cutting board, and plate she used to make her ham sandwiches last night. Wiping down the island counter, she wipes any crumbs into the basin before rinsing them down the drain, along with the remains of her vomit.

Now that the kitchen is tidy, Sarah-Jane turns her attention to the lounge. She straightens up the cushions on the couch, folds the caramel blanket and places it on one end of the couch, making sure the room looks spotless before she heads upstairs. Halfway up the stairs Sarah-Jane can now smell the stronger odour of rotting flesh; Lance is starting to decompose. Whatever she is going to do with his body, she better do soon, before the flies appear.

Entering the bedroom, Sarah-Jane makes a dry retching sound as she gags at the smell. *I wonder if the cops could*

smell Lance's body from the front door, she thinks to herself. His body has now turned a purple black colour.

Sarah-Jane ties a t-shirt around her nose and mouth, taking shallow breaths as she tries to avoid inhaling the vile smell coming from Lance's corpse. She rolls his body in the duvet and pulls it onto the carpet. It hits the floor with a heavy thud, and she drags the duvet-wrapped package along the hallway to the bathroom, leaving it on the floor. Going back to her bedroom, she collects all of Lance's belongings – his trousers, shirt, socks, and underwear. In the trouser pockets she retrieves his phone and wallet, placing them on the dressing table.

She takes his clothes downstairs, collecting the cape hanging up on the coat rack as she passes, then carries the bundle to the basement; she wants to wash everything to get rid of any DNA evidence. Sarah-Jane mixes his clothes with hers in a full load of laundry, leaving them to wash while she goes back to her room to collects his phone and wallet.

Back downstairs, she heads to the kitchen to fetch liquid bleach, rubber gloves, a cloth, a hammer, and a plastic bag, then finds her car keys. *I have to drive away from here, somewhere deserted, and destroy his phone,* she thinks. *At least they can trace that he is no longer here. If the police come back and say that his phone registered its location as*

here even after they left, I will just say that he came back to collect his phone. I can say that I told him his flatmate had reported him missing but he left again and didn't tell me where he was going.

Sarah-Jane picks up her sunglasses which are lying on the long, thin table and puts them on before shrugging on her winter jacket. She removes the chain from the latch and unlocks and opens the front door, welcoming the fresh air that greets her immediately. She breathes deeply, hoping the rotting smell will leave her nose. Locking the front door behind her, Sarah-Jane walks to her car, pressing the remote for the electric gate, then climbs in, starts the car and reverses out the driveway.

Still feeling groggy from all the wine, Sarah-Jane drives cautiously and in silence, not wanting to draw attention to her or her car; she doesn't want to get caught by any speed cameras. She doesn't have any specific place in mind to get rid of Lance's phone or wallet, so drives to the outskirts of town to where all the derelict, abandoned factories are situated. She figures it could be a good place to destroy the phone.

In Sarah-Jane's fragile state of mind, she believes this will lead the police away from her and look somewhere else, or at someone else. It's an hour's drive from her house across town and then on to the factories and there is a lot of traffic, being a Monday. People are rushing around, going to

work, out on deliveries, housewives on their way back from the school run. And here is Sarah-Jane, on her day off, confusing the police over the whereabouts of Lance, trying to conceal evidence that he is still at her house, dead on the bathroom floor, wrapped in her duvet.

By the time Sarah-Jane arrives at the abandoned factories, some clouds have gathered overhead, and the sun makes only brief appearances in between the breaks. The clock on the dashboard says half eleven. Sarah-Jane stops, switching off the engine and gets out, taking Lance's phone and the cleaning products she collected from the house. She walks to an open entrance of one of the buildings. Squatting on the ground, Sarah-Jane puts on the rubber gloves, pours some bleach onto the cloth, and wipes the wallet and phone down, hoping the bleach kills any DNA.

Wrapping the phone in the cloth, Sarah-Jane lays it on the ground, then takes the hammer and smashes the phone, banging it repeatedly ten or more times. She picks up the remains of the smashed phone and places it inside the plastic bag, shacking the cloth to dislodge any debris. She then ties off the bag, gathers up her cleaning products and heads back to her car. Now she has to find somewhere to dump Lance's wallet and the remains of his phone.

She starts the car and drives off, leaving the abandoned factories to the ghosts of time. Sarah-Jane decides to leave

town completely, driving a further hour-and-a-half. The roads are quieter, and she only crosses paths with about ten cars in that time.

Finally, she pulls over and switches off the engine. Still with the rubber gloves on, she gets out and heads into the open field in front of her. She walks around for half an hour, trying to find the right spot to dump Lance's wallet and phone. When she comes across a hollowed-out tree, she bends down and places the items in the tree trunk, then picks up loose soil from around the tree and attempts to bury the items.

When she gets back to her car, the clock reads quarter-to-three. Feeling a little more at ease now the items have been disposed of, Sarah-Jane takes the long drive home and it's quarter past five when she parks her car back on the driveway. She hopes that the smell isn't too bad when she goes inside the house, but knows in her heart that it will be putrid and overpowering. Lance has been lying on the bathroom floor for over six hours wrapped in her duvet.

Sarah-Jane takes the cleaning products and the hammer out of the car with her, and stands at the front door for several minutes, dreading opening it. When she finally plucks up the courage and unlocks the door, the putrid smell hits her like a punch to the stomach. She quickly goes

inside, locking the door behind her. She leaves her keys and sunglasses on the long, thin table, takes off her jacket, then picks up her phone to check for messages. There are several missed calls, and five texts from Agnes. Sarah-Jane left her phone at home on purpose, as she didn't want her phone's GPS giving away vital information about where she has been for the last six to seven hours.

She reads the text messages. The last one says: *"Tried calling you, got no answer. Hoping you are ok. Please text back so I know you are okay."*

Sarah-Jane tells herself she will text Agnes back later, but first she has to do something with Lance's body. She has been mulling over what to do with him on the car ride back home, and the conclusion she has come to is she has to dismember Lance's body. It's not something she ever thought she would have to do, but there is no other alternative, His body is decomposing faster than she would have hoped for. Although she vaguely remembers some high school anatomy, she doesn't think that is going to help here so she decides she is just going to have to wing it and see how things go.

She knows the first step is to drain the blood from the body. Needing to build up the courage to slit Lance's throat and drain the blood, if it hasn't already turned to a slimy goo, she goes to the kitchen to fetch a chef's knife and the half

bottle of wine. Taking the cork out, Sarah-Jane takes a hearty swig of the wine, leaving about one-quarter of the bottle. Some wine drips down her chin as she takes the bottle away from her lips, and she wipes it off with the sleeve of her hoodie.

Sarah-Jane is still in the hoodie and sweatpants she fell asleep in. After the police showed up this morning, there was no time to mess about showering and putting on fresh clothes. In her mind, that wasn't important, but she is going to need a shower after dealing with Lance's body.

She finishes the wine, deciding it best to open another bottle to numb her to the gruesome job ahead. Leaving the kitchen with the wine and chef's knife, Sarah-Jane goes upstairs to the bathroom. Thankfully, there are no flies yet, but if she leaves his body any longer, they will appear. She places the bottle of wine on the basin counter top, not wanting to knock it over if something goes wrong.

Before Sarah-Jane unwraps the duvet, she takes off all her clothes; she doesn't want to soil them by getting blood and body fluids on them. As she unwraps the duvet, the smell hits her nostrils and makes her dry heave. She has nothing solid to throw up, as she hasn't eaten since last night's pizza. Sarah-Jane pushes Lance's corpse over onto his stomach which is now bloated, filled with gas from his decomposing body.

Once she has him on his stomach, she places her arms under his and lifts the body over the edge of the bath with his stomach sitting on the edge and his head touching the bottom of the bath. Holding the knife in her left hand, she uses her other hand to lift his head by grabbing a handful of his hair, then puts the knife to his throat. Her hand is shaking uncontrollably, and she doesn't know if she can go through with the deed.

Leaving his body hanging in the bath, Sarah-Jane drains half the bottle of wine, making her numb and giving her the courage to finish what she has started. Grabbing his hair and lifting his head, Sarah-Jane nervously slits his throat, leaving hesitation marks on the skin until the blade makes it mark. As the skin opens, Lance's blood runs down the plug hole. It doesn't take long for the blood to stop.

It takes Sarah-Jane three-and-a-half hours to separate the body, partly because it is hard to cut him up, and also because she has to stop at least ten times to throw up. Even with an empty stomach, the grizzly job makes her vomit. She decides to wrap the pieces of his body in black bin bags and put them into one of the deep freezers in the basement.

Realising she didn't bring black bags with her, Sarah-Jane quickly jumps in the shower, rinsing Lance's fluids from her, then towels herself before she runs downstairs to fetch the bags from the kitchen. On her way back from the kitchen,

she switches on the basement light and goes down to switch on the power to the deep freezers. There is an electrical buzz as they jump to life.

Back upstairs, she tears off six black bags and wraps up the body parts before sealing each bag and placing them on the floor next to each other. She is exhausted but knows she has to finish what she is doing. First, she has to take Lance's remains to the deep freezer, then clean and bleach the bathroom, and finally wash the duvet cover and the duvet. She hopes the bedding won't hold the smell of decomposing flesh after it's been washed.

Armed with a plan of action, Sarah-Jane gets busy, and it is almost eleven o'clock by the time she has finished cleaning and had another quick shower. Her room still holds the smell of death, so she slightly opens the windows in the room so she can air it, and hopes the smell will go.

She decides to sleep downstairs on the couch. Closing the bedroom door behind her, she takes the duvet from her childhood room down to the lounge and leaves it on the couch before going to the kitchen to get another bottle of wine. *I deserve this wine. It's been a long day and one I don't want to remember*, she thinks. *I just want to drown it out.*

Having not eaten the whole day, Sarah-Jane nibbles on dry bread as she can't face making anything. She picks up an

apple from the bowl and bites into it, immediately spitting the mouthful into the bin. There is half a worm in the apple, and it is still moving. She dumps the rest of the apple in the bin and takes the bottle of wine back to the lounge.

Suddenly she realises she forgot to reply to Agnes. *Fuck it, she can wait*, she thinks. *I'll message her in the morning. I'll just say I fell asleep, was delirious, sweating, didn't know where I was.* Dimming the lounge lights, Sarah-Jane prepares the couch for sleeping. She props up the pillows at one end of the couch, lays down the duvet, then places the caramel blanket to form a cocoon over the couch, the ends of the blanket not quite touching the floor. Turning down one corner of the blanket and duvet, exposing the couch beneath, Sarah-Jane picks up the now three-quarter full bottle of wine and takes a deep drink. Some wine escapes her mouth the drunker she gets, this little line of red liquid growing in length as it snakes it way down her chin, along her throat, collecting on her right breast until gravity pulls the wine over the side, plunging down between her breast and falling on her stomach as she sits there naked.

Sarah-Jane hasn't bothered to dress since her shower, but her new motto is "Fuck it, I just don't care!" After all the shit life has thrown at her in the last couple of years, she just wants to throw shit back at life. Looking down at her wine-stained body, she tries wiping the wine off with her free hand, shaking it as little droplets of wine fall to the

cream carpet below. She watches the drops falling in slow motion like the first spots of rain hitting the ground as the clouds breaks.

Knowing she should try to get the wine out before it permanently stains the carpet, Sarah-Jane stumbles to the kitchen and gets a bowl. She pours in some dishwashing liquid before adding hot water, then takes the bowl and a sponge back to the lounge, spilling the soapy liquid as she walks. Sarah-Jane places the bowl on the carpet and gets down on her knees to scrub the stains. After rubbing furiously, she realises she is making a right mess; the soapy water is now a sea of red foam. "FUCK, this is all I need after the day I've had today!" she mutters aloud.

Getting slowly to her feet, she heads to the kitchen and fetches some dishcloths to mop up the red foam. She dabs the carpet with the first cloth, which soaks up most of the foam, then takes another and gently massages the carpet with the cloth. Having cleaned away the sea of red foam, Sarah-Jane can see that she has successfully gotten the wine out the carpet. Placing a third cloth over the wet patch of carpet, she stands on top of the cloth, stepping in place as if she is marching, trying to draw the last of the moisture from the fibres of the carpet. The wine is making it hard for Sarah-Jane to keep her balance, so she finally gives up, leaving that cloth where it lies, taking the now red-stained cloths and the bowl of foamy red water back

to the kitchen. She leaves them in the sink to deal with in the morning.

On the way back to the lounge she realises she hasn't brushed her teeth for another night, but can't be bothered trying to go upstairs. *It will have to wait till the morning,* she thinks. *I should leave a toothbrush and toothpaste in the guest toilet; that way at least I could do the bare minimum.*

Sarah-Jane is finding it harder and harder to walk in a straight line, and as she approaches the lounge, she stops to steady herself by leaning against the staircase. Once she feels she can walk the rest of the way, Sarah-Jane sets off for the lounge. The couch looks so inviting as she walks through the door, but first Sarah-Jane puts the bottle to her lips, draining the last of the wine. Leaving the wine bottle on the table, she flops onto the couch, her naked body slumped like a ragdoll.

"Fuck!" she shouts out. Sarah-Jane needs to pee, but all she wants to do is pass out. Rolling off the couch onto the carpet, Sarah-Jane crawls on all fours to the guest toilet as she doesn't have the energy in her drunken state to get off the floor. Stretching up, she pulls the handle down, pushing the door. It swings open and she crawls the rest of the way to the toilet, lifting the lid before using the toilet as leverage to lift herself up.

After peeing Sarah-Jane flushes the toilet but can't be bothered to wash her hands. She uses the basin to steady herself as she gets off the toilet, her knees feeling weak beneath her drunken weight. After what feels an age, confident she is ok to stand unassisted without the help of the basin, Sarah-Jane finally stumbles back to the lounge and the awaiting couch. This will be her new bed for a while, as she won't sleep upstairs till the smell of death is gone, and even then, she knows she will opt for her childhood bed. It will take some time before Sarah-Jane can sleep in that room again without feeling uneasy about the fact someone died on that bed by her hands.

She is struck by a sudden thought. *I forgot to take the duvet from the washing machine and put it in the tumble dryer. I'm going to have to wash it again, as the smell of damp will have settled in!* These are her last thoughts before the vale of sleep falls upon her exhausted, drunken wreck of a body.

It's three in the morning when Sarah-Jane bolts upright screaming, sweat seeping from her pores, the duvet is soaked through. She wakes abruptly from a nightmare. All she can remember is she was being chased by Lance's lifeless corpse, his left arm raised pointing at her, and in a raspy, dry voice says, "YOU DID THIS, YOU KILLED ME! His eyes were gone, now just hollowed-out black voids, as a thick gooey substance poured from his mouth, dropping to

the ground before it morphed into snakes that slithered after her, hissing and striking at her heels.

It takes her a minute or two to realise where she is and slow her breathing. After a few minutes, having gained her senses, she goes to the kitchen to drink some water. Her mouth feels dry, her tongue like sandpaper. Going to the toilet on her way back to the lounge, this time she washes her hands after peeing. Sarah-Jane returns to the couch, dumping the sweat-soaked duvet on the floor. *Another thing to wash tomorrow*, she thinks to herself, before she falls asleep again.

In the morning, she wakes with a nasty hangover as the last two days of heavy drinking settle in. Her stomach queasy, her head throbbing, Sarah-Jane looks for her phone, then remembers she left it on the long, thin table before she went to take care of Lance's body. Wiping the sleep from her eyes, she goes to fetch her phone and unlocks it to find further missed calls and text messages. This time, they aren't all from Agnes. Jenny and Amanda have tried calling.

Needing to pee, Sarah-Jane writes her reply while on the toilet. *"Sorry, all, slept all day, was delirious and didn't know where I was half the time. I'm still feeling horrid, but I'm fine. No need to worry, I'm still alive."* She sends it as a group text to the three of them, but all she can think to herself is, *Hope they stop messaging, they are starting to*

bother me. It's like being mothered by someone who isn't even your mother.

Still naked, she goes upstairs to the bathroom, where a heavy smell of bleach still hangs in the air. Sarah-Jane brushes her teeth and takes a shower, then goes to the bedroom to get dressed. Opening the door of her room, she feels a cold chill against her body. The smell of death is still present but not as strong; it might take a week or two for the smell to go completely. She gets dressed then goes to finish the cleaning up, taking out the duvet cover and clothes from the tumble dryer, washing the duvet a second time.

After breakfast, Sarah-Jane takes the duvet and puts it in the tumble dryer, before she washes the sweat-laden duvet from her nightmare. By two o'clock she has finished all the cleaning and laundry, but she still has to get rid of Lance's clothes. Taking some wood from the basement, Sarah-Jane starts a fire in the lounge.

As she throws his Halloween outfit on the fire, she wonders why she bothered to wash his clothes when she has ended up burning them. *I should have just done this yesterday, it would have been less hassle,* she thinks. The smell of burning fabric fills her nose as she pokes them with a metal poker, throwing his boots onto the fire once the clothes have disintegrated in the intense heat, only leaving smouldering ash behind.

Lance's boots are made from leather, and take longer to burn, so Sarah-Jane adds more wood to the fire. Flames engulf the boots as the new logs catch fire, but the smell of burning leather makes Sarah-Jane gag. She can't think why burning leather would smell like wet dog, but it does.

Sarah-Jane orders an Indian takeaway and goes to the kitchen to get a fresh bottle of wine while she waits for her chicken korma and naan bread, which should arrive in 40 minutes. Sarah-Jane has put the caramel blanket on the two-seater couch with its back to the window, leaving the three-seater free of clutter to air. She hopes her sweat will dry before she needs to sleep tonight.

Sitting on the couch facing the window, she sips the wine while watching the world go by. Her food arrives just before four o'clock, and she opens the door, takes the food, and tips the delivery driver, then closes the door without saying a word. Back in the lounge, Sarah-Jane turns on the television, scrolling through the channels to stop on a movie channel. Rob Zombie's *House of a Thousand Corpses* is on, which she has never watched before. The film is fast-paced, violent, and has loads of extreme gore. Normally, Sarah-Jane would watch thrillers, as she has never been into extreme horror, but after the events of yesterday this feels tame in comparison to what she did, and she is no longer grossed out by the gore.

Having finished the bottle of wine, she goes to fetch her second bottle. Remembering she will need to brush her teeth this time before going to sleep, she goes to the bathroom to fetch the toothpaste and her toothbrush and leaves them in the guest toilet.

Without realising the sun has set, she goes back to the lounge with her fresh bottle of wine. The television is still on, and Clive Barker's *The Midnight Meat Train* is playing. She walks into the room just as a man with a mallet hits another man in the back of head so hard that his eye flies across the train car, a spray of blood following it.

Sarah-Jane drinks the bottle of wine a lot slower, finishing it as the film ends. As she puts the empty bottle on the table, she thinks, *Maybe tonight I should go to sleep early, hopefully without passing out from being drunk.*

"Right then," she says out loud, and she gets off the couch to brush her teeth. She pees while brushing, holding the toothbrush between her teeth to flush the toilet, before washing her hands, rinsing out her mouth, then drying her hands and mouth with the hand towel.

She goes back to the lounge and to sleep.

Chapter 12

It has been two weeks since that fateful morning and Sarah-Jane hasn't left the house. She has been surviving on takeaway food and wine, hasn't showered in ten days. Her hair is matted and she smells really bad.

Sarah-Jane is still wearing the same clothes since her last shower, and there are food stains down the front of her hoodie from spillage while eating drunk. Her days are spent walking around the house drinking, mumbling incoherently while she walks, pacing back and forth from the lounge to the kitchen. With each passing day, Sarah-Jane is slipping further and further away from sanity to the hell that is a psychotic break from reality. Deep in thought she mumbles something then, without warning, lets out a gut-curdling screech before blurting out a coherent sentence. "They must pay for what they have done, men must die!" she screams, then goes back to her mumbling as she paces.

As the days begin to blur together, the hours are spent in delirium – only broken with short moments of clarity – and

the kitchen is now a hive of takeaway boxes and empty wine bottles: fried chicken, Chinese, pizza, Indian, kebabs, and burgers. Before the string holding Sarah-Jane's sanity intact snapped, she left strict instructions that all food should be left outside on the white wicker bench and she would pay online, including a tip for the driver. She didn't want any human contact.

Her other deliveries have been the essentials: crisps, chocolate, and sweets. Sarah-Jane has been drinking so heavily she has almost finished the wine in the basement, so has placed a weekly order of 24 bottles to be left on the porch by the front door.

When she bothered to check her phone, there were a slew of missed calls and text messages. All her friends were worried as she hadn't messaged Agnes about coming back to work after the first week. During the past two weeks, Sarah-Jane has heard voices at the door, but she didn't know if they were real or part of her alcohol-induced delirium. Occasionally she would be jerked out of an alcohol blackout by someone knocking at the door, but most of these times she would be slouched on the entrance hall floor, her legs outstretched in front of her, her back against the wall, head flopping forward, drooling at the mouth, her saliva running down her hoodie, with the cold from the tiles seeping into her bones.

Dark thoughts of despair and abandonment run wild as she

slowly loses touch with reality. More and more Sarah-Jane distances herself from her friends and her cousin Mike. During one of the moments of clarity, she hears Mike banging on the door and he tries peering through the yellow glass window panes in the door. But he can't make anything out as the house is in total darkness.

Now the middle of November, it is getting cold. During a moment of clarity, Sarah-Jane realises she hasn't taken a shower. In fact, she doesn't remember how many days it has been since her last shower. Going upstairs, she opens the bedroom door and pauses. The smell of death has dissipated, almost completely gone.

Sarah-Jane catches sight of herself in the dressing table mirror. She looks horrible. Taking her paddle brush, she tries to brush the knotted mess that is her hair, but it has thinned due to the extreme stress she has been going through. By the time she has finished brushing, there are two big balls of hair sitting on the dressing table.

She peels the rank smelling clothes from her body, taking fresh clothes with her as she goes to have a shower. When she washes her hair, the water dripping off her and down the drain is black in colour. Afterwards, Sarah-Jane feels more human, and she puts on fresh clothes then goes in search of her phone. It is under the couch, but when she tries to unlock it, she realises it is dead.

For a few minutes she tries to remember where she last left her charger, then vaguely recalls using it in the kitchen. She finds it there, and plugs in her phone, waiting for enough power to switch it back on.

For the first time in two weeks Sarah-Jane is clear-headed and sober. Taking in the bombshell of takeaway boxes and rubbish in front of her, she decides to clean up. Sarah-Jane tears off two black bags and checks each box to see that there are no food remains left behind. A couple of the boxes have a rotten smell coming from them, and in one she finds the remains of a burger that has gone green and mouldy, with maggots squirming around the meat. Another box has the remains of a half-eaten chicken korma; its orange mustard colour plagued by spots of blueish green with white fur sprouting out of it. Sarah-Jane scrapes the food into the black bag in the bin, flattens all the boxes one at a time, then piles them into a separate black bag. She then collects up all the empty wine bottles and places them in another black bag.

Turning her phone on, she waits for it to boot up, needing to unlock her phone with a code instead of her finger, for security purposes. Sarah-Jane lets out a loud gasp when she realises that two weeks have gone by in a blur. She can't remember much of what has happened in those two weeks, but she is sure that she isn't going to like what she has done. One thing she is sure of is that she wants revenge.

One thought keeps playing over and over again in her mind: *Men are scum, men must die, revenge is what I seek.*

During this time of her psychotic break from reality, the one thing that kept playing out in her mind each day is Tom's attempt to molester her when she was five years old, and it has sparked a deep sense of hatred towards men. *How am I going to get my revenge?* That is the only thought Sarah-Jane is sure of in her new-found mental reality.

While she is cleaning up, she decides that the only way she knows is to use sex. So she will lure them to her bed and to their death. She recognises that the one time she felt utter power over a man was during the intense orgasm she had on the night Lance died. She had never felt such ecstasy before, and she wants to feel that level of intense power running through her again. Sarah-Jane comes to the conclusion that death by strangulation is the only way she will fulfil that feeling she experienced.

Knowing two weeks have gone by, she remembers she didn't let Agnes know that she wasn't going to come back to work after the week she said she was sick. Sarah-Jane has a flashback to the night of her birthday, at Giorgio's, when she told her four friends how lucky she was to have them as family, that they would do anything for each other, and they would die for each other. But that is now gone, all in the past. With her new-found insanity, Sarah-Jane no

longer needs their sympathy, their help, or their love. For all intents and purposes, they are all dead to her.

She sends one last group text to the four girls: *"This text message is notice of my intention to resign with immediate effect. Refrain from contacting me again, I won't reply. Sarah."* There is a real coldness to her text.

After sending the text to the girls, Sarah-Jane writes a final text to Mike: *"Cousin, sorry for anything I have done in the past. Please don't contact me again, I won't reply. I won't be home; I'm going away for a long time."*

Sarah-Jane only continued working at the library after her parents died to occupy her time because she enjoyed her work. She didn't need the money, as her parents left her the house and they had a life insurance policy each, with her as the only beneficiary. Her inheritance meant she didn't need to work another day in her life, but at the time her job had been really fulfilling and brought joy to her day. Now it felt like a chore.

With the text messages sent, for the first time Sarah-Jane feels a sense of freedom. The bonds that bound her to others is slowly dissolving, and soon there won't be any left. In case she is going to go into a dark place again, Sarah-Jane decides she must set up direct debits for her bills, so she won't need to worry about them again. At least that way she will be sure of having electricity and water.

Now there are two thoughts in Sarah-Jane's mind: revenge, and attaining that feeling she had when she orgasmed as Lance's last breath left his body. Over the next week her drinking becomes less and less; she wants to stay lucid, and all she can think about is how intense that orgasm was and how she needs to experience that again. The urge grows stronger with every passing day, and there is now this compulsion deep inside her, like a junkie needing a fix of drugs. She will do anything to get that fix, though it is sex that has become her drug of choice. Every day she sits fantasising, seeing herself having that full body-shaking orgasm.

The master bedroom is no longer the den of delight Sarah-Jane had thought it was on that night she led Charles to her bed. To her it is now the Den of Death, and any unfortunate soul that enters this room won't be leaving it with a heartbeat. "How do I get someone up to the 'Den of Death'?" she says out loud. "I need to think of a way to lure them there, tie them up, and have my way with them. I need to have that feeling again. Without it, I feel dead inside."

On the third week anniversary of Lance's death, she comes up with the solution. Talking aloud to herself, she says, "I've got it. I need four pieces of rope for this to work. Two pieces of rope tied at the bottom of the bed to secure their feet, and two pieces of rope tied to the headboard to secure their arms. That way they can't wriggle free, and it will

make it easier to get the silk scarf around their neck." Still deep in thought, she goes on, "Now I need to find a way to subdue them so they won't be able to fight me off and I can get them tied up."

Twenty minutes later, Sarah-Jane shouts triumphantly, "I'VE GOT IT! I will spike their wine. We can drink the wine while we engage in foreplay, then they will fall asleep. When they wake, they will be restrained, and I can do what I need." An evil smile breaks across her face as she revels in having devised her plan to kill. She will lull them into a false sense of security before they are bound and can't move, then she can enjoy that feeling of control before she gets to experience that intense sexual gratification.

"I will need sleeping pills, the liquid ones that come in a gel casing," she tells herself, still planning out her idea. "That way they will dissolve in the wine. Using a pill made of compressed powder will leave a residue that could be seen floating in the wine. I need to go to a pharmacy to get some over-the-counter sleeping pills."

Sarah-Jane hasn't had a drink in three days, and she is feeling a lot better since her psychotic break. And now she has a new sense of self-purpose. She gets up from the couch, collects her car keys, wallet, and winter jacket, then locks up and heads out to her car. Sarah-Jane reverses out of the driveway, the electric gate closing behind her.

"I need to withdraw cash before I get the sleeping pills," she tells herself as her car pulls away from the house. "I don't want any electronic trail of the purchase. I will go to the closest bank machine, then drive to a pharmacy on the far side of town where no-one knows me. I've got to cover my tracks, so it's a good job I've left my phone at home."

While she is driving, she thinks to herself. *Maybe while I'm out I will go to a shop that sells sim cards but doesn't take personal details with the purchase. I need a new number. I don't want anyone I used to keep in contact with getting hold of me, but I still need a phone to communicate with my victims-to-be.*

It takes Sarah-Jane an hour-and-a-half to get to the far side of town, having already stopped off to withdraw the cash she needs. Parking her car at the far end of the shopping mall's parking lot, she gets out and heads for the electric doors at the entrance. Inside, she checks the information board to search where the pharmacy is located, as she has never been to this mall before. It is located on the ground floor, on the other side of the food court.

"Good day, how may I be of assistance?" a helpful employee asks as Sarah-Jane enters the pharmacy.

"Hi, could you please help me. I am trying to find sleeping pills, but the liquid-based ones. I can't swallow the tablet ones; they make me gag. I was told by a friend to get some

as I have had insomnia for the last month. I just need something that will knock me out, but not leave me drowsy in the morning," explains Sarah-Jane.

"Ok, please follow me. Let's see if we can't get you sorted with a mild sleeping pill," says the shop assistant, who can see dark rings under Sarah-Jane's eyes.

They walk down the third aisle, stopping halfway down. The assistant picks up a blue plastic bottle with the words "assured sleep, non-drowsy" written in large black letters. "This one should do the trick," she says, passing the bottle to Sarah-Jane.

"How many should I take to get a normal night's sleep? Also, if I only need to sleep for two to four hours, should I take less than the normal amount?" she asks the assistant.

"Normally you need two tablets to have a full night's sleep. That is the recommended dose, though some people have told me they need three pills because these are mild strength. If you want a short, deep sleep, then I recommend you take one pill before bed time, but make sure you take them on a full stomach, otherwise you could damage your stomach lining," the woman tells her.

"Can you drink alcohol and take these pills?" Sarah-Jane asks the assistant.

"They recommend only taking one pill if you have any alcohol," the woman replies. "They make you drowsy when mixed with alcohol, and taking a normal dose mixed with alcohol could make you vomit."

"Thanks for your help. Where do I pay?" asks Sarah-Jane.

"You can pay at the counter. It's at the back, and two aisles over."

Sarah-Jane thanks the assistant and pays for the sleeping pills then heads out of the store. Once outside, her stomach rumbles. Sarah-Jane has not eaten today, so she walks back to the food court, not sure what she fancies to eat. The court has the usual fast-food eateries, and she eventually decides on a fried chicken burger, fries, and an extra piece of chicken, with a chocolate milkshake to wash it all down. Enjoying her breakfast – even though it is two in the afternoon – sitting at a table bathed in natural sunlight, Sarah-Jane begins to feel a warmth inside herself. She hasn't felt like this since Lance died.

Knowing she is only going to feel this warmth briefly before it dies for good, Sarah-Jane decides to savour the moment as she eats. There is a stillness in the air, as though time itself has slowed while she is lost in thoughts of happier times. She finishes the last bite of her food, takes a drink of

her milkshake, and gets up to leave, throwing the bones of her chicken in the closest bin.

I still need rope, Sarah-Jane thinks to herself. *There's bound to be a hardware store here, but I don't know if I should buy it here or somewhere else. Buying two things I need from the same mall is one thing too many to link together. I think it's maybe best to go somewhere else no-one knows me. And I still have to get that sim card. I will need to go to three different locations today, which means lots of driving. It's a good thing I haven't had any wine in three days.*

Sarah-Jane walks back to her car, finishing her milkshake before she gets to the exit, throwing the empty cup in the bin as she walks through the electric doors. Stopping briefly next to her car. Taking a deep breath, Sarah-Jane takes in the cold late November air. It hits her lungs like a cold fire as it spreads, waking her and giving her energy. She takes another deep breath and then a third. For the first time in a long time, Sarah-Jane feels alive.

Driving off, she considers where she should go to buy the rope and sim card. Deciding on the sim card first, Sarah-Jane knows there are several dodgy stores in the centre of town. It takes longer than expected to get to the centre of town, due to an accident between two cars slowing down traffic, and any warm, joyful feeling Sarah-Jane had when she left the shopping mall has now gone, replaced by

frustration building to anger. She knows she shouldn't feel angry, but what should have been a half hour drive has turned into an hour-and-a-half.

Finding a parking spot adds to her anger, and she ends up having to park ten streets away from the store she has in mind. Clouds are forming overhead, covering the sun as they congregate, closing in on the sun and bringing a chill to the air. It mirrors the warmth leaving her body as the frustration takes over and the anger builds. Sarah-Jane is mumbling while she walks the ten blocks to buy the sim card. "It's ten blocks one way, then ten blocks back. Makes me mad." The veins at her temples are throbbing by the time she finally reaches the store.

Sarah-Jane goes inside and asks the person behind the screen for a pay-as-you-go sim card. Unfortunately for her, the only way to get a sim without any questions is to buy a cheap throwaway phone. She pays for the throwaway phone, but the added purchase just fuels her growing anger. Sarah-Jane is starting to feel the urge to drink, but forces herself to calm down. Leaving the mobile store, she walks back to her car. "Not yet. When I get home. Can't lose my judgement while in public," she says in her mind, hoping she hasn't spoken the words out loud.

Deep in thought while walking to her car, Sarah-Jane doesn't hear someone calling her name. "Sarah! Sarah!"

Eventually she hears and stops, looking around to locate which direction the voice is coming from. Recognising the face running up to her slightly out of breath, Sarah-Jane puts a smile on her face. She needs to be polite and happy. It's Ken.

"Sarah, thought it was you. I was visiting an art gallery nearby and was on my way to get the bus home," he says, trying to catch his breath. "I didn't know if I was ever going to see you again. I haven't heard back from you in about two months."

"Sorry, Ken, it's been a really busy time. I was meaning to text you. I've had to get a new sim card," she explains. "I've had someone stalking me since we last met. Don't worry, it's not from We Play; it's my ex-boyfriend from university. We bumped into each other and things got a little steamy. I told him it was one night, and he has been stalking me since," Sarah-Jane lies.

"Oh, I didn't know. Sorry for rushing to judgement," says Ken.

"Don't worry about it, how were you to know? I've still got your number on my phone. I'm going to text you soon, promise," she assures him with a smile. "I'm sorry I'm in a bit of a rush, got to be somewhere shortly. Hope you understand."

Ken replies, "Don't be silly. I'm keeping you here. Hear from you soon." He leans in for a kiss and Sarah-Jane opens her mouth as Ken's lips meets hers, their tongues twirling around each other, before they walk off in different directions.

She thinks to herself, *So gullible, men! Got to keep them interested. Give them hope that you will fuck them, and they are putty in the palm of your hands.* Back at her car, she tosses the throwaway phone onto the passenger seat as she climbs in, closing the door. "Ken, poor Ken," she says out loud. "You will be my first since Lance. You don't know what you are in for. It will be the ride of your life, that's for sure." She has a sinister smile on her face.

Deep in thought as she is pulling out from the parking spot, a loud honk from a passing car snaps her back into the moment. Narrowly missing the other car, she slams on the brakes. *That was close!* she thinks to herself. *Fuck, I need to be more focussed. I can't let my fantasising get me killed.*

Checking her side mirror to see if there are any more cars coming up from behind, Sarah-Jane pulls out from the parking spot. "One last thing to get," she says out loud, "just got to find a hardware store. Now this is where having a smart phone would come in handy. I could just run a search, and in a matter of seconds I would have a result showing the nearest hardware store to me. But that records the

location I'm at using my GPS, so we can't have that. I'll just need to drive around looking, and see if I come across one."

Sarah-Jane drives through six neighbourhoods before she sees a sign advertising a hardware store a mile down the road. Pulling into the side parking lot for the store, Sarah-Jane notices a car reversing out of a spot at the end of the first row. She heads for the now vacant spot and parks, noticing the time on the dashboard clock is now twenty past five. Sarah-Jane feels a rumble in her tummy. *Yikes, that's the time already. I need to hurry up. Starting to get hungry,* she thinks to herself.

Sara-Jane walks to the entrance, the door slides open as she nears it. Inside, she can hear the chatter of people going about their daily lives, asking questions, or giving answers. She catches the eye of one of the shop's employees, and he walks towards her.

"Afternoon, my name is James. How may I be of service today?" he asks her.

Sarah-Jane replies, "I need ten metres of rope cut into four equal lengths. I need rope that is a centimetre in thickness, please."

"What type of rope do you need, nylon or cotton fibre?" James asks.

"Cotton fibre, please," she replies with a smile. A host of thoughts run through her mind as she tries to be polite. *What I could do to you!* she thinks, looking him up and down. *You're lucky I'm trying to cover my tracks, or I would have you strapped to my bed.*

"I'll just get that for you. If you wait here, I won't be long," James tells her. Sarah-Jane nods as he goes off to get her the rope.

Ten minutes later, James reappears with her rope. "Here you go. You might want to dip the ends in white glue then let it dry, this will help to stop the ends from fraying. I brought a pot of glue just in case you will need it," he explains.

"Okay, thanks for the information. I will need the pot of glue as well. Is there any specific way I should apply the glue?" Sarah-Jane asks.

"Holding the rope six inches from the end, slowly dip it in the pot of glue, making sure to cover at least an inch in glue. Let it dry, then do the other end, that way you don't end up gluing the two ends together."

"Thanks, I'll keep that in mind." She smiles at him. "How much do I owe you for the rope and glue?"

"That will be 17.50, please," replies James, having scanned her items. "Cash or card?"

"Cash, please." She hands him a 20, adding, "Keep the change. Put it in the animal welfare box."

"Thanks for visiting DIY World," James replies. "See you again soon."

The night sky greets her as she leaves the hardware store. The days are shorter at this time of year, and as she breathes out Sarah-Jane can see a plume of mist leave her mouth. A cold chill hangs heavy in the air. Her stomach is no longer grumbling, it is screaming at her. She can feel the hunger pains in the pit of her stomach, and considers what she should have to eat. She definitely doesn't want to cook, so she will get takeaway.

Driving off, she looks for the first drive-through. Sarah-Jane doesn't care what she will be eating, as long as it is close by so she can quell these hunger pains. Halfway home she comes upon a burger restaurant, so slows her car down before turning off into the drive-through lane. There are only two cars in front of her. No longer feeling agitated, Sarah-Jane is deciding what she will eat as she inches her car closer to the ordering intercom.

"Welcome to Jimmy's Burger Barn. What would you like to order?" a voice greets her.

Knowing she has to decide quickly, she replies, "Can I have the Jimmy's special, please? Medium size with orange soda. Thanks."

"Your order will be with you shortly. Drive to the pick-up window, and your order will be there when you pay," says the voice coming from the intercom.

Sarah-Jane's car slowly rolls forward till she is at the pick-up window. The window slides open, and a staff member says, "That will be 8.50 for your meal."

Looking through her wallet, all she has left is a 20. She passes the note to the cashier, who takes it from her then returns the change before passing her the bag of food and her orange soda. "Enjoy your meal. Come again soon to Jimmy's Burger Barn."

Sarah-Jane rolls up her window after taking her food. She is now starving but has to drive away from the window to avoid holding up other hungry customers. Pulling around the building, she looks for a place to park and eat. There aren't many available spaces left, as Jimmy's is well known and is always busy, but eventually she finds a space right at the back in the corner.

"Finally, food. I'm starving," she says out loud as she opens the paper bag. Inside she sees her burger sitting on top of a cardboard box which has her fries inside. Taking the straw and serviettes from the bag, Sarah-Jane plunges the straw through the hole in the lid of her soda, then places the serviettes on the passenger seat next to the throwaway

phone. She takes a long sip of her orange soda before placing it in the cup holder, then she takes the burger and fries from the bag. Flattening the paper bag, Sarah-Jane places it over her lap and puts the box of fries on top. Then she unwraps the burger and removes the waxed paper wrapper to find a double patty burger with lettuce, sliced tomato, and raw onions. It has ketchup, yellow mustard, and yellow cheese. Some of the melted yellow cheese has stuck to the wrapper, and as she tries to remove it with her teeth, some of the oil from the burger drips down her hand.

She crumbles the wrapper, leaving it on the paper bag, and with both hands cradling the burger Sarah-Jane sinks her teeth deep into it, taking a large bite. Feeling so hungry, Sarah-Jane wolfs down the burger in no time at all. Opening the box, Sarah-Jane can see steam rising from the fries, which look to be lightly salted. She thinks it best to let them cool down, so she drinks her soda. Unfortunately, they forgot to give her ketchup for her fries.

"Oh well, never mind, I will have to eat them naked," she says to herself, placing her soda back in the cup holder. Picking up the box, Sarah-Jane tries taking some of the fries but drops them back in the box; they are still too hot to eat. She puts the box of fries back in the paper bag, next to the throwaway phone, and takes a couple of serviettes to wipe the burger juices from her mouth and hands. I'm going to have to either wait here for my fries to become eatable, or reheat them

when I get home, she thinks to herself. Opting for the second option, reheating, she finishes her soda before driving home.

Sarah-Jane parks her car on the driveway, the electric gates shutting behind her. The time on the dashboard clock is quarter past seven. It has been a long day of driving. Sarah-Jane collects all the things she has bought before she gets out and locks her car, then walks to the front door, first checking if there is any post before she goes inside. To her delight there is no mail.

As she unlocks the front door, she has a feeling she is being watched. Sarah-Jane turns around, scanning the street in the dark to see if she can make out anything out of the ordinary, but nothing catches her eye. Other than if someone sees that she has been out, there is no evidence to say otherwise, she decides. Her phone is still in the house, and the GPS would say she hasn't move from her current position. Once inside, she locks the front door and leaves all her new purchases on the long, thin table then goes upstairs to change and take a shower.

Feeling refreshed from her shower, she goes downstairs and takes her fries to the kitchen where she reheats them in the microwave for two minutes. Sarah-Jane collects her purchases, leaving them on the dining room table, before collecting her fries when the microwave pings. She empties the fries onto a plate and squeezes ketchup over them before she unplugs her phone from the charger and takes it

with her. Sarah-Jane has to exchange the sim cards to ensure no-one she knows will bother her again, unless she chooses to get in contact with them.

Placing the plate on the dining table, Sarah-Jane unlocks her phone. "Fuck!" she explodes. "Don't these people get the message I don't want anything to do with them!" She looks in disgust at the 15 missed calls and slew of texts. "It doesn't matter any more, I'm not even going to read them. Once I have destroyed the sim, they don't exist to me."

Sarah-Jane powers down her phone and removes the sim card. Picking up the throwaway phone, she opens the packaging, takes out the new sim card, then inserts it into her own phone before switching it back on. It takes a few minutes to reboot. Her new number pops up, saying 'emergency calls only' beneath it. Leaving her phone to sync with the new sim, Sarah-Jane takes the pot of glue and removes the lid, breaking the paper seal that keeps the contents fresh. It's similar to the seals on a ketchup bottle, the one you have to peel off before first use.

Holding the rope six inches from the end, as James instructed, she dips the first inch of the rope slowly into the glue, making sure the ends are covered properly before she slowly pulls the rope out, letting the excess glue drip back into the pot. Having completed one end, Sarah-Jane takes the rope to the kitchen and leaves the end hanging over the

edge of the basin in case the glue continues dripping. She repeats this process while eating her fries, until there are four ropes lying side by side, their ends hanging in the basin waiting to dry.

Sarah-Jane's fries are finished, the remnants of ketchup long dry by the time she has completed all eight ends of the four pieces of rope. As she waits for the last four ends to dry, she picks up her phone to see the time. "It feels so nice not seeing any notifications," she says as she unlocks the phone. It's quarter-to-nine, and Sarah-Jane realises she hasn't had any wine since she came home.

"Now that I've got all that out the way, I can finally have a drink," she says, getting up from the table to open a bottle. Still not bothering with a glass, Sarah-Jane sips from the bottle while she checks on the four rope ends, which are almost dry. She thinks to herself, *Once they're dry, I will go upstairs and tie them off to see how it looks*.

At nine o'clock Sarah-Jane checks the ropes. Satisfied they are dry enough, she takes them and the wine upstairs to the den of death, taking a swig of the wine before she leaves the bottle on the bedside table. The smell of death has now left the room, and Sarah-Jane climbs on the bed to remove the pillows from the headboard so she can tie a rope on either side. Using a knot she learnt many years ago as a girl scout, Sarah-Jane yanks on the

rope to test if the knot holds. She repeats the process on the other side before she kneels on the floor, tying a rope around the left leg of the bed frame. She yanks it hard, making sure the knot holds then ties the last rope around the right leg.

Happy with the results, Sarah-Jane rolls up the ropes at the foot of the bed, tucking them under the frame so they aren't in view. She rolls up the headboard ropes and places the pillows over them, so they too are out of view. Thankfully, Sarah-Jane has managed to get the smell of death out from the duvet and duvet cover, so the room is now back to its former state before that fateful morning.

Picking up the bottle of wine, she goes back down to the dining room to clear up. She is feeling quite tired from the day's excursions. Sarah-Jane is still sleeping on the couch; she isn't ready to sleep upstairs, even if it is in her childhood room.

Once she has finished tidying up, she decides to watch a film while she drinks the rest of the bottle of wine. *I will only drink the one bottle today*, she thinks to herself, knowing she needs to slow down on the drinking if she wants to take her revenge. Being drunk and sloppy makes for mistakes.

It is quarter-to-twelve when Sarah-Jane switches off the television, the wine bottle long empty. Wearily, she goes to

the guest toilet, brushes her teeth, then turns off the lounge lights and navigates her way to the couch in the dark. She climbs under the covers of her makeshift bed, drifting off to sleep quickly with the help of the wine.

Chapter 13

The only people Sarah-Jane has given her new number to are Ken and Charles, as she text them two days after getting the new sim card. Ken already knew the reason for the new number, but Charles was surprised to receive an anonymous text from a number he didn't recognise so, being cautious, didn't open the message for three days.

Sarah-Jane has arranged to meet Ken. It's the last week of November, and with the weekend approaching, Sarah-Jane is feeling a little excited and nervous. She is excited at having Ken strapped to the bed and is curious whether her experience was a one-off or if she can achieve the same explosive orgasm she had the night Lance died. She is also a little nervous as the days count down to their meeting, in case something will go wrong. Last time was an accident; this time, however, she is going to end Ken's life on purpose.

Since Sarah-Jane got her new sim card, she has been flirting with both men. Ken has been easier to control as she has seen and had some physical contact with him recently, and

she knows that kiss on the street when they bumped into each other would have been running through his mind. Charles, on the other hand, has taken a little bit longer. They had a good time together and he had been looking forward to seeing her again, so he wasn't happy that Sarah-Jane hadn't kept in contact when she said she would.

It took a few days of messaging for Sarah-Jane to convince Charles that her ex had been stalking her and she was afraid of what he might do. But as each day passes, Charles opens up to her and finally accepts her story. From then on, it has been plain sailing and he has been putty in her hands. Sarah-Jane has asked Charles if he wouldn't mind texting for a few more weeks as she is waiting for the restraining order to be granted, which he completely understands as he has been through a similar experience. She has promised Charles that by early December she should be free of the whole nightmare she is going through, and they can meet up then if he would still like to. They agreed to wait till the restraining order but to text every day.

A lot of their texts have been very hot and steamy. Some of the ones Charles has sent her make her wet while she reads them, and on occasions Sarah-Jane felt so horny from reading the texts that she would rub her fingers over her moist pussy, her juices covering her fingers. Rubbing her swollen clit, feeling it throb between her fingers as she squeezes it, gently biting her bottom lip as she inserts her

middle finger inside herself, she moves her middle finger in and out, back and forth, over and over. With each passing stroke, Sarah-Jane increases her pace, and with each plunge her finger makes, the deeper she tries to push it. Rubbing her clit with her other hand, she gets closer to coming, then, only rubbing her clit as she orgasms, Sarah-Jane feels a rush of juices running down her leg.

Sarah-Jane has told Ken that she is making lasagne for dinner on Saturday and that it's a family recipe handed down from generation to generation. He is looking forward to their date and thinks he is going to have another great night of sex. The last thing he would ever think of is that Saturday night will be the last night of his life. She tells Ken that he should get a cab or use the bus system. Although a cab will be quicker, it will cost more, so Ken says he will use the bus system; he has a weekly bus pass and doesn't want to waste it. All he needs is her postcode so he can plan his journey to her.

Ken and Sarah-Jane agree that Ken should be at her house by six o'clock. She has told him that the earlier he arrives, the more time they get to fuck. But she still needs time to make the lasagne and get herself ready. *I'll wear some sexy underwear under a kitchen apron,* she thinks while cooking the mince for the lasagne. *When I answer the door, the first thing Ken will see is me with virtually no clothes on. That will get his motor running; the rest will be easy.*

It is midday and Sarah-Jane has finished making the lasagne. She just has to put it in the oven for 30 minutes once Ken arrives, leaving them time to have a few glasses of wine before they eat. "I'll make sure to drink slowly to keep my wits about me," she says aloud. "I'll keep plying Ken with wine to make him more than tipsy and let his guard down."

A thought pops into Sarah-Jane's mind. *Tipsy. How I find that word to be inaccurate in its description. I think 'tipsy' should be replaced with a word like slanted; at least slanted gives a more accurate description of someone. The drunker they get, the more slanted they feel.*

Even though Sarah-Jane has cut down her drinking to almost nothing, she is still ordering a case of wine a week, so the wine racks look less empty when she goes down to the basement to fetch a couple of bottles. Since she put Lance in the deep freeze, she has only been to the basement to do laundry, or to unpack or fetch wine. At first, she tried to avoid the basement, but now she feels nothing every time she goes down there.

Sarah-Jane has been doing a bit of online shopping in the lead-up to meeting Ken this evening, and has bought herself some sexy lingerie. She has purchased two identical sets — one in black, and the other in red. The bottom of each set has a crotchless area for easy access, while the top half has cut-out sections, allowing the nipples to be free. She has

also bought garter belts in matching colours. She has decided to wear the black set this evening.

I'm sure two bottles will be enough, she thinks to herself as she selects the wine. *If I need more, I can easily fetch another two. Let's hope it doesn't take that much to get Ken intoxicated but not sloppy drunk.*

"I'll open the first bottle just before Ken arrives. That should give it enough time to breathe, and the second bottle I'll open just before we go upstairs," she talks to herself as she takes the wine to the kitchen and places it on the island. "I can tell him that it needs to breathe before we drink it, and that gives enough time for the sleeping capsule to dissolve in his glass. If he drinks it while we have foreplay, hopefully he will fall asleep quickly, allowing me to tie him up."

It is a dull day; cold and bleak; the clouds heavy and dark. You can feel the moisture in the air, but the clouds aren't yet ready to burst. With nothing more to do, Sarah-Jane goes to the lounge to relax. There is no longer any clutter, as Sarah-Jane is back sleeping upstairs. Although her bed in the master bedroom is bigger and more comfortable, she still sleeps in her childhood room. The master bedroom has now become her den of death, but she still keeps her clothes there as it is just too much hassle to move everything.

Turning on the television, Sarah-Jane no longer scrolls through channels. The horror channel is a permanent fixture; she is now completely desensitised to the violence and gore. Clive Barker's *Hellraiser* is playing, but she has unfortunately switched the television on near the end of the film. A man hangs in mid-air by chains, with hooks that dig deep into his skin. A woman runs from the room and the door closes. The man says, "Jesus wept" before the chains pull him apart, pieces of flesh exploding in different directions. Sarah-Jane watches the film till it ends. She has never seen *Hellraiser* before and decides she would like to watch it from the beginning.

The next film starts briefly, after some adverts. It is *Henry: Portrait of a Serial Killer,* which has been shot more like a documentary than a traditional film. It is loosely based on the serial killer Henry Lee Lucas, and as a film Sarah-Jane finds it more psychologically disturbing than gory. When the film finishes at half three, she switches off the tv and goes to take a shower, washing her hair and using a body scrub to make her skin feel softer.

After her shower Sarah-Jane wears her dressing gown while she puts on makeup then dries and straightens her hair. She sprays perfume in all the right places, making sure not to use too much that the scent becomes over-powering. If need be, she can spray a little more just before Ken arrives. At quarter past five, Sarah-Jane is almost ready. She puts on

her black lingerie, the garter belt, and a pair of black lace stockings.

Now ready, Sarah-Jane goes to the kitchen and fetches an apron. Putting it on, she ties the strap at the back. Now that it is the end of November, the heating in the house is on, so at least Sarah-Jane isn't feeling cold as she walks around in the lingerie and apron. At quarter-to-six she takes the lasagne from the fridge, removing the clingfilm covering it, and turns the oven on to preheat so she can put the dish in when Ken arrives. It's best not to put a cold lasagne in the oven.

Just before six o'clock, Sarah-Jane is uncorking one of the wine bottles when she hears knocking at the front door. Leaving the cork on the corkscrew, she puts it on the island counter before going to answering the door. Sarah-Jane looks through the peephole and sees it is Ken. She opens the door, peering her head around the side, and says, "Ken darling, welcome to my home. Excuse the way I answered the door, my outfit isn't weather ready." She opens the door wider to let Ken enter then quickly closes it behind him.

"Wow, that definitely isn't the right outfit to wear in this weather, though it is the right outfit to greet someone," Ken says, openly admiring her lingerie.

Taking off the apron, she says, "Now you can have a better look." Sarah-Jane can see a bulge starting to swell in Ken's

crotch. "Are you happy to see me, or is that a rocket in your pocket?" she jokes.

"It's my snake, and he is happy to see you," replies Ken. "Just seeing those crotchless panties has made me hard."

Sarah-Jane takes Ken's jacket and hangs it up on the coat hooks before she goes to kiss him, rubbing her hand along the length of his cock. "Glad we made the effort to meet again. You sure know how to use that snake of yours. I look forward to him burrowing deep inside my warm, wet pussy," she whispers teasingly.

"I look forward to my dessert after dinner." Ken rubs his fingers over her pussy lips, feeling her creamy juices covering his fingers. Her nipples harden as they grow like mountains sticking out of the holes in the lacey bra.

"More of that later," she promises. "First some wine. Let's go through to the kitchen."

He follows her to the kitchen where she pours half a glass of wine for each of them, and hands one to Ken.

"Here's to another great evening of sex," toasts Ken as they clink glasses.

"Cheers. Here's to another great night of sex," Sarah-Jane says in reply. As she smiles, she is thinking to herself, *Little*

do you know, it is going to be a great night for me. Unfortunately for you, it is going to be your last night alive.

She takes a sip of her wine before she puts the dish in the oven. "The lasagne will be ready in half an hour, let's sit at the dinner table," she suggests.

"What was the outcome? You said you applied for a restraining order against your ex, have you been granted it yet?" Ken asks as they settle themselves at the table.

"Not yet, but it should be any day now. Just waiting on the judge to finalise the paperwork, then he can't contact me, see me, or be within a hundred feet of me," she replies, flicking her hair over her shoulder.

Half an hour later, Sarah-Jane goes to check if the lasagne is ready. As she gets up, she sees her pussy juices have left a creamy residue on her chair. *There is probably going to be more of that before dinner is done,* she thinks, shrugging.

Having laid the table earlier, Sarah-Jane brings the lasagne and places it on a wooden chopping board. She takes Ken's plate in one hand, using the other to pick up the spatula. Slicing downwards, she cuts out a square of lasagne, scooping it out the dish before placing it on Ken's plate. "Hope, you enjoy the lasagne. Be careful, it is hot," she warns.

"From what you have told me about the lasagne, I'm really looking forward to it. Other than the great sex we will have later, your lasagne is the only other thing I could think about today," Ken admits, slicing his fork through the lasagne and scooping some onto his fork.

Ken blows on the lasagne, hoping to cool it down as steam rises off his fork. He chews slowly, trying not to burn his mouth. "Wow, that is hot. Think I'll let it cool down a bit before I carry on," he says.

"Sorry. I did warn you, though. Why not drink more of your wine?" Sarah-Jane fills Ken's glass almost to the top, then tops her own glass to the halfway point. So far, she has only had quarter of a glass.

"Are you trying to make me drunk?" he asks her.

She laughs. "Trying to get you well oiled. I'm drinking less as I want to treat you this evening as you treated me last time. I'm taking the lead this time."

"I look forward to seeing what you have in store for me," Ken replies, taking a large gulp of his wine.

The lasagne is now cool enough for them to eat, and silence falls over the table as they eat their food. Sarah-Jane can see by Ken's face how much he is enjoying his meal.

"This is the best lasagne I have eaten," he tells her. "Not even my mother makes lasagne as good as this. Can I have more, please?"

"Help yourself to more. Leftovers can be for breakfast in the morning," she replies with a smile. *Tell him what he wants to hear and make him feel at ease. He doesn't know what's going to hit him later,* she thinks to herself.

Pouring herself a larger amount of wine this time to avoid drawing any suspicion, Sarah-Jane empties the rest of the bottle into Ken's glass. "Let's finish our wine before we go upstairs to the den of delight," she tells him.

"Nice house you have here. How can you afford it on a librarian's salary?" asks Ken.

"My parents left me the house when they passed away over a year-and-a-half ago. I grew up in this house. If they were still alive, I would still be living in the apartment I was renting, which was walking distance from the library. I loved my apartment but there was no point in paying for a place to stay when I have this house to myself. Yes, it is too big for one person, and I have been thinking of selling it and getting something smaller for one person," she admits. "But there are so many good memories here, it is hard to leave."

"Sorry about your parents. I didn't mean to bring up bad memories," says Ken.

"Don't worry about it. I've finally gotten to a good place. It took me a long time to grieve them, but I no longer feel sad any more," she assures him, taking a sip of her wine.

Sarah-Jane can see that Ken likes to drink. "Do you have more?" he asks, as he drains the last of the wine from his glass.

"Yes, I have another bottle in the kitchen, and a wine collection in the basement if we need more. We will have to let the wine breathe before we drink it, though," she explains. "Here, have some of mine in the meantime." She leans over to pour some wine from her glass into his.

"Thanks," he says, taking a sip. Ken has a problem with alcohol; the drunker he gets, the faster he drinks, although he has a high tolerance for alcohol. It takes two to three times the amount of alcohol to get Ken drunk compared to the average person. "Where is the toilet, please? That is the problem with drinking alcohol, you need to go to the toilet more often," he laughs as he gulps the last of the wine in his glass.

"There is a door next to the long, thin table by the front door; that is the guest toilet. When you finish, come upstairs. I will be waiting for you in the bedroom, so just follow the light. I'll open the wine, pour us some, and take it to the bedroom."

Sarah-Jane can see that the wine is doing its job, as Ken is starting to stumble a bit as he walks off to the toilet. She leaves the lasagne and empty plates on the table and goes to open the bottle of wine. Taking a sleeping capsule, she drops it in Ken's glass, before filling it halfway. She feels she has almost got to her safe limit so she can remain as clear-headed as possible, so pours herself just a quarter of a glass.

Holding the glasses between her fingers, and the bottle in the other hand, she heads upstairs to the den of death, placing the glasses and bottle on a bedside table. Sarah-Jane lights all the new candles; their fragrance is peach and orange.

Ken appears at the door. "Nice, candles, they give off soft light, making the experience more intimate," he says, slurring his words a little. "Is that half glass of wine mine?" he asks.

"Come, get comfy on the bed." Sarah-Jane taps the bed a couple of times with her hand, before she continues, "The wine needs more time to breathe; at least another ten minutes, so let's have a little bit of fun first, then we can have more wine. Take your clothes off. You can leave them on the dressing table stool."

I hope he's not too drunk, she thinks to herself, teasing her nipples as she watches Ken undress. *I still need him to*

perform. I need his hard cock. I need to reach that special place, that explosive orgasm

Finally naked, Ken lies on the bed next to her. Sarah-Jane takes the lead this time and climbs on top of him, leaning forward. They kiss, their mouths open, their tongues twirling around each other with an urgency of lust. She presses her body into his as the heat of their kiss spreads over them, then she plants little kisses from his mouth down his chest, towards his cock. With each kiss, Ken's cock grows, getting harder until it stands firm like a pole in the ground.

Sarah-Jane takes his cock into her mouth, its length disappearing until his balls are all that can be seen. Her head bobs up and down, getting faster with every stroke. Ken's breathing is shallow and fast as he arches his pelvis, shooting his load down her throat. She slows her pace as she sucks him dry, sending shivers up his spine.

"I haven't been sucked off like that in a long time," says Ken with a smile on his face.

Sarah-Jane passes him the glass of wine; the sleeping capsule has completely dissolved now. Ken takes a large swig of the wine, almost emptying the glass, then drains what is left.

"Your turn," he says. "Lie back and let my tongue do its trick."

Sarah-Jane lies back, her panties still on. Ken dives straight in, his tongue splitting open her pussy lips to seek out its target. Her clit swells as his mouth sucks it in deeply, making her moan. But the sleeping capsule is taking effect, and Ken suddenly passes out with her clit in his mouth. Sarah-Jane was enjoying being eaten out and was close to orgasm, so she is a little disappointed she didn't get to come, but glad she can stop pretending.

Ken is heavy and it takes her 15 minutes to wriggle out from under him; he feels like dead weight even though he is alive. Pushing his body to the centre of the bed, Sarah-Jane secures one rope at a time, until all four of his limbs are tied up. There is no slack in the rope which would allow Ken to wriggle around, making it harder for her to achieve her desired outcome.

Knowing that she is going to have to wait until Ken is awake to have her way with him, Sarah-Jane decides to clean up the mess from dinner. She puts her dressing gown on before she goes downstairs, leaving a sleeping Ken naked and tied up on the bed. She places a clean sheet of clingfilm over the lasagne before putting it in the fridge, then rinses the plates of any leftover food and slots them into the dishwasher.

Sarah-Jane is waiting to hear Ken's screams; that is when she will know he is no longer asleep. By the time she has

tidied up from their dinner, she still hasn't heard a noise from upstairs. *I hope these sleeping capsules don't last too long*, she thinks, *I don't want to fall asleep myself.*

The time on the microwave is nine o'clock when she finishes cleaning. Sarah-Jane goes to the lounge and switches on the television to watch a film while she waits for Ken to wake. *Hollow Man* with Kevin Bacon has just started playing. As the film ends, she hears what she thinks is a faint murmuring from upstairs. She switches off the television to hear if it is Ken waking up.

"WHAT THE FUCK!" she hears him scream. "HEY, YOU CRAZY BITCH, COME UNTIE ME!!"

Sarah-Jane makes her way upstairs quickly, not wanting his screams to draw too much attention and alert her neighbours to what is going on.

Ken yells, "WHAT YOU DOING THIS FOR? WHEN I GET FREE, I'LL KICK YOUR ARSE!" as she comes through the door.

Sarah-Jane takes one of his socks and shoves it into his mouth to shut him up. "There, there, no need to shout," she soothes. "You aren't getting out of these ropes, no matter how much you try to wriggle. So you might as well stop struggling." She can see the fear creep into his eyes as he stops fighting.

Ken knows he is in deep trouble. He can see the joy leave her face, only to be replaced by a look of anger and hatred; a look of pure evil.

"Tonight, you are going to fulfil a desire I thought I would never again achieve, but unfortunately for you, it requires you to die in the process. Nothing personal," she assures him, "you were just the person who stepped into my web of death first."

As tears roll down his cheeks and onto the bed, she goes on, "On Halloween, I met up with someone from We Play. We hit it off, and there was a chemistry between us that neither of us had felt with anyone else before. We were going to see if a relationship could blossom between us." She strokes Ken's leg with the silk scarf as she continues talking. "He suggested that we try autoerotic asphyxiation, as he had tried it twice before. He said he trusted me and wanted us to experience a sexual high that most people would never experience in their lifetimes. I was hesitant at first, but he reassured me everything would be fine, and we agreed on a safe word and a safe gesture."

She sighs and goes on, "Unfortunately, as I climaxed, unbeknownst to me, he had died, unable to breathe, unable to speak, his hands unable to perform the safe gesture we had decided on. His hands were gripping at the silk scarf that we had used – this silk scarf." She shows him the scarf.

"It was the most intense full body-shaking orgasm I have ever had, and tonight you and I are going to recreate that experience. I want to feel what I felt before I opened my eyes and saw him dead. Poor, poor Ken. I know you wish you were anywhere but here right now, but alas, you *are* here. I will give you some pleasure before the pain, so at least you go out with some satisfaction... even if it is brief."

Ken's eyes betray him. She can see fear and despair in his eyes, like the fear of a cornered animal knowing it is going to die. Sarah-Jane climbs on the bed kneeling next to him and strokes the silk scarf lightly over his crotch back and forth, watching, waiting for his cock to grow.

The only thing going through Ken's mind is, *Soft cock, soft cock, if it stays soft, she won't kill me.* But just like his eyes betrayed him, so does his cock, growing, hardening with each pass of the scarf.

"That's right, Mr Snake, get hard. You have work to do," Sarah-Jane says to Ken's cock.

Taking a condom from the box, she tears it open with her teeth, spitting out the foil as it comes free. Holding Ken's cock at the base of the shaft with one hand, she unravels the condom with the other hand and rolls it down Ken's erection.

"That wasn't so bad now, was it?" she says to Ken, who is unable to answer.

She knows he is trying to be as unresponsive as he possibly can, so she is going to have to get them started. Sarah-Jane rubs her pussy with her free hand while stroking Ken's cock, keeping him hard. By the fifth stroke, her fingers are moist as she rubs her swollen clit, taking deep breaths with each stroke before she shoves her middle and index fingers inside her pussy. In and out she thrusts her finger, a little faster and deeper with each thrust, her thumb massaging her throbbing clit.

By this point, Sarah-Jane has dropped Ken's cock as she squeezes her nipples with her free hand, her breathing now shallow, short breaths. She knows she is close to coming, and stops. "How unfair of me," she tells a bewildered Ken. "You are meant to be helping me on this journey. Let's take care of you for a bit. You seem to have gone soft."

She takes Ken's cock and puts her lips to the tip, slowly opening her mouth to take it in her mouth, then moves her head up and down in a circular motion. Ken's cock jumps to life, swelling, growing twice the size in her mouth, her saliva running down his balls. Sarah-Jane can feel the change in Ken's body as it goes from rigid to relaxed as he begins to enjoy the last sex he is ever going to have.

"That's better. Rather enjoy your last moments; why fight it?" Sarah-Jane says.

She takes the scarf and wraps it around his neck, just as Lance had done, laying the ends on either side of Ken's body. "I won't lie," she admits. "I enjoyed our time together. It was special, but alas, all things must come to an end."

Sarah-Jane climbs on top of Ken, slowly lowering her body as his hard cock slides inside her wet pussy. Kneeling with her legs either side of Ken, she leans forward placing her hands on his chest for support, slowly rocking her pelvis back and forth as her pussy slides up and down his cock. Letting out a soft moan each time, Sarah-Jane can feel Ken's cock throbbing inside her as her pussy muscles contract, tightening with each stroke she makes, her breathing becoming shallow as she gets closer to coming

Taking the ends of the scarf in her hands, she uses it as support to lean back. She makes sure there is no slack in the scarf then closes her eyes, grinding her body into Ken's, each time moving her body faster and faster. Sarah-Jane arches back hard as she comes. She can feel Ken's cock explode while she pulls hard on the scarf, making his body stiff as the oxygen is cut off. She hears him trying to gasp for air, the sock in his mouth making it harder with each attempt he makes.

Shaking from the full-body orgasm, Sarah-Jane eyes are still closed as she enjoys the wave of ecstasy rushing over her body and the tingling in her brain. "Thank you, sweet Ken, you helped me achieve ecstasy for the second time," she whispers. "Let go. The pain will soon be over."

Sarah-Jane is calm when she opens her eyes to focus on Ken's dying face for the first time; the shock and fear she felt after Lance died isn't there this time. Ken's eyes gaze back at her, as she watches his final moments as his eyes glaze over and he lets out his last breath.

She slowly removes Ken's cock from her as she get off his dead body, still feeling the waves of ecstasy rushing through her body. Sarah-Jane doesn't waste any time. She gets dressed before she unties the ropes binding Ken to the bed, knowing that she needs to move fast before rigor mortis sets in.

She tries pulling his body off the bed and onto the floor, but due to Ken's weight it takes her half an hour to get the body to the bathroom. Exhausted from her effort, she leaves his body on the floor and goes to the kitchen to fetch the sharp kitchen knife she used to dismember Lance. This time she remembers the black plastic bin bags.

Armed with all she needs, Sarah-Jane goes back upstairs and puts on rubber gloves to collect all of Ken's belongings,

trying not to get any of her DNA on his things as she places his clothes, wallet, shoes, and phone in a black bag. Sarah-Jane has kept his keys. Knowing where Ken lives, she is going to take his stuff back to his apartment, so that if the police question her about his disappearance, she can say they met for sex, but then he left and went home. She will tell them to check his phone's GPS to see where and when a cell phone tower last picked up his signal.

Leaving Ken on the bathroom floor, she drives to his apartment and parks her car a few streets away. Taking the black bag with his belongings, she gets out and heads towards Ken's apartment block. Initially, she intended to take his belongings and leave them in his apartment, but she now realises that she will be caught on the CCTV inside the apartment block. As she walks past a large dumpster at the entrance to an alleyway, she lifts the lid with a gloved hand and shakes the contents of the bag into the dumpster. She then throws his keys on top and slowly closes the lid back as quietly as possible to avoid arousing anyone to her presence.

The clock on her dashboard shows quarter-to-one in the morning when she gets back to the car, and she drives home, knowing she still has to take care of Ken's body. Parking her car on the driveway, she unlocks her front door and quickly goes inside, hoping that none of her neighbours have spotted her coming home.

She immediately goes back to the bathroom and lifts Ken's body over the edge of the bath, then strips naked to ensure she doesn't get any of his blood on her clothes as she dismembers him. It takes half the time to break down Ken's body, as she has learned the lessons dismembering Lance. This time, her cuts are straight and true, and she is more confident with each slice of the blade. This time, there is less mess.

At least cleaning up is going to be easier this time, she thinks to herself. *Even though Ken is a large man, knowing what to do and where to cut certainly makes things smoother.* Placing the last of his body parts in a black bag, she wraps and seals it, laying it next to the others on the floor. "Glad that's done," she says out loud as she gets up off the floor. "Just got to shower, tidy up, and then to sleep."

She checks to see that she won't trail any blood through the house when she takes the body parts to the freezer to join Lance. Satisfied she is clean enough to do so naked, Sarah-Jane examines each bag to make sure no blood is leaking out, then takes the smaller bags of limbs down to the freezer before returning for Ken's torso and head.

Having cleaned the bathroom, Sarah-Jane takes a shower to wash away the last of Ken's body fluids then puts on her dressing gown. Finally, she cleans the den of death before going to her childhood room. Within minutes of getting into

bed, she falls asleep, exhausted from the events of the night.

Sarah-Jane has the best sleep she has had in a long time, and definitely since Lance died – maybe even since her parents died. Sleeping soundly, Sarah-Jane dreams of nothing. She is content, a smile on her face, a warmth in her heart.

Chapter 14

Sarah-Jane and Charles have been texting each other at least once or twice a week since she got her new sim card. It's now two weeks since Ken met his untimely demise, and Sarah-Jane and Charles have organised to meet at her house on the weekend. Charles has been really busy at work, and this will be his first free weekend. It is mid-December, and the weather has gotten worse with each passing day.

Charles has said that as Sarah-Jane paid for dinner last time, he is going to cook for her. As she likes lasagne so much, he is going to make a salmon and mixed vegetable lasagne. Sarah-Jane insists that if he is going to cook, she will provide the wine. When Charles asks if she has any white wine to go with the meal, Sarah-Jane informs him she only has red but is due to order a mixed case of wine so can swap out four bottles of red for some white. Those four bottles are sitting in the fridge chilling, waiting for Saturday to come.

Sarah-Jane has asked Charles if it would be ok if they drank wine instead of smoking some weed like last time. Although

she enjoyed the experience with him, she needs Charles to drink, otherwise she won't be able to give him the sleeping capsule which makes it easier to tie him up. There is no way she wants to be denied the satisfaction she craves.

As the lasagne takes so long to prepare, Charles is coming to her house at two, and says he will need to park his car in her driveway. He would have taken a taxi to her, but has too much stuff to bring with him, including the ingredients for the meal and his wok. Unfortunately, Sarah-Jane doesn't have a large enough wok; hers is small and only makes enough food for one person. It means Sarah-Jane is going to have to get rid of his car later, after Charles is dead.

She has been thinking of ways to speed up the process of dismembering and disposing of Charles. One of the ways is to keep a roll of black bags, rubber gloves, and the knife in the bathroom, next to the laundry basket in the cabinet under the sink, with the knife wrapped up in a smaller plastic bag. She also wants to be able to get the body from the bedroom to the bathroom faster, but she is still trying to figure that one out.

Sarah-Jane wants to make herself look sexy for when Charles arrives. The more his senses are aroused, she knows he will be putty in her hands. Being well aware that she doesn't want a repeat of last time, Sarah-Jane has placed a gag under the pillow. If Charles happens to find it, she can

say that she wants to experiment a little with bondage. If he wants to try it with her, he can gag her and spank her, lifting her endorphins levels. She can then suggest to Charles that he might like to try it as well. Last time, Ken's screams probably could be heard by her surrounding neighbours, so she doesn't want to draw attention to the goings on inside the house. The less people know, the better for her.

It's late Saturday morning and Sarah-Jane has enjoyed a lie-in. Getting out of bed, she goes to have a shower, washing her hair, shaving her legs, and underarms. She already groomed her pubic hair a couple of days ago in preparation for this evening. Even though she is going to kill Charles, she still wants to enjoy herself. She reckons Charles deserves one last good fuck before he shuffles off his mortal coil.

Sitting at her dressing table after the shower, her dressing gown is unstrapped and opened, exposing her naked body. Sarah-Jane rubs lavender scented body lotion over her breasts, up her neck and along her arms, massaging it in as she moves along her body. She then squeezes some lotion onto one leg and then the other, spreading it with one hand and then the other.

Sarah-Jane wants Charles to feel totally at ease. The more relaxed he is, the less he is going to suspect that this is his last evening alive. In her mind she equates this dinner to

the last supper of Jesus; both Charles and Jesus being betrayed before they die.

Taking her favourite perfume from the dressing table, Sarah-Jane squirts some perfume on her neck, then on either wrist, rubbing them together. She lifts her right wrist up to her nose, inhaling deeply, the scent of wild flowers bursting inside her nose. She puts on eye makeup – just enough to highlight them without making them the dominant feature of her face – and applies a little light rosy blusher to bring a little warmth to her cheeks. Tonight her lips must be the main feature, as she wants to draw him in, so she applies a high gloss red lipstick after her eye makeup and blusher.

Taking the towel off her head, Sarah-Jane brushes her hair through with her paddle brush before finishing it off with a round brush and hairdryer to provide body and bounce. She is left with soft, flowing curls, but knows that by the time Charles arrives her hair will have dropped and lost some of its bounce. That's fine with her, as her hair isn't meant to be the focus of attention.

Her skin has soaked up all the body lotion, so Sarah-Jane rubs more on her breasts, massaging it in. Her nipples tingle as her fingers glide over them, sending the sensation down her spine and awakening her pussy. Feeling horny as she massages the lotion, Sarah-Jane hates to waste any sexual

desire so uses her free hand to rub her pussy lips. Parting them as her fingers get wet from her juices, she massages her swelling clit while she pinches her hardening nipples with her other hand.

Looking at herself in the dressing table mirror, Sarah-Jane sees the desire in her eyes. She picks up one of her perfume bottles. It is made of glass and is smooth, long, thin, and round, with a screw-on lid shaped like the head of a penis — one of the reasons she bought the perfume in the first place. She rubs the bottle up and down between her pussy lips as her creamy juices coat the glass, she then inserts the bottle, slowly moving it in and out, back and forth. The bottle glides inside her with ease as her juices drip onto the leather stool. With every passing stroke, Sarah-Jane twists the bottle in her hand, building up pace as it glides in and out. Her breathing matches the pace of the bottle, getting faster and faster, building, becoming stronger until she lets out a moan, squeezing her legs together as her body shakes, a small taste of what's to come later.

Sarah-Jane goes to the bathroom. Standing at the basin, she puts on the tap, adjusting the temperature not to scald herself, and wipes away her juices with a damp facecloth. When she has finished, she rinses the facecloth, twisting it in her hands to make sure there isn't any water left, and leaves it hanging over the edge of the basin. Taking the hand towel, she wipes her crotch dry before washing and

drying her perfume bottle then takes it back to the den of death where she carries on getting ready.

She looks at her phone; it is one o'clock. Not long till Charles arrives. She puts on the red lingerie, adjusting the panties so the crotchless bottom is sitting properly – she doesn't want it giving her a wedgie. The bra doesn't need much adjusting as it sits firmly covering her breasts, the nipples sticking out the front. Then she attaches the garter belt to the matching red stockings and is almost ready.

As Sarah-Jane puts on a pair of black jeans with a purple long-sleeved t-shirt, she thinks how wrong it feels to be wearing such nice lingerie with casual clothes. She would prefer to wear it with her black silk dress, but that outfit is more suited to fancy restaurants, a night at the theatre, or going out to a nightclub. It would look too formal for a dinner at home drinking wine and eating lasagne.

Nonetheless, she looks stunning. Her skin-tight jeans show off the curves of her arse, and the t-shirt is slim fitting, hugging her waist at the bottom, her breasts pushing out at the top. She is confident this will drive Charles wild.

She puts on a pair of trainers to finish off the outfit, but every time Sarah-Jane walks, her pussy rubs up against the skin-tight jeans. She hopes this won't be too much of a problem, as she doesn't want to soak the jeans with her juices.

Sarah-Jane tidies up the makeup on the dressing table before she goes downstairs to the kitchen. Taking the ice bucket out of the cupboard, she fills it with ice and gets a bottle of white wine from the fridge. She opens it and puts it in the ice bucket to chill before Charles arrives. The time on the microwave blinking back at her is one thirty-seven.

Her phone vibrates in her back pocket. Unlocking it, she sees a text from Charles: *"Afternoon, I'm running a little bit early. Should be at yours in ten minutes."* Sarah-Jane has left her car in the garage, giving Charles the space on the driveway.

Glancing out at the backyard, she decides she will have to let Henry come to take care of it. The lawn is no longer well-manicured, and there are apples that have fallen on the ground and almost rotted away. She hasn't been in touch with Henry since she sent out those texts telling everyone not to get in contact with her. She will have to tell him that she lost her phone and has a new number. She knows he won't question her on it. But she needs Henry to do his magic before the weather gets worse and the snows come.

While she waits for Charles's next text to say he is outside and can she open the electric gate for him, Sarah-Jane decides to send Henry a message: *"Hi Henry, this is Sarah-Jane Morley. I have a new number as I lost my old phone and they can't seem to be able to give me my old number.*

Sorry for not getting back to you sooner. Could you please come and work your magic, as the gardens are starting to look shabby? Would it be possible for you to come early next week? I will be home, as I have taken time off work. Look forward to seeing you if you can come. Have a great weekend." She reads over the text then sends it.

Placing her phone on the island, she gets the wine glasses from the cupboard. Her phone vibrates with a reply from Henry: *"Hi Sarah, no worries about not getting in touch. Yes, I can come on Tuesday to look after the gardens. There is snow coming and it will be harder to look after them once the snow arrives. See you Tuesday. Enjoy your weekend, too. Henry."*

While still reading Henry's text, her phone vibrates again. This time it is from Charles, saying he is outside. She walks to the front door, picks up the remote and pushes the button to open the electric gate. Charles drives in, parking his car as the gates close behind him.

Sarah-Jane peers through the yellow glass. She can see Charles collecting the wok and ingredients from the boot, then locking his car with the push of a button on his keychain. When he reaches the porch, Sarah-Jane unlocks and opens the door and ushers him inside. He heads straight to the kitchen, with Sarah-Jane close behind, and places the wok on the stove and the ingredients on the island counter.

"Can I have a chopping board, knife, and some empty bowls? It is easier to chop up all the ingredients before the cooking starts," he says, then gives her a hello kiss on the lips. "You look dashing," he adds.

Sarah-Jane fetches him everything he has asked for, placing them on the island. It has started raining. The clouds that have been threatening to burst all day have broken, heavy rain hitting the oak patio with force. The large raindrops look as if they are being pushed back into the air as they bounce off the oak boards before they fall back and break in a splash.

"You were lucky. Good thing you arrived early, or you could have been drenched in this rain," she tells him, placing the bowls on the counter.

"I wouldn't have wanted to be caught in that rain, as I would have been soaked to the bone. I would have had to make the lasagne naked while my clothes dried," he laughs.

"Nothing wrong with cooking naked," she replies with a cheeky smile on her face. "Maybe you want to anyway. Would you like a glass of wine while you are chopping up the vegetables?" She takes the bottle out of the ice bucket and pours him half a glass.

"Thanks," he says, taking the glass from her. He lifts it up to his nose and sniffs the aroma of the wine before he takes a

sip. "Nice and flavourful, but dry. I like it," he decides, placing his glass on the counter. "I need to take it slow with the wine, though. Don't want to chop off a finger!"

Sarah-Jane smiles at the joke, but thinks to herself, *No, we don't want you to chop off your finger. But later I will chop you up, after you give me what I need.*

Placing the bottle back in the ice bucket, she takes a sip. "I see what you mean about the wine," she comments. "Very flavoursome and dry. I like it, too. I asked the person on the phone, when placing the order, to give me in his opinion the best white wine they sell. I don't know much about wines; I tend just to drink them. But I'll take note of this one, so I know what to ask for next time."

"Could you put the lasagne sheets in the fridge, please?" Charles hands Sarah-Jane an unopened packet of fresh lasagne sheets. "They need to be kept cold so they don't dry out."

It takes Charles 45 minutes to chop up all the vegetables and place them in the empty bowls Sarah-Jane has given him. Each bowl has a different vegetable: diced red onion in the first; thinly sliced chestnut mushrooms in the next; diced red, green, and yellow bell peppers in the third; and diced courgette in the last bowl. Next to the bowl is a can of garden peas, alongside one vegetable stock pot. Charles

likes to be prepared; he has brought everything he needs to make the lasagne with him.

He pours olive oil into the wok, adding salt, pepper, mixed herbs, paprika, thyme, sage, and fresh garlic, which he scrapes off the chopping board with the back of the knife. Opening the stock pot, he plops it into the wok and turns on the stove, waiting for the oil to heat up as he stirs the herbs into the oil. Taking more oil into a frying pan Sarah-Jane has provided, he turns the heat low. He adds the rest of the garlic, salt, pepper, thyme, and rosemary to the last remaining empty bowl and pours in some olive oil, which he mixes together with a teaspoon. Taking the salmon out of its packaging, Charles lays it on the chopping board and rubs the oil and herb mix onto the side of fish before he places it in the frying pan, turning up the heat slightly.

Charles places the onion in the wok with the sliced mushrooms, mixing them in with the herbs. Then he waits for the mushrooms to release their liquid before he adds the mixed peppers and courgette, and lastly the peas, mixing them together. He then lowers the heat to allow the vegetables to simmer in their own liquid. Fifteen minutes later, the salmon is ready, so he turns off the heat. He places the salmon on the chopping board, letting it cool down before he flakes it.

Sarah-Jane is watching everything he is doing, as she decides she would like to try and make this dish for herself.

Charles finishes cooking the mixed vegetables and turns the stove off. He has to wait for them to cool down, as he doesn't want to burn his hands assembling the lasagne.

"How has your week off been? Have you done much, or have you done as little as possible?" he asks her, taking a larger sip of his wine. "This is dangerous. The wine is so tasty, I can drain my glass in a blink of an eye."

"My week off has been relaxing, as I haven't done anything. Wake up late, get out of bed even later. With the weather being so shit of late, I haven't even been out for my not-so-regular runs," she tells him.

"It sounds like you have had a good time," he replies. "I can't take any time off before Christmas, as I'm getting ready for a trip to see some sea turtles. I fly out on the twenty-seventh."

"Wow, that sounds awesome. You must be looking forward to some hotter weather. Don't forget your swimming trunks," she says jokingly. But she is thinking to herself, *You won't be making that flight.*

Charles makes a white sauce, stirring it to avoid any lumps, before he adds half the grated cheese. Turning off the heat, he asks Sarah-Jane for the lasagne sheets from the fridge.

As she hands them to him, Sarah-Jane asks if he'd like his wine glass filled up.

"Yes please, that would be great. I will have to buy a case of this wine, I'm really enjoying it," he says, taking a small gulp before he starts assembling the lasagne in the dish she has provided. First, he glazes the bottom with some of the sauce, before placing large blobs of salmon, vegetables, salmon on top of the sauce, then lasagne sheets on top of that. He repeats the process until there are three layers, lashing sauce on the top before sprinkling the rest of the cheese to finish it off.

Sarah-Jane sets the table while Charles puts the lasagne in the oven. "Forty-five minutes till we can sink our teeth into the lasagne," he tells her. "We have to let it cool down first."

"I know just the thing to pass the time," she replies, pulling out the chair at the head of the table. "You come sit at the table, take that juicy cock of yours out, and I will suck you dry."

Charles unbuckles his belt, unbuttons his trousers before unzipping them, slides both his trousers and underwear down, letting them fall to his ankles. He then kicks off his right shoe, his trousers and underwear now loose from his leg, and sits back in the chair with his legs outstretched. Sarah-Jane kneels between Charles's legs and takes his cock

in her hand. Easing it into her mouth, she moves her head up and down as his cock hardens. With every third stroke, Sarah-Jane picks up the pace until Charles starts to arch his back, pushing his cock deep down her throat.

"I'm going to come!" he says, as he explodes inside her mouth. She swallows his cum as she sucks him in deeper, all the way to his balls.

"After dinner I will return the favour," Charles promises as he puts his clothes back on.

They sit down to eat at half five, by which time they have finished the first bottle of wine. Sarah-Jane has already changed the ice and opened a new bottle, leaving it on the table while Charles dishes up their meal. The pair sit in silence as they enjoy their food, only letting out the odd murmur of satisfaction.

Finishing their dinner, Sarah-Jane clears the plates, rinsing them before putting them in the dishwasher. There is a full load, due to all the bowls Charles has used, so she switches on the dishwasher then walks back to the table to fetch the lasagne. She leaves it on the counter, covering it with clingfilm; she will put it in the fridge later, once it has cooled down.

They sit sipping their wine and chatting while they let their food digest. At quarter-to-seven they decide to make

their way up to the master bedroom. Charles drains his wine. "I'm going to piss before we go upstairs. Can you fill my wine glass, please?" he asks, as he gets up from the table.

"Ok," she replies. Once Charles is in the toilet, she takes his glass to the kitchen. Taking a sleeping capsule, she pricks it with the point of a sharp steak knife, squeezing the liquid into the glass, then returns to the table and fills the glass halfway. The sleeping capsule wouldn't have had time to dissolve fully by the time he comes back from the toilet, so she hopes this method will still work.

Taking the ice bucket in one hand and the two glasses in the other, Sarah-Jane is met by Charles just outside the guest toilet, and he takes the ice bucket from her as they go upstairs. Charles places the ice bucket on the dressing table as he takes off his clothes, folding them as he puts them on the stool. Sarah-Jane hands him his wine.

"I look forward to some drunken, sloppy sex," he says.

Sarah-Jane can hear in his voice that he is quite drunk. "Go lie on the bed and I will be there shortly," she tells him, taking a sip of her wine before placing it next to the ice bucket. She proceeds to light the candles in the room before turning off the lights, leaving shadows dancing on the walls from the flickering flames.

Returning to the dressing table, she uses the front of her left foot to pull her trainer off at the heel, and repeats the same for the left trainer. Facing Charles, who is lying on the bed watching her undress, she takes off the purple t-shirt and drops it on the floor.

"Nice lingerie. I like the holes," he comments as she removes her jeans. There is a wet spot where her pussy has been rubbing up against her jeans.

"Here is a better view for you," replies Sarah-Jane, as he sees her crotchless panties. Her moist pussy is glistening at him as she rubs her hand over her lips, the creamy juices sticking to her fingers.

"Bring yourself over here. I still owe you for the blow job earlier," says Charles, as he moves over giving her space on the bed.

Sarah-Jane hopes this time she can come. *Last time Ken fell asleep while eating me out,* she remembers. Unfortunately, she has no better luck this time. Charles is skinny compared to Ken, so the fast-acting sleeping capsule has worked quicker than she was expecting. As the liquid was mixed directly into the wine, it didn't have to dissolve as it normally would in the capsule. Plus Charles has drunk over two-thirds of a bottle of wine by himself.

Sarah-Jane watches as Charles passes out. "FUCK, can't a woman catch a break!" she grumbles out loud as she puts on her dressing gown instead of getting redressed, leaving her clothes in a pile on the floor. Sighing, she walks to the bed and, one by one, ties a rope to each of his limbs. Sarah-Jane remembers Charles telling her that he smokes weed to help him sleep because sleeping pills knock him out quickly but don't work for long.

Having finished tying him up, Sarah-Jane places the gag in his mouth and then goes downstairs, finishes cleaning up, and unpacks the dishwasher. Then she goes to the lounge to watch something on the television while she waits for Charles to wake. Two-and-a-half hours later, Sarah-Jane hears a rustling upstairs, which must be Charles struggling, but at least this time there isn't any screaming or shouting.

Sarah-Jane can see the anger in Charles's face when she enters the room. "You must be wondering why you are tied up with a gag in your mouth," she tells him. "Well, the short answer is tonight you're going to die. The long answer is that I have stumbled – accidentally at first – onto a sexual high I never thought possible. You look as if you don't have a clue in the world about what I am talking about.

"You see, my first accidental murder was on Halloween," she explains. "I was talked into performing autoerotic asphyxiation, and the person died, but the sexual high I felt

was like nothing before I can compare it to. So, a few weeks ago I committed my first premeditated murder, and you will be my second. I need to feel that high again, and you are going to help me."

She takes the silk scarf from under the pillow and wraps it around his neck, laying the ends on either side of him. "I'm going to ride you till I'm close to coming, then I'm going to take these ends and you will slowly lose consciousness until your life is no more," she continues.

She strokes his cock, watching as it hardens in her hand. "Look on the bright side, at least you get some pleasure before you die. Now, try not to struggle. Why fight it? Rather enjoy what moments you have left."

She takes his cock in her mouth, giving him a wet, sloppy blow job. She takes off her dressing gown, taking a condom from the box, sheaths his hard cock before she climbs on top of Charles. She rubs his hard cock along her pussy, back and forth, her creamy juices covering the condom as she slips him inside her.

Sarah-Jane can feel the tension in Charles's body as she rocks back and forth, her pussy sliding up and down his throbbing cock. It doesn't take long before Charles accepts his fate, and his body relaxes. Sarah-Jane takes the ends of the scarf in her hands as she is nearing her destiny, her

pussy muscles tightening around his cock. She leans back, the scarf taking her weight. Grinding her body into his, Sarah-Jane pulls on the scarf harder and harder, cutting the air flow to Charles. He is starting to black out, but before he does Sarah-Jane can feel him come. The throbbing of his cock inside her makes her come, squeezing her legs tight as she leans back, her body shaking from the explosion within her, the waves rushing over her. This time, Sarah-Jane has not closed her eyes; this time, she wants to see the life leave Charles's body as he struggles for air. His eyes roll back in his head, all she can see is the whites of his eyeballs as they bulge out, turning red before her, then he finally goes limp as his heart stops beating.

"Whoa, what a rush!" she says out loud. "That is the best one so far. From now on, I have to watch as the last breath leaves their bodies."

She climbs off Charles, his cock still hard as it flops out of her pussy. Finding her jeans and t-shirt on the floor, Sarah-Jane puts them on and goes to the bathroom to fetch the rubber gloves and a black bag. She puts all of Charles's belonging in the bag and leaves it on the bed while she drags his body to the bathroom.

"Thank fuck he is lighter than Ken," she tells herself as she leans Charles over the edge of the bath. Pulling up the sleeves on the long purple t-shirt, she takes the knife from

the plastic bag and slits his throat. Rinsing the knife under the bath tap, she washes the blood off the gloves and leaves Charles to drain.

Sarah-Jane puts her trainers on, takes the bag on the bed with his belongings and goes downstairs to fetch his car keys and the remote for the electric gate. Opening the front door, Sarah-Jane is thankful that it has stopped raining; the night sky is clear, not a cloud in sight. She pushes the button on his key chain to unlock Charles's car, opening the electric gates as she gets in, then reverses out of the driveway onto the road. The gates shut behind her as she pulls away slowly to avoid drawing attention to herself.

After she has driven ten miles from her home, Sarah-Jane leaves the car at the side of the road with the keys in the ignition and his clothes strewn alongside the vehicle. She folds the black bag, placing it in her back pocket, then starts walking back home to the job awaiting her. Half way home it starts raining again. It is quarter-to-twelve when Sarah-Jane gets home, drenched to the bone. Sarah-Jane can see her breath in front of her as she exhales, her jacket is soaked through.

Glad to be home, she locks the door behind her and strips off her wet clothes, leaving them at the front door. Shivering, Sarah-Jane goes to the bathroom and switches the shower on, adjusting the temperature to a little hotter

than she would normally have it. She needs to warm up quickly. Feeling the chill in her bones, she stands under the spray for ten minutes as the hot water thaws her out. Staring through the misted glass, she can see Charles's body slumped in the bath.

She roughly dries herself off before she gets to work on dismembering Charles. The hot shower has helped, but she knows she will need a second shower after dismembering Charles, to wash the last of him off her.

Separating him turns out to be a lot quicker than expected. Now skilled in the art of body dismemberment, there is the added bonus of Charles being slim. She packs each body part one by one, sealing the bags and placing them on the floor of the shower. Although Charles is slim, he has made more mess on the floor between the bath and the toilet, but thankfully she had the good sense to leave the bucket and mop upstairs after cleaning up after Ken.

She cleans the bathroom thoroughly, leaving Charles in the now clean bath while she rinses the last of his liquids off her, then she takes the already wet towel and dries herself as best she can. After three trips to the freezer, she can finally have a proper shower to remove the stink of death.

It is half past two when Sarah-Jane can finally relax. Having worked up an appetite while cleaning up after Charles, she

goes to the kitchen and removes the clingfilm from the lasagne dish, then scoops a large portion onto a plate. As she waits for the food to heat up in the microwave, she opens the third bottle of wine; the second one is still on the dressing table where Charles left it.

Pouring herself a glass, she takes a sip of the wine as the microwave pings. Sarah-Jane lifts out the plate and takes it with a fork and her glass of wine to the table, and sits down to eat. "One thing I can say is he makes one hell of a salmon and vegetable lasagne," she says out loud. "Hope I can replicate it." She sinks her fork into the lasagne, scooping it up and enjoying a mouthful of goodness.

Still not feeling tired from the adrenalin rush of the evening, she finishes her food and rinses the plate before placing it in the dishwasher, then takes the bottle of wine with her to the lounge to watch a film until she feels tired enough or drunk enough to sleep. She chooses to change things up and watch a comedy, instead of the usual horror movies. She chooses *The Hangover*, which she has watched around 20 times and has always found really funny, but not this time. She sniggers at one or two funny bits, but otherwise she has a deadpan look on her face.

Picking up the now half empty bottle of wine, she decides the only way for her to come down is to drink more wine. She downs the rest of the bottle then goes back

upstairs to get the remainder of the second bottle from the bedroom. She takes the water-filled ice bucket to the kitchen, dumping the water down the drain and leaves the bucket in the sink.

Sipping the wine from the bottle, she switches the lights off in the kitchen and dining room on her way back to the lounge, then turns the television back to the horror channel. *The Thing* with Kurt Russel is halfway through, and she drinks the wine as she watches it to the end. Sarah-Jane downs the last of the wine just before the film ends, squeezing her legs together trying not to pee just so she can watch the ending. As the credits roll, she is off the couch like a lightning bolt, running for the guest toilet. Pulling down her pyjama bottoms with one hand, she lifts the lid of the toilet with the other, and sits down just in time as pee gushes from her. The sound her pee makes as it hits the bottom of the bowl is like the rushing water of Niagara Falls, and Sarah-Jane lets out a huge sigh of relief as her bladder no longer feels like it is going to burst.

I feel pumped. I'm not sure what to do to get to sleep, she thinks. *Maybe I have to drink that last bottle of white. Hopefully that will do the trick.* She flushes the toilet and washes her hands before she heads back to the kitchen for the fourth bottle. She opens the bottle and immediately downs a quarter of it before she stops to take a breath. Feeling light-headed, Sarah-Jane knows that sleep is not far

behind, so she corks the bottle and puts it back in the fridge.

Stumbling a little, she makes her way upstairs to the bathroom to brush her teeth. But before she gets the chance to brush them, Sarah-Jane feels a rush to her head and a pain in her stomach. Dropping to her knees and lifting the lip on the toilet, she throws up, heaving as the wine and lasagne leaves her body faster than they went in. Dry heaving a few times before she is sure she isn't going to vomit any more, she flushes the toilet and tries to pull herself off the floor. Her vision is now blurred. Using the basin for support, she tries again to brush her teeth.

Thankfully, her bed is right next door. Using every bit of energy just to stay up straight, Sarah-Jane stumbles into her room and collapses on the bed. She tries to pull the duvet over her just before passing out, the duvet covering half her body as one leg dangles on the floor.

Sarah-Jane is dead to the world, blind drunk, and all that can be heard in the quiet of the night is her drunk snoring.

Chapter 15

Sarah-Jane has been keeping to herself since she killed Charles, barely leaving the house other than to buy groceries. She has noticed she has put on weight recently, probably from eating so much takeaway and drinking too much wine. She decides to try eating healthy again and only to have two glasses of wine with her dinner.

Every morning she wakes up early to exercise; she can't go out for a run as it has been snowing. She was glad to see Henry the other week, and the front and backyard are looking pristine again. He was lucky, it started snowing two days after he had been to her house. After Henry had finished taking care of the gardens, they shared a cup of coffee and a lovely conversation. She hugged him goodbye as he left, closing the door behind him, leaving the last of her joy at the door.

Sarah-Jane knows that with today being New Year's Eve there will be lots of opportunities out there to coax some poor drunken man away from his friends. Even better for

her if he is alone. She decides to go around town to the many different bars, scouting for her prey. Having had dinner already, Sarah-Jane has a shower, washes her hair, shaving the important areas and leaving them silky smooth. She dries and straightens her hair before she puts on her clothes.

Yesterday was the first day it stopped snowing, and thankfully it isn't meant to snow again for a few days. Tonight is a full moon new year, and there is not a cloud in the sky. Sarah-Jane puts on her bra and panties before putting on her black thermal leggings and matching long-sleeved thermal top. She knows it won't look sexy, but she doesn't want to freeze either. Putting on her leather trousers and a plain, long-sleeved black hoodie, she finishes off the outfit with calf-length, flat-soled biker boots and a black leather biker jacket.

After Henry left, she felt she wanted a change of appearance, so on one of the few days that she left the house to go grocery shopping, she bought the leather trousers and the boots. She already had the jacket.

By the time Sarah-Jane finishes getting ready, it is ten. She hasn't had any wine to drink today, as she is trying to stay as sober as possible so that it will be easier for her to control the situation. Trying to manage a drunk person when you yourself are drunk is impossible.

Most bars only start getting busy after half ten. She isn't going anywhere near Jonestown tonight, as she knows that Mike will definitely be working and the last thing she wants is to bump into anyone she might know. Instead, she is going to the far side of town where the concert halls are. She has been checking the events pages on the internet and knows there is a Slipknot concert on at the local arena. Drunk metal heads. There is always some guy who is trying to get it on with some unsuspecting young woman, so that will be her target, her prey.

There are quite a few bars that will fill up once the concert lets out, and seeing Slipknot live leaves every fan pumped up with adrenalin, desperate to carry on the party. Those bars will stay open late as it is New Year's Eve.

Sarah-Jane knows she will have to have a drink or two during the course of the night, but will stick to soda water and orange juice. If she is offered any shots, she will just say no. *Best laid plan always go awry when you deviate from them*, she thinks to herself. Now ready to leave, she checks that the windows and the patio door are locked, takes her purse, and locks the front door behind her. There is a blanket of snow covering the lawn as she walks to her car, opening the electric gate as she gets in. Sarah-Jane reverses out the driveway, the electric gate closing as she heads off.

Her dashboard clock says 20 past 11 when she finds a parking spot. Sarah-Jane is glad to be out; she was starting to feel cooped up in the house. If she had stayed in one day longer, cabin fever would have set in, driving her crazier than she is already. Although she hasn't wanted any human contact, it is the one thing she really needs.

As the concert finished at 11, the area is a hive of black-clothed people all making their way to the bars. Depending on the genre of music being played at the arena on any given night, the bars tend to cater to the tastes of their fans for the after-parties, so tonight every bar is a metal bar. Going to the first bar, Sarah-Jane can see there is a queue to get in, so she decides to walk down the street to find one that hasn't got such long queues. With each bar that she passes Sarah-Jane's temper is starting to build. Everywhere is busy and there are huge queues everywhere. She should have expected it, being New Year's Eve.

She doesn't care if she isn't inside a bar when midnight comes. She isn't here to celebrate the New Year; she is here to find her prey. She couldn't give a fuck that it is New Year's Eve; to her it is just another day, though a much busier night than usual. Getting to the last bar in the street, Sarah-Jane is now fuming, and she turns around to head back in the direction she came. She is mumbling to herself incoherently as she walks, and doesn't hear her name being called. "Sarah! Sarah, SARAH-JANE MORLEY!"

It's only when she hears her whole name being spoken that she stops and looks around to see who is calling. It is Mitch, Dan's best friend, who is running up to her.

Taking a few deep breaths, he says, "Sarah-Jane, are you okay? Everyone is worried about you. Dan told me you stopped going to work. Jenny and all your colleagues don't know if they have done anything wrong to make you cut them out of your life, and even Mike feared you had taken your own life. Once your phone got cut off, they knew something was wrong. I'm glad to see you are okay."

"I'm fine," she says with a gruffness to her voice, still angry about the queues. She needs to be inside a bar; this is wasting precious time. "Sorry, Mitch," she goes on, forcing a smile. "I shouldn't have spoken to you in that tone. I'm fine, but I have been going through some stuff lately and decided to move on with my life, going in a different direction to the people I once knew."

"As it's New Year's Eve, would you like to join me and my friends for a drink to celebrate?" Mitch asks her.

"Okay, why not? Lead the way." Sarah-Jane trying to fake another smile.

Mitch leads them back to where his friends are waiting in the queue, they are almost at the front. It is quarter-to-twelve

when they eventually get their first drinks at the bar. One of Mitch's friends buys a double round of tequila, which is the first time Sarah-Jane has had one since Halloween. They pick up their shots, and one by one Mitch and his friends put the salt on their hands ready to drink. For the first time Sarah-Jane doesn't put salt on her hand or take a piece of lemon. "CHEERS!" they all scream together over the loud music.

Sarah-Jane knocks back the shot. As the tequila goes down her throat, she sucks in slowly, letting the aftertaste of the alcohol do its job, just as Lance described to her so many weeks ago. It seems like a lifetime ago to Sarah-Jane.

"I like your new look, it suits you," Mitch says, leaning close to her ear so she can hear him over the loud music.

"Thanks," she replies as they take their second shot. "Like I said, I'm on a different life path now, and that means as my inner self changes so does my outer self." She speaks close to Mitch's ear, her hair tickling him as she leans in.

Her soft, low voice sends shivers up Mitch's arm, giving him goosebumps. He has always had a crush on Sarah-Jane. She is the older girl fantasy he had when they were young. Mitch is five years younger than Sarah-Jane, but knew that hanging out at Dan's house he would get to see her whenever she came to visit Susie. Mitch was always shy as a child and sometimes hid so he didn't have to speak to her.

But as he got older, Sarah-Jane was the first girl he jerked off to.

Mitch would give anything to fuck Sarah-Jane. He never believed he would ever get the chance. *Maybe tonight might just be the night I get to fuck the woman of my fantasies,* he thinks to himself.

"Would you like a beer?" Sarah-Jane asks him. "I'm having one and don't want to drink alone."

"Sure, I'll have a beer with you," replies Mitch, as she orders two beers for them.

One of Mitch's friends leans in to ask quietly, "You going to hit that later?"

He smiles. "I hope so. Remember I told you about the older girl fantasy I had as a kid? Well, this is her."

His friend claps him on the shoulder. "Well then, go get some. What are you doing hanging around with us? Go off with her and have fun. We will see you later," he tells Mitch.

When Sarah-Jane gets back with their beers, Mitch suggests they hang out together as his friends are going to another bar.

Midnight comes and everyone in the bar is singing. Mitch says Happy New Year to Sarah-Jane, and as she stretches up towards him to reply, she gives him a kiss on the lips. Her tongue licks his lips, and there is a spark of sexual energy between them. Closing his eyes, Mitch opens his mouth as her tongue slides inside his mouth, finding his tongue, and they twirl around each other, their saliva mixing as they kiss.

For Sarah-Jane, it is an opportunity to have sex; she is feeling horny after those two tequilas. Mitch is also an easy target for her later. After their kiss, Mitch leans close to her ear and says, "I don't know if I should tell you this, but..." He pauses nervously.

"Say what you need to say. Life is too short to be shy. You never get the things you want without speaking up," replies Sarah-Jane, as she grabs his cock with her free hand, rubbing it up and down as he gets hard.

"Ok," he goes on. "When we were young, I used to have fantasies about you, and you are the first girl I jerked off to. I have always wanted to be with you, even if it is only for one night."

She smiles at him. "Mitch, tonight is your lucky night. Being New Year's Eve, I'm feeling especially horny, so you are going to finally fulfil your wildest dreams. I'm going to take

you home and fuck your brains out. Do you need to say goodbye to your friends before we go?"

Mitch is smiling from ear to ear. "No, they said they would see me later, so let's get out of here." He downs the last of his beer, while Sarah-Jane does the same.

She has missed drinking beer. The icy cold bubbles tickle her throat as the drink goes down. Since Halloween, she has been drinking nothing but wine, mostly red. Only those four bottles she had with Charles were white.

It takes them ten minutes to get out of the bar, pushing their way through the crowd of people. "Where you parked?" Mitch asks her as they walk up the road.

"Not far. It's over there," she replies, pointing in the direction of her car. Before they climb inside, Sarah-Jane pulls Mitch towards her and kisses him again. "This is going to be the night of your life," she promises. "You will remember this till the day you die."

"Do you have any music for the journey back to yours?" he asks as she starts the car.

"I only have radio, or if you have any music on your phone, you can connect via Bluetooth to the sound system," Sarah-Jane replies.

Mitch takes his phone out of his pocket, searching for Sarah-Jane's sound system. Finding it, he connects and plays some Metallica. Mitch has chosen their *Master of Puppets* album, and they sit in silence enjoying the music until they arrive at Sarah-Jane's just after one. The clear night sky is no more. There is only a bright shadow of the moon highlighting the passing blanket of clouds,

It starts raining as they get out of the car, so they run for the front door, Sarah-Jane unlocking it to let Mitch in first, then she follows quickly behind.

"Do you have anything alcoholic to drink?" he asks.

"All I have is lots of red wine. The basement is full of wine," she laughs. "Let me go get a couple of bottles."

There aren't any bottles left in the kitchen, as Sarah-Jane had been trying to stay sober before heading out, so had avoided bringing any wine up to the kitchen.

Switching the light on in the lounge, she tells Mitch, "Make yourself comfortable and I'll get us some wine and two glasses. You can put on the television and find us some satellite radio. There will be a better choice of music than the tv music channels."

"Don't bother with the glasses," he replies. "We can drink straight from the bottle."

Sarah-Jane goes to the kitchen first to fetch the corkscrew then heads down to the basement to get the wine. She is glad they will be drinking from the bottle, as it means less for her to clean later. Placing the corkscrew in her back pocket, Sarah-Jane picks four bottles. Taking two in each hand, holding the bottle necks between her fingers, she walks up the stairs, turning off the light with her elbow. She can hear Slayer's *God Hates Us All* as she is closing the basement door.

"Here we go, I brought four bottles just in case," she announces with a genuine smile. "We don't know how much wine we will drink."

"I'm not sure we will need that much, but ok," he laughs.

Sarah-Jane opens one bottle and passes it to Mitch. He takes a long sip, expecting to pass her the bottle to share, but she has already opened her bottle by the time Mitch takes his away from his lips.

"I thought we were going to share, but well, cheers!" he says, clinking his bottle against hers. They drink in silence for a while, listening to the music.

When he has drunk half his bottle, Mitch is starting to feel lightheaded so puts the wine down on a table. Sarah-Jane is still drinking; she is three-quarters through her bottle before she puts hers down. Getting up to stand in front of

Mitch, she kneels on the carpet between his legs and unbuckles his belt before she unbuttons his jeans. Slowly she pulls down his zip, taking both his jeans and underwear in both hands and pulls on them. Mitch lifts his arse as Sarah-Jane pulls his clothes around his ankles, then takes his shoes off one by one.

As Sarah-Jane relieves Mitch of his jeans and underwear, she leaves his clothes in a pile on the carpet next to her. Taking his flaccid cock in her hand, she looks up into his eyes. As he watches her stroking his cock, it starts to swell in her hand. Now that he is hard, Sarah-Jane teases the tip of his cock with her tongue before she takes it in her mouth, slowly moving her head downwards. Mitch's cock disappears in her mouth, all the way down to the base, while she fondles his balls as she sucks him off. His throbbing, hard cock is all the way down Sarah-Jane's throat, and she is moving her head up and down. With each passing stroke her mouth makes, she increases the pace until Mitch arches his back, lifting his arse off the couch, his arms outstretched with his head leaning back. She knows he is close to coming, and before Mitch get the words out of his mouth, he shoots his load. As it goes down her throat, Sarah-Jane sucks in hard, her mouth going up the shaft of his cock, making sure not to waste a single drop of his cum.

"Fuck me, that is the best blow job I have ever had," he groans. "No woman I have ever been with has deep throated me before. I hope to have that again in the future."

"Your turn," she says, standing up to remove her leather trousers. "I want you to eat my pussy like it is your favourite thing in the world." As she removes her thermal leggings and top, she drops them on the floor beside Mitch's clothes. "Sorry for the unattractive look," she says.

Naked, she sits on the couch, rubbing her pussy while she waits for Mitch to kneel on the floor between her open and waiting legs. Her fingers are moist from her juices. Mitch takes over from her fingers, rubbing his thumb along her lips, his thumb splitting them apart in search of her clit. He massages her clit as he licks her pussy and Sarah-Jane opens her legs wider. Mitch pushes his face deeper into her pussy as he licks her slowly, making her sigh with pleasure.

Sarah-Jane is leaning against the back of the couch, slightly slouched down with her arse on the edge as Mitch licks her, only stopping to insert his middle finger inside her warm, creamy pussy. Moving his position slightly, Mitch moves his fingers faster and faster, pushing deep inside her. He can feel her pussy muscles tighten around his finger as she comes, leaving his hand covered in her cream.

"Let's go upstairs to the bedroom," she pants. "I hope you're ready. That cock of yours has a job to do."

Mitch stands up and takes a large gulp from the wine bottle. Getting off the couch, Sarah-Jane looks to see if she has left

a wet spot from her juices, but thankfully there doesn't seem to be one. Mitch did a good job but didn't make her squirt. She enjoys it more if she leaves a puddle, but she has no doubt she will squirt later when he fucks her upstairs. *Let's see, maybe I won't kill Mitch,* she thinks to herself. *It all depends on how well he fucks me.*

Sarah-Jane switches off the lounge light with her free hand when they leave the lounge, her bottle of wine in her other hand. Mitch is hugging his bottle as they make their way upstairs. When they reach the bedroom, she switches on the lights.

"Take the rest of your clothes off and lie on the bed," she tells him, placing her bottle on the dressing table. She goes around the room, lighting all the candles. "Don't you think that candles make the sex more intimate?" she asks, as she turns the lights off.

Mitch is lying on the bed stroking his cock as he waits for her, his bottle of wine on the bedside table next to him.

"Take a condom from the box and sheath your beast. I'm hungry to have him inside me," she instructs with a naughty smile, as she rubs her pussy while walking over to the bed.

Once Mitch has sheathed his beast and is kneeling on the bed, Sarah-Jane climbs on beside him. She goes on all fours,

positioning herself in front of Mitch as he rubs his hard, throbbing cock along her exposed, moist lips. The tip of his cock parts her lips as it finds it target, and he holds onto her thigh with his one hand while the other slowly pushes his throbbing cock millimetre by millimetre inside her wet pussy until he is all the way inside her.

Sarah-Jane leans back slightly, pushing into Mitch until he is balls deep inside her. Holding her other thigh with his now free hand, Mitch rocks his body back and forth as he fucks his fantasy girl. He slowly pulls back all the way, almost but not quite pulling out, then grabs her thighs towards him as he slams his cock deep inside her. Sarah-Jane lets out a loud "AHH" with every slam of his cock, picking up the pace with every fourth slam.

"I'm coming!" she screams, as her body shakes and her legs buckle beneath her.

Mitch's cock flies out of her pussy as Sarah-Jane squirts her juices on the bed. She is rubbing her clit fast as she comes, intensifying her orgasm, then flops over shaking as the full body orgasm rushes over her in waves. Not quite finished, as he hasn't come, Mitch flips Sarah-Jane on her back. Holding her legs at the knees, he opens her legs wide, lifting her back off the bed, then he slides his cock into her as he holds her legs at the top of her thighs. He rocks back and forth, slamming deep inside her, as Sarah-Jane rubs her clit.

Mitch slows down a little, changing position, his hands now cradling her arse, a cheek in each hand. With his cock balls deep, Mitch slowly rocks back and forth, back and forth, keeping the rhythm smooth and slow, their bodies as one. Slowly Sarah-Jane keeps in sync with Mitch's rhythm as she rolls back and forth, then together they increase the pace as their bodies move together. They are looking deep into each other's eyes as they both come. Exhausted and totally spent, they fall asleep.

Sarah-Jane wakes first. "Mitch, Mitch," she whispers to see if he is awake. Mitch turns onto his back and snores. *Perfect*, she thinks, *I can tie him up. I know I said it would depend on how well he fucked me, and he fucked me really good, but alas I don't feel complete if I haven't had my special ending.*

She slides off the bed, trying not to wake Mitch. When she has tied three of the ropes, Mitch moves slightly. Fearing that she has woken him, Sarah-Jane waits to see if he says anything. After what seems an eternity, she ties off the last of the ropes.

Knowing that Mitch is secure and can't move, Sarah-Jane gags him to stop any screams or shouting when he wakes. As she hasn't given Mitch any sleeping capsules, she is sure he will be easy to wake so she won't have to wait.

Climbing on the bed to straddle Mitch, she twists his nipples and he wakens instantly with the pain. With a look of fear

and dread, he realises he has been restrained and knows something isn't right. He feels deep in his stomach that he is fucked; he is going to die.

All Sarah-Jane can hear is Mitch's muffled pleas for his life.

"I know we have known each other most of our lives," she tells him, "But that means shit to me. Any man, no matter who they are, makes it into this house and onto this bed, is never going to see the light of day. Sorry, Mitch, you are just the next victim to fall onto my bed of death. I'm going to ride you until I'm close to orgasm, then I'm going to strangle you as I come."

Sarah-Jane can see tears run down his cheeks and onto the bed, reminding her of when Ken lay there doing the same. Rubbing her pussy with one hand, she strokes Mitch's cock with the other, her fingers wet with every stroke of his cock. Not bothering with the silk scarf this time, Sarah-Jane decides she isn't going to wait. She needs him inside her now, and this time she wants to feel flesh on flesh, without a condom. She wants to feel Mitch shoot his load deep inside her as he takes his last breath.

Sliding his cock inside her, Sarah-Jane rocks back and forth. There is no finesse in this act as she rides him faster and faster, trying to come as quickly as possible so she can hit that sexual high she is craving. She is almost there. She can

feel the orgasm building, waves tingling through her body. Leaning forward with her arms straight out and her hands clasped around Mitch's throat, Sarah-Jane twerks her pelvis up and down, up and down, her pussy sliding along Mitch's cock. Tightening her grip with every stroke, she looks him deep in the eyes as she comes, taking his last breath from him as he blows his load deep inside her. His eyes glaze over, and he is no longer Mitch.

Feeling the high she has craved since Charles left this earthly realm, Sarah-Jane is no longer experiencing the intensity of sexual arousal she felt before. Deciding she needs another victim to feel the warmth, she drags Mitch's body to the bathroom and dumps it in the bath before having a quick shower to get the smell of sex off her.

When she is finished, Sarah-Jane gets dressed in the same clothes, dumping Mitch's belongings into a black plastic bag to be disposed of later.

Chapter 16

Leaving her house, she puts the bag with Mitch's clothes in the boot of her car, then goes in search of her next victim. The clock on her dashboard reads half four. She wonders where she will find the next fly for her spider web, as the only places open now are the fast-food joints serving food to hungry drunk eaters.

It doesn't take long for her to find her next victim. Stumbling along on the other side of the road is a guy eating a burger while he walks home.

"Hey, you," she says to him. "Are you ok? Do you need a lift home?"

Turning slowly to see who is talking to him, he squints with one eye to focus before he replies, "Please. My friends left me, and I don't know where I am. You would be helping me out. I can give you my address."

Sarah-Jane turns her car around to pull up next to him and opens the passenger door. "Hi, my name is Carly," she tells him.

"Hi, my name is Paul," he replies, taking the last bite of his burger before he gets in the car.

Rolling down his window, Sarah-Jane says, "If you are going to vomit, try do it out the window, even though it is freezing. There is nothing worse than the smell of vomit."

Paul manages to tell her his address before he sits back and closes his eyes.

Parking her car back home, Sarah-Jane wakes him. "Sorry, I was on my way to your house when my car started to play up, so I thought it best to get home. We can call you a taxi when we are out of the cold."

"Cool, no worries," replies Paul.

Once they are inside the house, she locks the door behind her.

"Do you have anything to drink? I mean alcohol wise," asks Paul.

"I have some red wine in the lounge," she tells him. "Let's go in there. Would you like a glass, or are you ok with drinking from the bottle?" She switches on the light.

"Out of the bottle is fine by me," he replies, sitting on the couch facing the window. "As long as I get it in my body, I don't care how it gets there." He slumps back on the couch. "Would it be ok if I crashed here? I don't think I'm going to make it all the way home before I pass out."

"Sure, that will be fine, but you don't have to sleep on the couch. There is more than enough room on my bed upstairs. I'm sure you will be more comfortable," replies Sarah-Jane.

Paul looks surprised. "Are you sure you are okay with me sleeping next to you? Aren't you worried I might try and rape you while you are sleeping? You have only just met me; you know nothing about me." He downs half the bottle of wine before passing it back to her.

"I'm sure," she tells him. "I don't feel uncomfortable around you, and who knows? Maybe I want to fool around. I broke up with my boyfriend last week, so this is the first New Year I have been alone in a long time. Do you want to fuck me?"

Paul is startled by her straightforwardness, but pulls himself together quickly. "Hell, I'm all up for free pussy," he laughs.

"Follow me then." Sarah-Jane leads the way out of the lounge and up to her den of death. It is just after five o'clock and she can hear the tweeting of the morning bird song as they go upstairs.

The bed is still a mess from when she killed Mitch. She hopes Paul won't ask any questions about the state of the room.

"Nice room, awesome bed," says Paul, who is too drunk to see straight. All he can think of is warm comfy bed to pass out on.

"Why don't you make yourself comfortable? Get undressed, lie on the bed, and I will be with you shortly," Sarah-Jane tells him as she lights the candles, setting the atmosphere.

Paul is super eager to get it on and almost falls over trying to get his trousers off. Using the bed for support, he drops his trousers on the floor, then off comes his long-sleeved hoodie, t-shirt, and base layer, all in one. Paul drops them on top of his trousers. Last to land on the pile of dishevelled clothes is his underwear.

Jumping on the bed, he lies back, stroking his cock, waiting for her to come and fuck him.

Sarah-Jane has her back to Paul while she is getting undressed, folding her clothes as she lays them on the stool. "Hope you're ready for a wild time," she says, turning around to find Paul has passed out with his hard cock in his hand. "Great, just great. That is the second time I have been

cheated out of sex," she says to herself, as the only other person in the room wouldn't hear a foghorn going off if it was right next to him.

Feeling sleepy herself, Sarah-Jane decides she will nap, too, but first she will tie Paul up. She starts with his legs before she ties up his arms then places the gag in his mouth. After blowing out the candles, Sarah-Jane climbs into bed next to Paul. She is curled up in the foetal position on the edge of the bed as Paul takes up most of the space.

Pulling her pillow down towards her, she makes herself more comfortable and pulls the duvet over herself, finally succumbing to sleep. After such an active night, she has used up all her energy and needs to recharge so she can have her way with Paul in the morning. It will be her first murder in daylight hours, but she has reached the point of no longer caring. Sex and death are now her only driving force, and she needs to reach a new high as the old one no longer seem to satisfy her.

Sarah-Jane is rudely awakened hours later to Paul struggling next to her. She can hear the muffled screams for help through the gag, but she knows no help will be coming. His day of reckoning has arrived. He is thrashing his arms and legs trying to free himself, in the hope that the ropes will loosen their grip on him, but instead they are cutting into and burning his skin.

Feeling groggy as she opens her eyes, Paul's arm slams into her back. "Hey, fuckhead, you woke me up!" she snarls. "Calm the fuck down. Those ropes are tight. They are not coming undone until I untie your dead body."

It's clear by Paul's expression that he now realises the shit storm he has wandered into, but he tries the rope one last time before he stops.

"You see, this is the situation," she tells him. "I found a sexual high I never knew existed two months ago, but the problem is that that high is no longer as intense as it was the first time. I need to change something. I need to feel that intense warmth rush over my body just like the first time, so I need to think what to do to get that intense high back.

"Unfortunately for you that means you will be tied up here, lying there waiting with the knowledge that sometime today I am going to kill you. It sucks, doesn't it? Such rotten luck." Sarah-Jane gets out of bed naked, an excited look on her face. "I'm going to have breakfast and a nice strong coffee while I sit and think of ways to heighten the experience to get that intense sexual high again."

Leaving Paul tied to the bed, Sarah-Jane makes her way downstairs to the kitchen. *What should I have for breakfast?* she thinks. *I'm feeling quite hungry this morning. Toast or cereal isn't going to cut it. I need something heartier to eat;*

I need the energy to kill. Sarah-Jane decides she will have a fry-up.

Taking all the ingredients out of the fridge for her fry-up, Sarah-Jane puts two slices of bread in the toaster ready to toast later, then fries up the bacon and sausages, some tomato, sautéed mushrooms, and onion. She heats baked beans in the microwave then makes her instant coffee, leaving it next to the empty plate waiting to be filled. Just before everything is ready, she makes the toast. Switching off the stove, Sarah-Jane plates her food and butters her toast, then takes her food and coffee to the dinner table, constantly thinking of new ways to achieve that high again.

It is ten in the morning when Sarah-Jane has finished her breakfast. She takes her empty plate and cup back to the kitchen, rinsing them before putting them in the dishwasher. Still feeling hungry, Sarah-Jane takes the milk out of the fridge, the cereal from the cupboard, and fetches a large mixing bowl and spoon. She fills the bowl halfway, adding milk until it covers the cereal; all she can see is a few bits of cereal peeking out of the top of a sea of white.

Sarah-Jane can't be bothered walking back to the table, so she leans against the island, staring at the snow-covered backyard, deep in thought as she devours the cereal. Feeling content after finishing her food, she rinses the bowl and spoon before placing them in the dishwasher. Still no

closer to coming to a decision, Sarah-Jane makes another cup of coffee using the same mug, which she retrieves from the dishwasher. Deep in thought, she sips her coffee as she tries to come up with a solution.

It has started snowing again. At first, Sarah-Jane can see small flakes, but as the minutes pass they become larger, as they rush to the ground, covering the backyard. By the time Sarah-Jane has finished her second coffee, she is still no closer to solving the problem of how to achieve that high. The only thing she has come up with, she is reluctant to do, because it will make so much mess and she doesn't want to spend her day cleaning up afterwards.

The time on the microwave clock is showing quarter past twelve when she finally says to herself, "Fuck it, I have no choice." Rinsing her mug, Sarah-Jane walks upstairs to the bathroom, opens the cabinet under the basin, and retrieves the plastic bag with the knife before she walks back to the master bedroom and the waiting Paul.

"Unfortunately, I have come to the only conclusion there is left to me," she tells him. "Now, when I say unfortunate, I don't mean for you; I mean for me. You see, the last possible way for me to reach that peak again is the one I've been avoiding, only because it is going to make such a mess. I do try to keep my kills neat and clean. There is a saying – what is it? Ah, I'm keeping my house in order. But

this one time, I'm going to have to break my rules. Either way, you're still going to die."

The expression on Paul's face is a mix of fear, dread, and despair. Inside, he is praying for some way to stop this nightmare, as tears stream from his eyes. He doesn't want to die.

"You see, for me to reach that point of nirvana again, as I come, I'm going to have to slit your throat, and this is where the mess comes in," she explains in a matter-of-fact manner. "It's not that I'm afraid of blood, it's that I just don't want to spend my entire day cleaning up your blood, to be honest. But needs be that I go down this path with you."

She takes out the knife, dropping the plastic bag on the floor next to the dishevelled pile of Paul's clothes, then she climbs on the bed facing him and places the knife on the left side of his head.

Sarah-Jane thinks, *I'm not putting that cock in my mouth. I don't know where it has been.* Spitting in her left-hand, Sarah-Jane takes Paul's cock, stroking her saliva along its shaft, watching it harden and grow until it stands at attention, throbbing.

"Good, I'm glad you passed out last night. You were too drunk to be of any use to anyone. You wouldn't have been

able to get it up, let alone any chance of maintaining a rock-hard cock to fuck me," she says, spitting into her hand before stroking his cock again. "I need you hard, ready, and able to perform."

Stopping to get a condom from the box on the bedside table, she opens the package with her saliva-free hand and her teeth, spitting the foil on the bed, then rolls the condom down Paul's stiff cock. Desperate to get to the finale, avoiding her usual build-up, she spits in her hand again and moistens her pussy before rubbing Paul's cock along her lips. Sliding him inside her, she rocks back and forth as fast as she can to reach nirvana. There is no joy on her face; her body is cold.

She continues rocking back and forth, Paul's cock appearing and disappearing in the blink of an eye as her pelvis twerks up and down the length of his throbbing cock. "That's right, give it to me," she breathes. "I want to feel you explode. I'm almost there myself. Let's see if we can come together."

Suddenly Sarah-Jane hears a loud banging coming from downstairs. She tries to ignore it and carries on fucking Paul, but the noise gets louder and louder as the door knocker slams into the door.

"Sarah-Jane Morley, this is Detective Simons," calls out a voice. "Open up. We have a warrant to search these

premises. We know you are in there, so you have five minutes to comply, or we are coming in."

"Sorry, Paul," she whispers. "I would have liked more time, but as you can hear, the police are here, and I will not be denied my prize."

Picking up the knife with her right hand, Sarah-Jane can feel Paul come inside her as she holds his head down with her left hand. Grinding her pelvis back and forth, Sarah-Jane comes as she slits Paul's exposed throat. The cut straight, clean, and true, the knife severs the main veins in his neck and a large gush of red splashes across her body, hitting her in the face. She closes her eyes, squeezing her legs together as her body convulses, waves of ecstasy rushing over her.

Sarah-Jane can hear the front door being busted open and there is a rush of noise as about 20 police officers enter her home. Some run upstairs while others are checking the rest of the house.

Dropping the knife on the bed, Sarah-Jane rubs the warm red liquid over her breasts as she leans back, letting the warmth take her over.

Detective Simons bursts through the bedroom door shouting, "Listen here, Miss Morley" with Detective Brown close

behind. Shocked by the sight that greets them, Detective Simons has lost her voice; she can't get any words out.

On the bed in front of them are two people. A man is leaning over Sarah-Jane with his hands tightly clasped around her throat. Her eyes are bloodshot as they glaze over, the life draining from her body. The last image reflected in Sarah-Jane's eyes before her mortal coil snaps is Mitch above her, as he chokes the life from her. Paul was a figment of Sarah-Janes imagination, the last thoughts running through her head as she dies.

It is still dark outside. The police have been following Sarah-Jane for weeks, building a case against her. On one occasion, she almost caught them out; they didn't know if she spotted their car while they watched her from the street. But Detective Simons wanted to catch Sarah-Jane in the act.

There are three missing men, and Simons knew Sarah-Jane had met all three through the We Play website. Since Lance Rosemead's disappearance, Detectives Simons and Brown had discovered another two cases of missing men, both users of the website. After gaining a warrant to search for connections between the three men, they found out that Sarah-Jane Morley was the person joining this whole case together.

An officer bursts into the room. "Detective Simons, Detective Simons, we found them. They are in a deep freeze

in the basement. It's horrible; she dismembered them," says the officer. "We will have to wait till they thaw before we can properly identify them."

Mitch is still tied to the bed by his feet, his legs twisted around, his bare arse pointing at the ceiling, lying on his stomach, while another police officer is trying to untie him.

Detective Simons and Detective Brown had been tailing Sarah-Jane the entire night, from her house to the bars and back. They had been waiting outside her house for the rest of the squad to arrive before she knocked on the door. The 15-person strong unit, including two dogs trained to smell out dead bodies, were being given their instructions in the cold night air when they heard a loud smash coming from the house.

Smashing in the front door with a sledge hammer, they rushed in, many running upstairs towards the direction of the noise: the master bedroom. When they entered the bedroom, they immediately saw that a wine bottle had been thrown at the wall, smashing the long-boxed mirror hanging on the wall. Shards of mirror and bottle cluttered the cream carpet, which had turned red as the wine soaked into the surface. Mitch had thrown the bottle at Sarah-Jane as they struggled.

Now free from the ropes, Mitch explains to Detective Simons what has happened. "I have known Sarah almost all my life. My best friend is her best friend's brother. She has

been missing for two months, but I was out with my friends to see a Slipknot concert at the Arena, and I bumped into her outside one of the bars."

He pauses briefly before continuing. "I have had a childhood crush on her for years. When midnight arrived, we kissed and one thing led to another, and we came back here and had great sex. We fell asleep and the next thing I know is my legs and one arm are bound. As she was trying to bind my free arm, I lunged at her best I could, grabbing her by the hair. I smacked her head into the bedside table, but that only dazed her for a moment. As she stumbled back, I managed to free my other arm and pick up the wine bottle that had fallen off the bedside table and landed on the bed next to me. I threw the bottle at her, but she jumped out the way, so it smashed the mirror.

"I was still on my back, but I knew I had to turn over or I had no chance to fight her off. Sarah lunged at me as I managed to twist my legs. The ropes were tight as they cut into my skin, but I had to forget about the pain or I was going to die. Sarah's head hit me in the chest, briefly knocking the wind out of my lungs. The only thing I could think of was to lie on her head to pin her down. She was struggling, fighting to get free, and tried to push me off her.

"I was lucky enough to get my hands around her throat and I squeezed for dear life. I knew if I didn't kill her, she was

going to kill me." Mitch is still naked, as he recounts the events.

"Where are your clothes?" Detective Simons asks. "I'll get an officer to get them for you."

"My top is on the floor next to the bed, but the rest of my clothes are on the floor in the lounge," he replies.

"Johnson," says Detective Simons to one of the officers in the room. "I want you to go downstairs and retrieve this young man's clothes from the floor in the lounge."

Sarah-Jane is still lying naked on the bed, finally at peace with the world. Her tongue is sticking out of her mouth as saliva trickles down her cheek, dropping into her matted hair.

An officer unzips a body bag, while another straightens her arms, lifting the body off the bed so they can slide and lower her into the bag. Placing her arms and legs inside, they zip her up.

"Detective Simons?" one of the officers asks, "Should we leave her here?"

"No, take her downstairs. You can leave her on the floor near the front door until the meat wagon arrives. They will

take her to the morgue with the rest of the body parts." She sighs. "It's going to be a hell of a job trying to match the parts in the freezer to the right bodies."

Detective Simons turns her attention back to Mitch. "We have been building a case against her for two months now," she tells him. "Three men have gone missing with no trace of them. We interviewed Miss Morley a couple of days after her first victim went missing. She said she met him on Halloween. It seems they met on We Play, which is a sex hook-up site, and they went to a party at Jonestown. According to her, they came back here, had wild sex, and in the morning when she woke up, he was gone.

"We followed that up with his flatmate and the mobile phone company. Unfortunately, there was a delay in getting the information until we secured a warrant, but once we did and checked the mobile phone records, we realised that Miss Morley had lied to us. The phone records showed that the GPS on his phone said he was still at this address.

"Then victims two and three disappeared," she went on. "It took us a while to figure all three men had one thing in common – they had all met Sarah-Jane Morley."

"I work at Jonestown on weekends as a DJ," Mitch told the detective. "Have you spoken to her cousin Mike Sloan? The last time he saw her was on Halloween. In fact, the last

anyone had heard from her was a couple of weeks after Halloween, when she sent texts to Mike and her closest friends that she worked with. She told them all not to bother trying to get in contact. Both Mike and Dan, my best friend, told me. Dan's girlfriend is one of Sarah's best friends from the library where she worked."

"Do you have a way to get home, or do you want me to organise one of the officers to take you?" Detective Simons asks.

"I'll try to phone Dan and Jenny, see if they can fetch me. If not, would it be possible for one of your officers to drive me home?"

Johnson comes back into the room with his clothes and hands them to him.

"Sorry, but before you get dressed, we need to take some photos of your injuries while they are still fresh," she apologises. "We need them as evidence."

Holding one hand over his crotch, Mitch cups his cock and ball in his left hand as the flash of the camera almost blinds him.

"Can I see the rope marks on your right arm, please?" says Johnson, as she takes a series of photos of Mitch's right arm. "Now the left, please."

Mitch cups his privates with his right hand so Officer Johnson can take a series of photos of the rope marks on his left arm.

"Now we need photos of the rope marks on your legs." Still seated at the foot of the bed, Mitch lifts one leg while she takes the photos, then he lifts the other. "All done, you can get dressed now," she tells him.

Mitch gets dressed, not caring that there are people present. He has endured a shocking ordeal tonight and is still shaking as he puts on his clothes. He finds his phone in his jeans pocket, and dials Dan's number. The phone rings for a few minutes before a groggy-voiced Dan answers.

"What the fuck, Mitch! Do you have any idea what time it is?" Dan grumbles.

"Sorry to wake you," Mitch tells him. "It is an emergency, otherwise I wouldn't have phoned you. Can you come and fetch me? Something terrible has happened."

"God, what's happened, have you been in an accident?" Dan asks, sounding more awake.

Mitch can hear Jenny on the other side of the phone asking Dan what is going on. He explains nervously, "It's Sarah-Jane. I'm at her house. She is dead and the police are here.

Please come fetch me. I'll tell you all about it when you get here."

"What! Say that again, Sarah-Jane is dead?" repeats Dan.

Mitch can hear the shock in Dan's voice then there is a scream from Jenny in the background followed by crying.

"Dan, I don't know if you should bring Jenny with you," Mitch tells him. "I don't think she should hear what I'm going to tell you. She is freaking out already, and this is going to hit all of you like a ton of bricks. Maybe the police will speak to the girls and Mike."

"Dude, she's my girlfriend," Dan replies. "We don't keep anything from each other. If you don't tell her, I will. We will be there as soon as possible. We just have to throw some clothes on and then we will be on our way. It will be about 45 minutes before we get there."

Mitch ends the call and turns to the officer. "Detective Simons, my friend Dan and his girlfriend are coming to fetch me. They should be here in about an hour. Do you still need me, or can I go downstairs to wait for them?"

"You can go wait for them downstairs, but give your phone number to Johnson before you leave. I will phone you if I need any further information from you. We still have a lot

of work to do here." She shrugs wearily. "The sun will be high in the sky by the time we leave."

Mitch leaves the police to comb the crime scene and goes downstairs. Lying near the front door is the body bag with Sarah-Jane's corpse, along with three more bags. Officers are bringing black plastic bags up from the basement and putting them inside the body bags.

He goes into the lounge to wait for Dan and Jenny to arrive. It's quiet in the room and the television is switched off, but time seems to be standing still as Mitch gazes blankly at the screen, unaware of all the police activity going on in the house. An hour feels like an eternity for him, and he is finally brought out of his daze when he hears Dan's voice.

"Mitch! I'm looking for my friend, Mitch, can you tell me where he is?" Dan asks a police officer who is putting a black bag into one of the body bags.

"He is in there," says the officer, pointing towards the lounge.

Dan and Jenny rush into the lounge to find Mitch still staring at the blank television screen. "Mitch, you okay?" asks Dan, as they sit down on either side of him on the couch. "What happened tonight?"

"I was out with the guys – you knew we were going to the Slipknot concert. After the concert, we were waiting to get into a bar to have a few drinks to see in the New Year," Mitch explains hesitantly. "I spotted Sarah walking, mumbling to herself, she seemed angry about something. I called to her, and she came to join us. You know I've had a huge crush on Sarah since we were kids." Dan nods before Mitch continues, "At midnight, I said Happy New Year. We kissed and she came onto me, so I told her about my childhood fantasy. She told me that tonight was my lucky night, and she was going to fulfil that fantasy."

Mitch pauses briefly to clear his throat. "We came back here, drank some wine, and had amazing sex then we passed out. The next thing I know, I wake up with my legs and left arm bound. We struggled as she was trying to tie the rope on my right arm, and I got my arm free before she could secure it. I was fighting for my life. I slammed her head into the bedside table, giving me enough time to get my left arm free.

"There was a wine bottle that fell off the bedside table as she slammed into it, and it landed on the bed next to me. I threw it at her, missing her and shattering the mirror. I twisted my legs, which were still bound, getting me off my back just in time as she head-butted me in the chest. I collapsed on her, and she tried to push me off." Mitch stops again, then says quietly, "The only thing I could think

of doing was to strangle her to save my own life. As Sarah died, the police burst in the room. And now I'm sitting here, lucky but haunted by it all."

His two friends look totally shocked at what they have just heard. Eventually, Jenny asks him, "What's with the four body bags?"

Mitch shakes his head. "This is the bat-shit crazy part. The detective in charge, Detective Simons, told me upstairs that they have been building a case against Sarah. She had met three guys on a sex site called We Play, and the guy she partied with at Jonestown was her first victim apparently. They don't know what drove her to kill those three men, but I could have been her fourth victim."

Jenny claps her hand to her mouth in shock. "Oh my god," she wails, "the girls and I gave Sarah that subscription to We Play. Maybe she would still be alive if we had never given her that birthday present."

"Don't blame yourself," Mitch tells her. "You never know what turns some people bad."

"But it's so sad," Jenny sobs. "She was still fragile from the death of her parents. I don't think she ever really recovered from that."

"Are you allowed to leave?" Dan asks Mitch.

He nods. "I just have to find this police officer before we leave. The detective asked me to give my phone number to the officer just in case they have to ask me more questions."

"We will wait here for you while you give the officer your number," replies Dan.

Mitch gets up from the couch, leaving the lounge to find Officer Johnson. He finds her in the kitchen, dusting for fingerprints.

"Detective Simons asked me to give you my phone number just in case she needs to speak to me again. She might need to ask me further questions about tonight," Mitch explains.

Johnson takes down Mitch's details. "I'm sorry this happened to you," she tells him, "but you're safe now. You are one of the lucky ones."

"I don't feel so lucky at the moment," he admits. "I know you are right, but I just don't feel lucky."

"Here, take this." She hands Mitch a business card. "It is a group for survivors of trauma, they can help you through this difficult time."

"Thanks," Mitch says, as he take the card from her. "My friends have arrived, so they are going to take me home now."

"I know it will be hard, but try get some sleep when you get home," advises Officer Johnson.

"I'll try," he says. "And thanks again for all you have done for me. Goodbye."

"Bye." Officer Johnson gives him a sympathetic smile before she goes back to dusting for prints.

Mitch heads immediately back to the lounge. "Let's go," he says to Dan and Jenny.

The three of them leave 36 Strawberry Grove, never to return.